RETURN TO MARSEILLE

PETER CHILD

Benbow Publications

© Copyright 2007 by Peter Child

Peter Child has asserted his right under the Copyright, Designs and Patents Act, 1988 to be identified as the author of this work.

All rights reserved. No part of this publication may be reproduced, stored in a retrieval system, or transmitted in any form or by any means, electronic, mechanical photocopying, recording or otherwise without the prior permission of the copyright owner.

Published in 2007 by Benbow Publications

British Library
Cataloguing in Publication Data.

ISBN: 9780-9540910-7-1

Printed by Lightning Source UK Limited,
6 Precedent Drive, Rooksley,
Milton Keynes, MK13 8PR

First Edition

Characters and events portrayed in this book are fictional.

THE MICHEL RONAY SERIES

MARSEILLE TAXI

AUGUST IN GRAMBOIS

CHRISTMAS IN MARSEILLE

CATASTROPHE IN LE TOUQUET

OTHER TITLES BY THE AUTHOR

ERIC THE ROMANTIC

INSPECTOR HADLEY
THE TAVISTOCK SQUARE MURDERS

INSPECTOR HADLEY
THE GOLD BULLION MURDERS

NON FICTION

NOTES FOR GOOD DRIVERS

NOTES FOR COMPANY DRIVERS

VEHICLE PAINTER'S NOTES

VEHICLE FINE FINISHING

VEHICLE FABRICATIONS IN G.R.P.

ACKNOWLEDGEMENTS

Once again, I wish to gratefully acknowledge the help and assistance given to me by Sue Gresham, who edited and set out the book, and Wendy Tobitt for the splendid cover presentation. Without these talented and patient ladies this book would not have been possible.

Peter Child

INTRODUCTION

Marseille, the second largest city in France, is a bustling melting pot of humanity and hive of activity that basks in the brilliant sunshine of the Côte d'Azure. From the Vieux Port up La Canebierre, its main thoroughfare, to La Plein, everybody appears to be in the business of trying to make a good living whilst enjoying the sensual pleasures that the city has to offer. No wonder then, that Michel Ronay, a Marseille taxi driver, who left his home with his fiancé, Josette, to start a new life in Le Touquet, decides to return to the busy streets that he knows so well. His venture into business with his cousin, Henri, became a catastrophe in Le Touquet and Michel thought that in the end it was the right decision to leave and return to Marseille. He knew that that would make everybody happy, it's what Josette wanted, Monique, his second wife wanted and Gerrard, the Gendarme, wanted - not to mention Jacques and Antone at Ricky's Bar. So, all Michel had to do was leave Le Touquet, with Josette, drive down the Autoroute, around Paris and then home to Marseille, a simple journey to the south, what could possibly go wrong?

CHAPTER 1

As Michel Ronay swung his Mercedes onto the road out of Le Touquet, he leaned across and kissed his fiancé, Josette, lightly on her cheek.
"So, it's back to Marseille and a new life together" he said as he accelerated the big car towards the autoroute to the south.
"I'm so happy that we're going back, cherie" whispered Josette.
"I know, ma petite, it's all been a bad experience and we just have to forget about it" replied Michel.
"Oui, and I hope that you'll forget all about that Christiane woman, cherie..."
"Don't even mention her name to me" interrupted Michel in an angry tone, hoping that would stop any further comments regarding the elegant woman who had been his demanding mistress in Le Touquet. He smiled inwardly as he remembered the passionate love making on the beach and the sensual moments in her bedroom whilst her husband was away in Paris. Josette looked out of the side window and pulled a face, hoping that Michel would never again set eyes on the rich, spoilt and 'too beautiful for her own good', temptress. She put thoughts of the Christiane woman out of her mind and concentrated on their new life together back in Marseille where all their friends and relatives were. Thinking about relatives, Josette then remembered that before Michel could marry her, he would have to get divorced from his second wife, Monique, and that might be a slight problem, as Monique showed no signs of making it easy for her wayward husband. Still, as Michel was now living with his fiancé in their flat in the Rue du Camas, which luckily, had remained empty after they left to start their new life in Le Touquet, it would be easier, as it showed serious commitment on his part, something that Monique could not ignore. Josette felt content and she settled back to enjoy the long drive back to Macon, where they had arranged to stay the night with her Aunt, Eloise. They drove on, retracing the journey that had brought them so recently to Le Touquet, past Abbeville and on to Amiens, where they joined the autoroute A16 towards Paris. They stopped at a service area for a break and

something to eat before pressing on to eventually join the famous Paris Périphérique. The evening rush hour traffic slowed to a crawl and Michel became impatient as they were caught up with the Parisians trying to get home to their loved ones, or someone else's loved ones…

"Mon Dieu! They're all mad if they do this every day" he said with passion.

"Oui, ma petite."

"Where are they all going to?" he asked.

"Or coming from" said Josette helpfully.

"I'm glad it's not like this in Marseille" said Michel.

"Oui."

"I'd be dead in a month" he half whispered as the BMW in front slowed to a crawl and then stopped.

"What time will we get to Eloise, ma petite?" asked Josette.

"I've no idea, cherie, late I expect" replied Michel in a resigned tone.

"Never mind, cherie, she'll wait up for us" replied Josette.

"Oui" replied Michel as he inched the Mercedes closer to the stationary BMW.

"I expect we'll see Jules again" said Josette brightly and Michel smiled when he remembered the good looking restaurant owner who was one of Aunt Eloise's current lovers.

"Oui, ma petite, and if he stays the night, I hope we can get some sleep, he's so 'athletic' I'm sure that he'll keep banging away at Eloise for hours!"

"Oui" giggled Josette as she remembered the noisy love making of her attractive Aunt.

"I don't know how she puts up with it" said Michel and Josette smiled.

The traffic began to move and then speeded up considerably, which then relieved some of Michel's stress. He wanted to put as much distance as soon as possible between himself and Le Touquet. He was very glad that he had made the decision to leave behind the ill fated business venture with cousin Henri, not to mention the demanding Madame Christiane. Another week or so of her sexual harassment, high rolling gambling habits at the casino and heavy drinking would have rendered him a physical and mental wreck. Yes, he had escaped just in time and he looked forward to renewing all his sexual acquaintances with his Marseille mistresses, who were so much more gentle and understanding. When things became difficult in his complicated life, he knew that he could find solace and peace in that oasis of understanding, Ricky's Bar, where Jacques, the bar man, and Antone his philosophical mature lover, would dispense advice and wisdom, whether it was asked for or not. Michel felt more comfortable by the minute as he drove the Mercedes as fast as he could towards the turn off the Périphérique mark 'A, to the south'.

"I feel as if we are almost home" he said as the car joined the slip road onto the autoroute.

"Oui, ma cherie" replied Josette as he accelerated hard. Soon the sign for Melan appeared on the gantry above, then Sens followed by Auxerre. As they sped towards the south, Michel felt his heart lifting as each kilometre passed and he found himself humming quietly with pleasure. They stopped at the service area near Chalon for fuel and something to eat, although they decided to have only a cheese salad baguette and a coffee each, in case Eloise treated them to dinner at Jules' restaurant. Refreshed and re-fuelled, they hurried on down the A6 to Macon, eventually slipping off the autoroute and following the signs for 'toutes directions' and 'centre ville'. When they reached the road to Bourg-en-Bresse, they knew that they were very close to Rue Montrevel where Eloise lived. Michel sighed with relief when he stopped the car outside the neat corner house then Josette leaned across and kissed him.

"Not too late for dinner at Jules restaurant" he smiled as he glanced at the dashboard clock.

"Non" Josette said before she slipped from the car and made her way up to the front door.

Eloise welcomed them in with a big smile, kisses and hugs. Michel thought that she looked more attractive than ever with her neat page boy haircut, ample bosoms, tight waist and her full, red, kissable lips.

"Ma petites, ma petites" she cooed "come in, come in, it's so good to see you."

"It's good to be here, Eloise" said Josette.

"Bon, now, have you eaten?"

"Two cheese baguettes at Chalon" replied Michel.

"Mon Dieu! You must be starving, I'll phone Jules and tell him to expect us soon" said Eloise and Michel smiled. They followed her into the lounge and she waved them to a seat before asking "what would you like to drink, ma petites?" They both had a brandy and she joined them, wishing them good luck and bon voyage for tomorrow before phoning Jules.

"Now, before we go and eat, tell me all about Le Touquet" she said.

"It was a catastrophe" replied Michel, shaking his head.

"Why?"

"It started badly and got worse..." replied Michel.

"We were unhappy about everything" interrupted Josette.

"You poor dears, I'm so sorry for you."

"We were glad to leave the place" said Michel.

"Have you lost a lot of money in the business?" asked Eloise.

"Non, thankfully" replied Michel.

"Bon, well you're here now and I'm sure after a good meal and a nights rest, you'll feel better" smiled Eloise.

"Oui" nodded Josette.

"So, tell me, ma petites, what really happened to you in Le Touquet?" Now, as all men should know, a woman's curiosity cannot be satisfied with broad, general statements, so Michel launched into the detail of the catastrophe, whilst Eloise listened carefully. Josette added her little points of interest, not forgetting to mention at regular intervals, the dreadful Madame Christiane, who had far too many shoes for one person. Eloise suddenly looked at her watch and said "we must go and eat, Jules will wonder where we are, petites."

"Bon" nodded Michel.

"You can carry on telling me all about it over dinner" she said.

They arrived outside Jules restaurant in Eloise's black BMW and were just about to get out when she said "be extra nice to Jules tonight, ma petites, he's upset because he's having a little difficulty with his wife." Michel smiled and nodded, thinking 'what an understanding mistress Eloise is' before he said "c'est la vie." Josette pulled a face at that and slipped from the car. Jules welcomed them all with a kiss and suggested that the Coq au Vin was simply outstanding tonight, before a smart young waiter showed them to a table close to the spectacular open wood fire. The delicious smell of French cuisine invaded their sense as they sat and perused the wine list. Michel ordered a bottle of full rich Burgundy as Jules appeared and asked "can I recommend the Coq au Vin for you all?"

"Oui, Jules" replied Eloise.

"Bon, and to start?" asked Jules. Josette chose grapefruit, Eloise soup du jour and Michel decided on crevettes. With a "bon appetite" the elegant restaurant owner disappeared.

"Jules seems quite happy tonight" said Michel with a smile.

"He's hiding his despair" replied Eloise.

"Really?"

"Oui, I know him so well, when he comes home later, he'll break down in tears" said Eloise.

"Oh, shame" said Michel sympathetically.

"Oui, and when he's like this, he cannot sleep" she said sadly.

"Oh, dear" commented Michel, fearing the worst.

"Oui, I have to console him all night" whispered Eloise, confirming Michel fears of another disturbed night because of the needs of 'athletic' Jules.

The starters arrived and they settled down to enjoy their food. The starters were delicious, the Coq au Vin was extraordinarily good and Michel ordered another bottle of Burgundy to complement the meal. It was after they had finished their sweet dishes and were enjoying coffee that Eloise returned to the subject of the catastrophe in Le Touquet.

"So, ma petites, tell me more." Michel sighed and with helpful reminders from Josette, he relived the series of extraordinary events that befell them in the refined sea side town. At appropriate moments, Eloise 'tut tutted' and whispered "oh, la, la", confirming to Michel that he not only had made the right decision to leave but had the undying sympathy of Josette's desirable Aunt.

"Now here we are, on our way back to Marseille" said Michel proudly, when he felt that he had said enough about Le Touquet.

"Bon, you're doing the right thing" nodded Eloise.

"I'm sure of that" said Michel.

"So, is it a Spring wedding next?" asked Eloise with a smile.

"Possibly..." began Michel, as his mind rushed to cope with the unexpected, dreaded question.

"Oui, and we're both very excited about it" interrupted Josette brightly.

"Bon, you make a lovely couple and are so well suited" beamed Eloise as Jules arrived with l'addition, much to the relief of Michel. He thought 'in a difficult situation, any diversion is to be welcomed, even if it costs money.'

They arrived back at Eloise's house and sat drinking Brandy until Jules arrived. By then both Michel and Josette were feeling tired as well as a little drunk. Jules settled down on the sofa next to Eloise with a very large Brandy and asked "so, Michel, how is the business going
in Le Touquet?"

"It's finished."

"Why?"

"It was a catastrophe" replied Michel.

"Mon Dieu! Are you bankrupt?" asked Jules in a concerned tone.

"Non, we stopped everything before it got out of hand" replied Michel with the air of a confident business tycoon.

"But nevertheless, it must have been a loss to you" said Jules.

"Just a little, but my cousin Henri has covered that, his shoe shop business is very profitable and he is certain that he can put the overheads against tax" replied Michel with a smile.

"Bon, a lucky escape then."

"Oui."

"So, what are you going to do now, Michel?"

"Get back as soon as possible to Marseille, and carry on as before…"

"And get married in the Spring" interrupted Josette.

"Bon, I'm very happy for you both, marriage is a wonderful thing, provided you marry the right person…" began Jules.

"Oh, we're absolutely right for each other, aren't we, cherie?" said Josette with a smile. Michel winced slightly before he nodded his head and said "oui, ma petite."

"Luckily, we've managed to rent our old flat in the Rue du Camas" said Josette.

"Bon, so it looks as if everything is turning out well for you both" said Jules before he took a large gulp of Brandy.

"Oui" smiled Josette.

"I envy you, in love with each other, no worries, not like me, mon Dieu, my life is awful, just awful" said Jules wistfully.

"Why, mon ami?" asked Michel.

"Hasn't Eloise told you?"

"Non, not really, she just said that you were having a little trouble…"

"A little trouble! Mon Dieu! I didn't know what trouble was until I got married!" exclaimed Jules before he took another large gulp of Brandy.

"Oh, dear" whispered Josette.

"Without Eloise, I know I should die" and Jules took the hand of his misty eyed mistress and kissed it.

"Ma cherie" whispered Eloise.

"My wife will kill me if I don't get away from her soon, but divorce is out of the question, the restaurant is all in her name, the house, everything, all I've got is my car, and that needs replacing" wailed Jules.

"Mon Dieu" said Michel.

"Oui, it's her family you see, they've got money and they financed the business, making sure that Jacqueline owned everything."

"What can you do then?" asked Michel.

"Nothing, absolutely nothing, I am trapped, like a wild animal, trapped by a woman who doesn't love me and I know I'll only be free when I'm dead!" said Jules and he took another gulp of Brandy.

"Mon Dieu" whispered Michel.

"Oui, you are lucky, ma petites, you are so right for each other" said Jules with conviction but Michel was not so sure. He knew from his own experience that women usually change after they get married and he felt a touch of gloomy reality descend as he gazed at Josette and forced a gentle smile. She gave him a wink and suddenly he got the strong impression that he was in the bag with no hope of escape.

"You're overtired, ma cherie, let's get you into bed" said Eloise gently.

"Oui, ma petite" Jules nodded and then drained his glass. Eloise helped him to his feet and with a nod to Michel, Jules left the room with his mistress. Michel looked at Josette and shrugged his shoulders before finishing his Brandy. Eloise arrived back in the room and suggested that they have a lay in tomorrow before she wished them 'goodnight'.

Michel had made up his mind to make gentle love to his fiancé, but when they actually slipped into bed, he was just too tired. So, after protestations of love and several kisses they fell asleep, only to be awakened a little time afterwards by the sound of Jules rhythmic thumping as he relieved all his anxieties with his sensuous mistress.

"Mon Dieu, nothing stops him, does it?" asked Michel in a whisper.

"Non, cherie, as Eloise says, he's very athletic."

"Oui, and I'm sure she's grateful." Josette giggled and they waited for the climax which came some time later accompanied by the usual cries of "mon Dieu!" from both of them. Michel was truly glad when it was all over and he fell into a deep sleep with his arms wrapped around Josette.

The next morning, after coffee and croissants with the bleary eyed Jules and Eloise, Michel and Josette kissed them before saying their 'goodbyes'. Michel did not speak to his fiancé until they reached the slip road on to the autoroute A6.

"Marseille, here we come" he said as he accelerated the Mercedes towards Lyon and the south.

"Bon, not too far now" said Josette.

"Non, ma petite, we'll easily be home by this evening" he replied and he began to think about the future with his fiancé. The comments that Jules had made certainly struck a chord, after all, Monique was his second wife, so he knew firsthand what a disaster an unhappy marriage could be. He realised that once he married Josette she would not tolerate his many mistresses and all that wonderful, carefree, sensual fun around Marseille would be over. He wondered if he could cope with that. As they neared Lyon, Michel thought about Cyril Gerrard's warning regarding Monsieur Conrad Montreau, the 'Black Snake', who was a known gangster and rumoured to be trying to take over the Salvator's rackets in Marseille. A shudder ran down his spine as he thought of the arrest of Claude Salvator at his father's funeral. He hoped that silly Gerrard, the gendarme, would not involve him in any more of the dubious 'undercover operations' in an attempt to bring crooks like Montreau to justice.

It was on the long downhill approach to Lyon that the accident occurred. Michel was not sure what happened, he knew that he was not driving too fast and that he was overtaking the car towing a caravan quite safely. Whether it was a sideways gust of wind or the English driver losing control of his car at that moment, no-one will ever know. Suddenly the caravan swung out into the path of the Mercedes and with no chance of avoiding the collision, Michel ploughed straight into it with a mighty crash. Large pieces of shattered caravan rained down over the Mercedes as Michel slammed on the brakes, shouting "mon Dieu!" repeatedly as he did so. The impact from the rear of the caravan then forced the back of the English car upwards, off the road surface, whereupon the driver attempting to brake with only his front wheels on the road, caused the whole moving disaster to zig zag across the autoroute, colliding with two other cars. When the shambles at last came to a screeching halt, Michel jumped from the Mercedes and ran to the heaps of wreckage that once had been the Englishman's pride and joy. He was joined by a Renault driver, a short man in a Breton beret, who had lost a front wing in the disaster and a pale faced girl whose little Citroen had been damaged at the rear. The tall Englishman and his plump, blonde wife got out of their Volvo Estate and stood surveying the wreckage and shaking.

"Oh, my God, Jean, look at all this, whatever are we going to do now?" said the Englishman.

"I don't know, Frank, best call the police" she replied and began to cry.

"Are you hurt, Monsieur?" asked Michel.

"What?" asked Frank.

"Are you alright, Monsieur?"

"I don't know what you're saying, I don't speak French" replied Frank. Michel then held up his hands and dropped them down again.

"Mon Dieu! Can you understand him, Monsieur?" he asked the man with the Breton beret.

"Non, Monsieur."

"Can you speak any English, Mademoiselle?" asked Michel

and the pale faced girl shook her head and began to cry. By now the traffic on their side of the autoroute had come to a complete halt behind them, whilst on the other carriageway the drivers were slowing so they could observe the accident more closely, as it is such good fun! Michel guessed it was only a matter of time before the Gendarmerie arrived and he went back to the Mercedes to examine the damage. Josette was standing by the passenger door, pale faced, and asked "are they alright, cherie?"

"I think so, but they're English and don't speak French, so I don't really know."

"They look alright" she said as a motorist who had been forced to stop by the accident came up to them and asked if anyone was hurt.

"Non, Monsieur" replied Michel.

"Bon."

"You don't happen to speak English by any chance?" asked Michel.

"Oui, just a little" he replied.

"Go and see if they are alright, s'il vous plait" said Michel and the man nodded before heading in the direction of the bemused English couple. By now, more stranded motorists had left their vehicles and were gathering, en masse, to examine the scene of the accident. Michel heard 'tut tutting', 'mon Dieu' and 'oh la la' from the circulating crowd as he examined his beloved Mercedes. It did look a mess and despite the car's formidable structure, the caravan chassis had been rammed into the front of the Mercedes, demolishing the grill, front bumper and headlights. Both front wings were buckled and it was obvious that the car was un-drivable.

"Mon Dieu, what are going to do now, cherie?" he asked as he shook his head.

"Is it that bad?" Josette queried.

"Oui."

"Can it be repaired?"

"Oui, but it will take time, cherie" he replied just as he heard the wailing siren of the Gendarmerie approaching.

"Bon, the Gendarmes, at least they'll arrange to get all this clear and off the autoroute" said Michel as he picked up some of the clothes that had been scattered from the caravan as they collided. The police car stopped in the emergency lane and two officers got out. One approached Michel whilst the other went in the direction of the shattered caravan locked in torment with the Volvo, still perched up in the air. Michel caught a glance of the man in the Breton beret carrying the front wing of his Renault and pointing at it with a group of sympathetic motorists looking on. Just as the Gendarme was about to speak to Michel, the noise of a loud crash followed by the sound of tinkling glass was heard and they all glanced in the direction of the opposite carriageway where a grey Renault van, which looked like a large corrugated chicken coup on wheels, smashed into the back of a Citroen which had slowed just a little too much to observe the incident.

"Mon Dieu!" exclaimed the Gendarme as they heard the sound of another wailing siren.

"Much needed reinforcements, Monsieur Gendarme" said Michel with a smile.

"It is not funny, Monsieur, not funny at all!" exclaimed the Gendarme as the sound of skidding tyres followed by another impact and tinkling glass reached their ears.

"Mon Dieu! Are they all mad!" said the Gendarme and he rushed away towards the centre reservation and began waving at the traffic approaching the scene of the accidents from the south. Then as the second police car arrived, Michel could hear more distant sirens, the sound punctuated by tyres screeching coupled with tinkling glass, and soon there were four police cars, three police motor cyclists, two fire engines, one on either side of the autoroute and six ambulances. Michel had never before seen so many vehicles with flashing blue lights in one place.

There was much general excitement and the crowd of trapped motorists grew, all anxious to examine the many crash sites on both carriageways. They crossed from one side of the autoroute to the other like migrating birds, examining the disasters and 'tut tutting'. Then the vehicle recovery lorries appeared, three on Michel's side and two on the carriageway to the north. Men in white helmets moved purposely about the wreckage on the autoroute as drivers reversed the lorries, waved back by the men in helmets, into positions where their winches could be used to drag the wrecked cars up onto the back of their recovery vehicles. The caravan had to be cut free from the Volvo, which crashed down to the road surface and then rolled unceremoniously towards the wingless Renault, striking the rear door and causing considerably more damage to the vehicle.

The little man in the Breton beret did a dance of angry frustration as the men in helmets failed to stop the runaway Volvo. Then the pale faced girl, who was the driver of the Citroen, fainted and ambulance men rushed to her assistance before placing her on a stretcher and lifting her into the ambulance. The rear doors slammed and with its siren blaring, it sped away along the empty autoroute toward Lyon.

"Now, Monsieur, you will come with us, s'il vous plait" said the Gendarme who suddenly appeared at Michel's side.

"What about my car?" asked Michel.

"It will be safely recovered, Monsieur, and taken to the pound at the Gendarmerie in Lyon" replied the officer. Michel nodded and handed the policeman the clothes that he had recovered from the road. The policeman looked at them with surprise as most of them were ladies underclothes of the English flannel type.

When everybody was safely in custody at the Gendarmerie, the investigation began into the events that caused the A6 autoroute to be closed in both directions. Michel and Josette sat patiently in the interview room whilst the Gendarme looked carefully at his driving licence and vehicle documents.

"So, Monsieur Ronay, I see that you are a taxi driver from Marseille" said the Gendarme.

"Oui, that is correct" replied Michel.

"And is this lady with you a fare paying passenger?"

"Non, she is my fiancé, Josette LeFranc" replied Michel.

"But in your documents here, Monsieur Ronay, it clearly states that your next of kin is Madame Monique Ronay, is she your mother?"

"Non, she is my wife…"

"We're going to get married as soon as Michel gets a divorce" interrupted Josette.

"I see" mused the Gendarme before adding "a wife and a fiancé."

"That's better than having two wives" replied Michel in a serious tone.

"I wouldn't know, Monsieur" grinned the Gendarme.

"Look, how long are we going to be here?" asked Michel.

"As long as it takes, Monsieur, to find out how your driving caused a major accident that closed the main autoroute that virtually cut France in two! Paris was isolated!" replied the angry Gendarme.

"My driving?"

"Oui, Monsieur, according to the Englishman and his wife, you rammed their caravan at a recklessly high speed!"

"That's not true! I was just about to overtake them when he lost control of his bloody caravan and it swung out in front of me" wailed Michel.

"Monsieur Ronay, we know only too well how you taxi drivers behave! You're all the same, rush, rush everywhere, cutting other motorists up, oui, it happens every day in front of our very eyes" said the gendarme.

"I can tell you that's just not the case this time" replied Michel.

"So tell me what is the case, Monsieur?" asked the Gendarme. Michel drew a deep breath and said "my fiancé were returning from Le Touquet…"

"You have driven all the way from Le Touquet, Monsieur?" interrupted the Gendarme.

"Oui…"

"I put it to you, Monsieur Ronay, that at the time of the accident, you were exhausted and were driving without due care…"

"We stopped at Macon overnight" interrupted Michel.

"Can you prove that, Monsieur?"

"Oui."

"Where did you stay?"

"With my Aunt Eloise" said Josette.

"I will require her full name and address, mademoiselle" said the Gendarme.

"Oui, of course" replied Josette as Michel had a brainwave that he was later to regret.

"Monsieur Gendarme, as I believe that you have the wrong impression about my driving and good character, can I suggest you contact Monsieur Cyril Gerrard, who knows me well and is an important officer in the Gendarmerie, dealing with criminal activity in Marseille?" Michel smiled triumphantly. The officer sat for a moment and then nodded before replying "a good idea, he should know if you are a criminal or not, Monsieur Ronay, please excuse me while I phone him." Michel nodded and relaxed back in his chair. When they were alone, Michel said to Josette "I'm sure Gerrard will sort everything out."

"I hope so."

"In fact, as he wants me back in Marseille urgently, he'll probably send a car for us."

"Bon, I'm anxious to get home." They sat in silence until the Gendarme returned and sat down opposite them.

"I have spoken to Monsieur Gerrard and given him the facts of the matter and he has said that he knows you…"

"Bon" interrupted Michel.

"He wants you to phone him back in half an hour" said the Gendarme.

"Why?" asked Michel with concern.

"He said it was a police matter, you can use the phone in the office next door, Monsieur, and meanwhile, I want a written statement from you regarding the accident."

"Mon Dieu" whispered Michel.

The Gendarme provided writing materials before leaving Michel to commit to paper the events of the day. He and Josette went over the accident carefully and wrote it all down. When the statement was complete, the Gendarme returned, picked it up and then invited Michel to make his call to Cyril Gerrard in Marseille.

"Bonjour, Cyril" said Michel when he heard Gerrard's familiar voice answer the phone.

"It's Monsieur Gerrard, we're on police business, Ronay" hissed Gerrard.

"As you wish."

"Now, what mess have you got yourself into this time?"

"There's been an accident, which was not my fault…" began Michel.

"I know all that, Ronay, how badly damaged is your taxi?" demanded Gerrard.

"Quite bad, it'll need a new bumper, grill, front wings…"

"I don't need all that detail, just tell me how long it will take to get it repaired" asked Gerrard impatiently.

"Well, if a repair shop started on it straight away, perhaps three or four days, provided they could get the parts" replied Michel.

"Excellent, that will fit my plan very nicely" said Gerrard with enthusiasm.

"What plan?"

"I have just been to see my Chief and he has given the immediate 'go ahead' for operation 'Snake'."

"Operation 'Snake'?" repeated Michel.

"Oui, now the plan is for you to remain in Lyon whilst your taxi is repaired and infiltrate Conrad Montreau's gang…"

"What? You must think I'm mad!" exclaimed Michel.

"Non, you did it with the Salvators', now you can repeat it with Montreau, and your accident is the perfect cover for you, it is heaven sent!"

"It may be for you, but…"

"Leave it all with me, Ronay, I'll see that your taxi is taken to a good repairer and the parts are delayed until we can bring Montreau and his mobsters to justice before they try and take over Marseille…"

"Now, wait a minute" interrupted Michel.

"Book yourself into the Hotel Arnaux in the Rue Benoir, it's very cheap and I know the couple who own it, Monsieur Veron and his wife…"

"Listen to me, I've got my fiancé with me and she's very anxious…" interrupted Michel.

"Send her back to Marseille on the train, Ronay, we don't want her slowing down 'Operation Snake'…"

"You're talking about the woman I love…"

"Oui, oui, Ronay, now the Chief has approved expenses for you as well as a reward if we can get a conviction as a result of your undercover work" said Gerrard.

"Oh, a reward… how much?" asked Michel in a surprised tone.

"Er, I don't know at the moment, but it will be considerable" replied Gerrard.

"Just for a few days here?"

"At the most."

"And all expenses paid?"

"Oui, but don't go mad, we're on a tight budget this year" replied Gerrard.

"Alright, I'll do what I can" said Michel as he thought of the reward.

"Bon, now stay at the hotel until one of my undercover officers contacts you and then you will be exposed to Montreau" said Gerrard.

"Right, then what will I do?"

"You'll be told. Now, make sure you complain to everyone that you have been accused of causing the accident on the autoroute…"

"But I didn't!" interrupted Michel.

"Well, that's as maybe, luckily it's all been on the Television news, so everybody thinks it is your fault, not the English tourists with their caravan" replied Gerrard.

"Mon Dieu!"

"Now, send your fiancé back on the train and get along to the hotel."

"But…"

"I'll fix everything with the Lyon Gendarmerie, so just do as I say, Ronay, and all will be well" with that, Gerrard hung up, leaving Michel shocked.

"Mon Dieu, what am I to say now?" he whispered to himself before deciding not to tell Josette the truth but give her plausible reasons for her return to Marseille without him. He returned to the interview room and told Josette that he had to stay in Lyon.

"But why, cherie?" she asked with a puzzled frown.

"Gerrard said he would help us by getting the car repaired quickly because he wants me back in Marseille and I think I should stay here whilst that's done to keep an eye on things" he replied.

"I hope you're not getting involved in any funny business" she said firmly.

"Non, ma petite, I promise you" smiled Michel.

"Alright then, where will you stay?"

"Gerrard has some friends who have an hotel in the Rue Benoir, it's called the Arnaux, so I'll stay there, it'll only be for a couple of nights, then I'll be home with the car" Michel smiled.

"Ring me tonight, cherie" said Josette and Michel nodded. They went in search of the Gendarme and then out to the wrecked Mercedes to retrieve their cases. The Gendarme confirmed that Gerrard had made arrangements for the taxi to be taken to a large repairer in the zone industrie, after the police safety check on the condition of the Mercedes. Michel and Josette took a taxi to the station where they said goodbye with kisses before she boarded the two o'clock train to Marseille.

Hotel Arnaux looked a little shabby from the outside, confirming to Michel that it was indeed 'cheap'. He was not surprised however, because he knew that as the Marseille Police Department was paying his hotel bill as well as other expenses, everything had to be at the lowest cost. He determined to spend as much as possible on everything else to compensate for the poor hotel accommodation. Monsieur Jacques Veron gave him the key to room 12 after he had signed in and Michel made his way up the poorly lit stairs to the landing where the dark blue carpet showed signs of wear. His room was quite spacious with a double bed and an en suite with a shower, toilet and sink. The bed felt quite comfortable and the linen appeared clean. Michel unpacked some of his clothes and was busy putting them away when there was a knock at the door.

"Entre" he called out and the door opened. He looked up at the attractive middle aged woman with a good figure, blonde hair and big blue eyes, who entered his room.

"Bonjour, Monsieur, I'm Madame Veron, I've just popped in to see if everything is alright for you and to ask if you require dinner to-night?" she smiled.

"Thank you, Madame, no, I'll be eating out this evening" he replied.

"Very well, Monsieur, now, is everything to your satisfaction?"

"Oui, it is" he replied.

"Bon, and if there's anything you want, just ring down and I'll see to it personally" she smiled and Michel caught the glint in her eye as well as the lowering of her voice to a suggestive, husky whisper.

"Merci, I will" he replied with a smile. She nodded and left the room leaving the scent of her perfume lingering to remind him of her presence. He was sure that Madame Veron would supply additional comforts if he required, at no extra cost. He sat on the bed to review the events of the day before phoning his wife, Monique, to tell her all that had happened on the journey home to

Marseille.

"Hello" she said.

"Monique, c'est moi."

"Oh, cherie, where are you?" she asked anxiously.

"In Lyon."

"What are you doing there?"

"I've had an accident on the autoroute…"

"Mon Dieu! Mon Dieu! Are you alright, cherie?"

"Oui, perfectly alright but the car is badly damaged…"

"Oh, cherie…"

"So I'm going to stay here until it's repaired."

"How long will that be?"

"Just a few days."

"So it's not that bad then" she said suspiciously.

"Bad enough" he replied noting her change of tone.

"Are you alone?"

"Oui, and I'm staying here at the Hotel Arnaux in the Rue Benoir" he replied honestly.

"So, what happened to you, cherie?"

"I was overtaking a car towing a caravan when it suddenly swung out in front of me and I hit the back of it."

"Mon Dieu, was anybody hurt?"

"Non, but two other cars on my side of the autoroute were damaged…"

"Oh, non."

"Oui, and several cars on the other side crashed into one another whilst they were watching me."

"Mon Dieu" she whispered

"I've been blamed for it all" he said indignantly.

"Oh, cherie."

"What made it worse was that a stupid Englishman was towing the caravan, and because he's a tourist, the Gendarmes believed him and not me!"

"Oh, non."

"I mean, what's an Englishman doing towing a caravan to the south of France in January, are they all mad over there?".

"I expect so, cherie."

"We should never have let them join the EU" said Michel in a firm tone.

"Non, cherie."

"So, hopefully, I'll be home in the next few days, but I'll ring you and let you know when."

"Bon, come as soon as you can because I'm very worried about Mama" said Monique.

"What's wrong with her?"

"I don't know, neither do the doctors" replied Monique.

"Doctors?"

"Oui, she's in hospital."

"Mon Dieu" whispered Michel.

"She just says she feels all funny and peculiar…"

"She's always feels like that, it's probably trapped wind" interrupted Michel.

"She says she doesn't care whether she lives or dies…"

"I know the feeling."

"So come home soon, cherie, I need you."

"I will, I promise, ma petite."

"Au revoir, cherie, I do love you" she whispered.

"And I love you too" he replied before hanging up and sighing, wondering why his life was so complicated.

Michel sat on the bed and watched the television until almost six o'clock. He was just about to have a shower when there was a knock at the door.

"Entre" he called, hoping to see the statuesque Madame Veron enter, but a tall, dark haired young woman in a white raincoat stepped into the room.

"Monsieur Michel Ronay?" she asked.

"Oui, Madame."

She closed the door and looked about the room for a moment.

"I am Evette Ricard, your contact" she said and Michel smiled.

"Bon, Madame."

"It's Mademoiselle, I'm not married because I'm dedicated to my work" she said in a firm tone.

"I'm pleased to hear it."

"Now, I don't know what Gendarme Gerrard has told you about 'Operation Snake'."

"Not a lot."

"Bon, the less you know the safer you will be."

"That's a comfort."

"But everything revolves around you now" she said, her eyes glinting with excitement.

"Really?"

"Oui, your accident on the autoroute was heaven sent…"

"So everyone keeps telling me" interrupted Michel.

"Now, I will call back for you at about eight o'clock, then we will go to a little bar that Montreau owns and enter separately, then you will pick me up and take me to dinner…"

"This sounds good so far" interrupted Michel.

"Then we will go to Montreau's night club, the 'Jardine Bleu' on the Avenue Foche" she said.

"Bon."

"There you will be seen to play roulette and loose."

"I can do that easily."

"You will ask for credit and if you get it, lose it."

"If I don't get it?"

"Make a fuss, you'll be watched because Montreau already knows who you are."

"How?"

"We suspect moles in the Lyon Gendarmerie."

"Mon Dieu!"

"He is aware that you helped arrest Claude Salvator…"

"I see."

"And as Montreau is planning to muscle in and take over the Salvator's business in Marseille, he will see you as a useful, but expendable pawn, in the process."

"I'm so pleased for him" said Michel sarcastically.

"He is a dangerous man, mon ami."

"How do you know all this?"

"My sister, Nicole, works for him, she's a stripper at the club" replied Evette.

"Bon, I look forward to meeting her."

"You will meet her, when I say so, Monsieur."

"Oui."

"I'll be back at eight, so get ready for a night out and make sure you've got plenty of cash" she said before she disappeared from the room. Michel slumped back on the bed and thought that this undercover work was proving to be very agreeable, although he did not know what he was supposed to do to bring Montreau to justice, but he was sure that Evette would tell him over dinner. Luckily, he had the money that Eloise gave them, as well as the substantial sum that he had taken from his Bank Box in Marseille before the ill fated trip to Le Touquet. He hummed in the shower as he thought that perhaps the accident was heaven sent after all.

It was just after eight when Evette arrived back to collect him. She was still wearing her raincoat, but her hair and makeup were exquisite and Michel drew in his breathe when he saw her. They left the hotel and drove in her white Renault through the busy streets of Lyon to Toni's Bar in the Rue Napoleon. She parked some distance away and said "you go in and buy a drink for yourself and I'll join you in a while, make sure you sit at the bar."

"Right."

"I've got to make a phone call, so don't get impatient, and when you see me, make sure you act like a man hoping to pick up a woman for the night" she said seriously.

"I can do that" he replied.

"Bon, now go, mon ami."

"Please call me Michel."

"Non, it's best that we remain distant in case you get killed, now go!" Michel went pale and left the Renault in a worried state, nearly colliding with a passing Citroen as he crossed the road.

Inside Toni's Bar the usual early evening drinkers were well settled and through the smoke filled atmosphere Michel could make out several empty bar stools and he selected the one at the end of the high, glass topped bar.

"Bonsoir, Monsieur" said the young barman with a smile and a polka dot bow tie.

"Bonsoir, a scotch, s'il vous plait."

"Oui, Monsieur, with ice?"

"Oui, and better make it a double."

"Oui, Monsieur." Whilst the young man was attending to his scotch, Michel glanced around the bar. Nothing or no-one unusual caught his attention, except for a thick set, bald man, sitting alone at a corner table. Michel thought the man glanced at him more than once. The double scotch with tinkling ice was placed on the bar before him and he paid the barman before taking a good sip of the golden liquid. He just placed the glass down when he was aware of a female standing next to him. He glanced at the young woman as she asked "looking for some company, Monsieur?" His mind went into overdrive and he scrambled through all the unfortunate possibilities that this impromptu meeting would have on the planned pick up of Evette.

"Possibly" he said slowly. She smiled and asked "don't you mean probably?"

"Possibly" he fenced.

"Well, could you buy me a drink whilst you make up your mind whether it's probable or possible?"

"Oui, what will you have?"

"Martini, dry, s'il vous plait" she replied and Michel nodded to the attentive bar man.

"I'm Michel, Mademoiselle."

"Please to meet you, Michel, I'm Christine" she smiled. He looked at her carefully, she was about thirty, attractively dark haired, brown eyed and with a large pouting mouth. She smiled easily and obviously was a working girl. The Martini was placed in front of her and she picked it up, raising the glass to Michel said "cheers, mon ami."

"Cheers."

"Now if I sit beside you, I can listen carefully whilst you tell me all about yourself" she said as she wriggled up onto the bar stool next to him. Michel wondered how to get rid of her before Evette showed up. For the first time in his life he wanted the woman he was due to meet, to be very late! He was in a quandary and thinking fast he decided to offer Christine money to leave him for the moment and come back later.

"Look, ma petite, I've got to meet someone soon and…"

"I'm an embarrassment" she interrupted.

"Oui, I'm afraid so."

"It's the story of my life, I mean, when do I ever get a break?"

"I don't know, but here's a little something for you and if you'll come back later…"

"When?" she asked as she took the Bank note from him.

"Say about eleven, I should be free, and I will certainly need some company then" he smiled. She nodded and downed the rest of the Martini in one swallow, then kissed him on his cheek before sliding off the stool and making for the door. As Christine went out, Evette came in and Michel breathed a sigh of relief. She approached the bar with her coat undone, revealing a red, satin dress and a black choker around her neck. She looked very lovely and Michel could not take his eyes of her as she stood the other side of the bar stool, vacated by Christine. Evette looked straight ahead and ordered a glass of white wine from the bar man, who smiled at her before hurrying to pour the wine. She paid him and sipped at her glass before turning slowly round and surveying the drinkers seated at tables in front of her. She totally ignored Michel and he was unsure what to do next, but he noticed the thick set, bald man in the corner watching them both. Michel decided to let her finish her drink then casually offer to buy her another. He was sure that would work, so he relaxed and kept glancing at her in between sips of his scotch. He timed it nicely, because as Evette finished her drink he did the same and was about to ask her if she would like to join him in another, when a dark haired young man suddenly appeared and sat on the vacant bar stool between them.

"Mon Dieu" whispered Michel to himself.

"So, Mademoiselle, why are you all alone?" asked the young man.

"Because I'm just waiting for the right person to come along, Monsieur" she replied.

"Well, here I am, now what will you have to drink?"

"White wine, s'il vous plait" she replied.

"Barman, another white wine and a Brandy, s'il vous plait."

"Oui, Monsieur."

"I'm Pierre, Mademoiselle, and you are?" asked the young man.

"Evette" she replied.

"Ah, Evette, a lovely name for a lovely woman" said Pierre, Michel winced at that and wondered how he could get rid of the stupid man. The drinks were placed in front of them and they smiled and said "cheers" before they raised their glasses.

"Now, I can believe that you're really waiting for someone" said Pierre.

"Oui, but how did you guess?" she smiled.

"You're too attractive not to have a man chasing you."

"Well, your half right…"

"Go on."

"I am waiting for someone…" she began and Michel wondered what was coming next.

"Who is the lucky man, anybody I know?" asked Pierre.

"It's a woman, her name is Nicole" said Evette.

"Oh" said a surprised Pierre.

"Oui, you see, I'm a lesbian, and I hate all men with a passion!"

"Mon Dieu!" exclaimed Pierre.

"You're all the same, scheming, sex mad bastards who don't give a toss about anyone but yourselves, so I think you're wasting your time with me, don't you?" she asked in a firm tone.

"Oui, oui, I think I am" he replied nervously and Michel smiled and gazed at his empty glass before him.

"So, Pierre, now that you know, are you going to stay and buy me another drink or piss off and try to get into some other poor, unsuspecting woman's knickers tonight?" she asked with venom.

"I think I'll go" he stammered as he slid off the bar stool and hastened towards the door. Michel smiled and looked at Evette who glanced at him and winked. Michel waited a few moments before asking "another white wine, Mademoiselle?"

"Oui, merci Monsieur" she smiled and sat on the stool next to him. Michel nodded at the surprised barman and said "a white wine and another scotch, s'il vous plaît."

"Oui, Monsieur."

"Well, that was quite a show" whispered Michel.

"It always works with stupid men" she replied and Michel wondered if she was a lesbian. Perhaps Nicole, the stripper, was not her sister, he mused. The barman placed their drinks on the bar and Michel paid him before they said "cheers".

"We're being watched all the time, so keep talking and make me laugh" she whispered.

"Right, I will" he replied and then told her about being trapped on the boat at Boulogne as well as other events in Le Touquet. Evette laughed easily and Michel had the impression that she was genuinely amused by his stories. Several drinks later she said "it's time we went to dinner."

"Bon, I'm starving" he replied and they made their way out of Toni's Bar a little unsteadily, under the watchful eye of the thick set man in the corner.

Bistro Romaine in the Boulevard Chavre, was a delight and an example of all that is best in French cuisine. The interior was warm, inviting and with a Romanesque theme that consisted of busts of Caesars in lit alcoves, draped in red velvet, giving it an atmosphere of quiet sophistication. They were shown to a small, candle lit table in an alcove where the attentive waiter took Evette's coat, revealing her stunning red dress before placing the menus on the table. They sat down and Michel could not take his eyes of the attractive police woman in front of him. They perused the menus and Evette decided on a starter of Moules Marinières followed by Boeuf Bourguignon, Michel ordered Crevettes and Tournedos Rossini. He then ordered the House Burgundy, always safe in the very heart of the region. He smiled at Evette and relaxed, thinking that there were some positive upsides to undercover work, especially as it was all being paid for by the police in Marseille, with the promise of a reward on top. Michel wondered how much 'considerable' was and smiled to himself.

"When we have finished here, we must go straight to the Jardine Bleu" she said.
"Right."
"Now, you know what you have to do?"
"Oui, play the tables and loose."
"Oui."
"Then what?"
"Cause a fuss, make a complaint, say the wheel is 'rigged' anything you like…"
"Mon Dieu, that's a bit dangerous isn't it?"
"Oui, but it'll get you noticed and in front of Montreau" she replied and Michel suddenly felt distinctly nervous.
"If I live" he whispered as their starters arrived.
"Courage, mon brave" she smiled and he tried to return a smile but all he could manage was a nervous grin. During the meal, he told her more silly stories about his experiences as a taxi driver in Marseille, which helped him relax and made her laugh frequently. Then, for sweet, Evette ordered a lemon sorbet and Michel had a pear belle Helene. After coffee she looked at him with a glint in her eye and said "now, to the Jardine Bleu on police business!"

CHAPTER 2

As Evette drove through the busy streets in her Renault to the Jardine Bleu, she told Michel more about the club.

"On the ground floor is the bar and restaurant, upstairs is the gaming room and above that are the offices of the manager, Maurice Gabon and Conrad Montreau."

"Right."

"In the basement there's a strip club, strictly members only…"

"Is that where your sister, Nicole, works?" interrupted Michel.

"Oui, now when we get there, we'll have a few drinks at the bar and then go up to the gaming room where you'll play roulette."

"Oui."

"How much have you got to gamble?" she asked.

"I've brought ten thousand Francs and thought I'd play a thousand Francs a time" replied Michel.

"Bon, and for how many times?"

"Perhaps six or seven" he replied.

"Bon, that will be about right, then, when you've lost it all, you'll have to complain."

"Okay."

"Then, hopefully, you'll be taken up to see Monsieur Gabon."

"What about Montreau?"

"If you argue enough, Gabon will hand you over to Montreau."

"Why?"

"To frighten you off" she replied calmly and Michel shivered at the thought.

"What do I do then?"

"I expect Montreau will ask you questions about Salvator and you'll just have to play along and see what happens" she replied.

"If I give the wrong answers I might end up in the river."

"Possibly, but don't let that negative thought hamper your determination to bring Montreau to justice" she said firmly.

"Mon Dieu! What am I doing?" he whispered just as they pulled up outside the Jardine Bleu.

"Working for the police" she replied as she switched off the engine.

The outside of the building was floodlit and looked impressive as well as expensive. The sign in blue fluorescent lights on the façade announced to passers by that this was the Club Jardine Bleu, in all its glory. They climbed the marble steps to the imposing doors that were opened for them by a large man in evening dress. He wished them 'bonsoir' as they passed him whilst moving into the warm, plush interior of the club. They were greeted by another heavily built man in evening dress who welcomed them and enquired whether they intended to eat in the restaurant.

"Non, merci, Monsieur, we'll have a drink at the bar and then go upstairs, we're feeling lucky tonight" replied Michel. The man smiled, nodded and then helped Evette off with her coat. At the bar, Evette had white wine and Michel stayed with scotch. They chatted and looked around the ornate, subdued lit room with its blue drapes and semi erotic oil paintings.

"Quite a place" said Michel.

"Oui, decadent to the core" she smiled as she sipped her wine.

"But people like it."

"Oui, they do."

"Downstairs must be something special" said Michel with a grin.

"It is, but we're going upstairs tonight, so drink up" she replied. They eventually left the busy bar and made their way to the gaming room, where a smiling young man welcomed them.

"Bonsoir, Madame and Monsieur, what is your pleasure this evening?" he asked.

"I think we'll try the roulette" replied Michel.

"Certainly, Monsieur, please follow me, there's room for you on table two" he smiled and they followed him across the noisy room to the table and sat beside each other, close to the croupier, who nodded his acknowledgement.

"May I have chips for this?" asked Michel as he placed three, one thousand Franc notes on the table.

"Oui, Monsieur" nodded the croupier and placed the chips in front of Michel.

"Madams and Messieurs, place your bets, s'il vous plait" called the croupier and Michel put chips worth a thousand Francs onto red seven. The wheel was spun and Michel relaxed in the happy thought that this was police money which he had to loose, so nothing could be easier! The ball clattered for a long while before it settled.

"Rouge, sept!" exclaimed the croupier before he shunted thirty six thousand Francs worth of chips to Michel.

"Mon Dieu" whispered Michel and looked up from the pile in front of him to the very attractive woman in a low cut black dress sitting opposite. She smiled at him and heaved her substantial bosoms. He half smiled back as Evette whispered "you're not supposed to win!"

"I know, I know, I'll lose the lot now" he replied hastily.

"Madams and Messieurs, place your bets, s'il vous plait." Michel piled all his winnings on red twenty three and looked up at the woman opposite and winked. She smiled but her partner, a bald, fat man, smoking a cigar looked hard at Michel before blowing his smoke towards the surprised winner. The wheel spun and the ball clattered.

"Rouge, vingt trois!" called the croupier, Michel could not believe it, the woman opposite heaved her breasts again and Evette whispered "Michel, stop it!" as thirty six times his bet, one million, two hundred and ninety six thousand Francs worth of chips, arrived on the table in front of him.

"What can I do if I keep winning?" he whispered to Evette.

"I don't know, but just get rid of it!" she whispered back.

"Oui" he replied.

"Madams and Messieurs, place your bets, s'il vous plait." Michel put the whole pile on black thirteen, a loser for sure and glanced up at the woman opposite who then placed her chips on black thirteen as did a small dark haired man sitting next to Evette. The croupier looked at the enormous pile, shook his head and said to Michel "would Monsieur please lower his stake on black thirteen?"

"No need to, it won't win, I'm sure" replied Michel with confidence.

"But it might, Monsieur" persisted the croupier.

"Non, it stays" replied Michel. At that the croupier nodded to someone out of view, on the far side of the room and they all waited until the manager, Monsieur Gabon arrived. The croupier advised the manager of the extent of Michel's winnings so far and asked permission for the bet to go ahead. Monsieur Gabon looked grave before he nodded slowly, then the anxious croupier spun the wheel. The ball clattered for an age before it landed in black thirteen.

"Noir, treize!" exclaimed the croupier in a strangled voice. Monsieur Gabon went white, the woman opposite blushed and her breasts heaved, while Evette whispered "you fool, now look at what you've done!"

"I couldn't help it!" said Michel.

"Monsieur, I cannot allow you to place any more bets tonight" said Monsieur Gabon in a serious tone.

"Why not?" asked Michel.

"Because, Monsieur, you seem to be extraordinarily lucky" replied Gabon.

"Well I'm not usually."

"As I said, Monsieur, no more bets, and if you would care to follow me to my office I will arrange a cheque for your winnings" and Gabon gave a little bow before standing back from the table.

"Wait for me at the bar" Michel whispered to Evette and she nodded.

Michel stood up and the assembled players began to clap as he followed Monsieur Gabon across the room and through a door to a corridor with stairs that led up to his office. Michel was ushered into the imposing room, furnished with black leather seats, occasional tables and a large glass topped desk. Monsieur Gabon sat behind his desk and waved Michel to a seat opposite.

"Monsieur, as your winnings now total forty six million, six hundred and fifty six thousand Francs, I must advise you that I do not have the authority to sign a cheque for that amount…"

"I'll take in cash then" interrupted Michel with a smile. Monsieur Gabon looked pale and very serious.

"Monsieur, the only person who can authorise that amount is Monsieur Montreau, the owner of Jardine Bleu, and he will see you in a short while" said Gabon.

"Bon."

"While we are waiting, may I offer you a drink to celebrate?"

"Oui, a scotch, s'il vous plait" replied Michel, Gabon nodded and pressed a button on his elaborate telephone. Moments later a very attractive blonde in a revealing, tight fitting black dress entered the office and Gabon smiled and said "two scotches, s'il vous plait, Jackie." The blonde nodded and disappeared.

"Tell me, Monsieur, have you recently arrived in Lyon?"

"Oui, just today in fact, I had an accident on the autoroute, which closed it in both directions…"

"It seems that everything you do is on a grand scale" interrupted Gabon.

"Oui, it does."

"You will certainly be able to buy a new car after tonight's good fortune" said Gabon with a touch of menace.

"Oui" replied Michel and he began to think of a strategy that would ease the difficult situation that he was in. The amount of money that he had won was too much and he thought that Montreau would certainly try to retrieve it by fair means or foul. The blonde soon arrived back in the office carrying a silver tray with two crystal glass goblets and a petite ice bucket. Michel took a glass and she dropped ice cubes into the generous amount of scotch. She then placed the tray on Gabon's desk and left the room.

"Cheers" said Michel.

"Cheers, Monsieur, I was about to wish you good luck, but I think that would be both inappropriate and un-necessary at the moment" replied Gabon and Michel smiled. There followed an awkward silence with both men sipping their scotch and thinking. Then the telephone rang and Gabon answered it immediately and said "oui" a number of times before hanging up.

"Monsieur Montreau will see us now" he said. Michel nodded, finished his drink and then followed Gabon out of the office and along the corridor to a door at the end. The manager opened it and Michel followed him through into another corridor where two large men in evening suits stood outside another door. They nodded to Monsieur Gabon and one of them opened the panelled door to a palatial office suite. Michel marvelled at its opulence, it also was furnished with luxurious black leather chairs and settees with occasional glass topped tables. The subtle lighting gave a comfortable, relaxed feeling to the suite and Michel felt that it was hard to imagine that Monsieur Montreau was a viscous crook, until the 'Snake' glanced up from his enormous desk. His black eyes, pale face and moustache gave him a look of utter ruthlessness and Michel shivered as he tried hard to smile at the man who waved him to a seat.

"So, Monsieur, I understand you have been very lucky tonight" Montreau said with a crooked smile.

"Oui, I have."

"It is not often that we have a guest who wins more than forty six million Francs at Roulette in one evening" said Montreau.

"I'm sure."

"May I ask what you plan to do with such a large sum of money?" asked the Snake with a curl of his lip. Michel waited for a moment before he answered.

"Well, Monsieur Montreau, with your agreement, I'd like you to keep all my winnings here" said Michel. It was a master stroke and caught Montreau and Gabon completely by surprise.

"Here?" asked Montreau when he had gathered his composure.

"Oui, Monsieur, if you would kindly offer me credit to the value of my winnings then I can come to the club regularly and play Roulette until I've won some more or lost it all." The Snake looked stunned and he shook his head in disbelief but before he could reply, Michel added "of course, I'd like to dine in the restaurant each evening, drink the very best Champagne and visit your special members club in the basement." Montreau held up his hands and shook his head and smiled.

"Monsieur, you're a remarkable man" he said and Michel suddenly felt very relieved.

"I'm sure the Jardine Bleu will offer you everything that you could possibly wish for" said Gabon with a broad smile.

"Indeed it will and for a start, I think we'd better make you a life member" added Montreau.

"Bon, I'd like that" said Michel.

"Maurice, get a couple of bottles of Champagne in here, we must celebrate with our wonderful guest!" exclaimed Montreau. There is nothing more pleasurable to a gambling club owner than retaining over forty six million Francs that was thought to be lost, and Montreau showed it. As Maurice disappeared from the room, Montreau asked "I understand that you are the Marseille taxi driver that caused an unfortunate accident on the autoroute today, is that so?"

"Oui, I am the taxi driver but I did not cause the accident, that was the fault of a stupid Englishman towing a caravan!"

"Ah, the English, it's so hard to understand them" replied Montreau sympathetically.

"Oui, it is, God knows how they managed to build an empire."

"Oui, they always seem so 'vacant' when you try and talk to them, and of course, none of them speak French" added Montreau. Michel nodded as Maurice arrived back with the blonde in tow, carrying bottles of Moët Chandon and champagne flutes on a silver tray. The corks were popped, the sparkling drink poured to overflowing and Maurice with Conrad raised their glasses to the reluctant winner. It all could not have gone better for Michel and he was more than a little unsteady when he was eventually helped downstairs by one of the large men that had been standing outside Montreau's office. He managed to make his way to the bar accompanied by Maurice, and found Evette talking to the man and woman who had sat opposite them at the Roulette table. Evette was all smiles when she saw Michel.

"Ah, my hero" she said.

"Oui, I am here" nodded Michel, his words slurred.

"As I have other duties to attend to, please excuse me, Monsieur" said Gabon.

"Oui, of course, and thank you, Maurice" replied Michel and he gave a little dismissive wave of his hand.

"I wish you both a very goodnight, Madame, Monsieur" smiled Gabon and he gave a little bow before he disappeared.

"Mon brave, do tell us, did they give you a cheque?" asked the woman in the black dress, her eyes wide open with anticipation.

"Non, Madame…"

"Non?" she looked puzzled.

"They're filling a suitcase with the cash as we speak" grinned Michel.

"Mon Dieu!" exclaimed Evette as the woman and her partner's jaws both dropped in unison.

"Don't worry, ma petite, they're sending round to my hotel in the morning with an armed guard" Michel laughed and Evette did not know what to believe.

"You've had too much to drink and I think it's time we went" she said.

"Oui, take me home and let me make love to you all night long" replied Michel and Evette blushed as he put his arms around her.

"Don't be silly" she said to Michel.

"You're the silly one!" grinned the woman.

Evette ignored the remark, said 'bonsoir' to the couple and helped Michel out of the club, collecting her coat as well as the doorman on the way, to assist Michel down the steps. Evette struggled to get him to her Renault and then safely into the passenger seat. As they drove back towards Rue Benoir she asked "tell me what happened then?"

"Conrad, Maurice and me, we're like that" he said as he tried to cross his fingers and failed.

"What do you mean?".

"They think I'm wonderful, Conrad has made me a life member of the club, so what do you think of that, my little lesbian gendarme?" he asked in a slurred voice.

"Why?"

"Because, I gave the money back" replied Michel.

"What?"

"I gave the money back, well, not back actually, I asked Conrad to keep it for me and let me have it as credit…"

"That's very clever, mon ami" she interrupted.

"Oui, I know I'm clever and now you know, that means were practically married, so, let me make love to you…"

"Don't be silly" she interrupted.

"You keep saying that."

"We're on police business…"

"You sound like Gerrard" he interrupted.

"Pay attention, we have to plan what to do next, now that you've become close to Montreau."

"Oui, but I'd rather be closer to you."

"This is a heaven sent opportunity!" she exclaimed.

"I agree, so just take me to bed, will you?" he asked as Evette pulled up outside the Hotel Arnaux.

"Non, let's get you inside, mon ami."

"My name is Michel!"

They struggled up the steps to the front door, which was locked.

"Mon Dieu" whispered Michel as he pushed several times at the unyielding entrance. Evette rang the bell and eventually she heard movement before the hall light went on. Monsieur Veron peered round the edge of the door and swung it wide open when he recognised Michel.

"Monsieur Ronay" he said.

"Oui, that's me."

"I'm afraid he's been celebrating a little" said Evette as she helped Michel into the hall just as Madame Veron appeared.

"Oui, I won over forty six million Francs tonight, but I gave it all back" smiled Michel as Evette managed to get him to the foot of the stairs where Madame Veron was standing in her dressing gown.

"I think you're drunk, Monsieur" said Madame Veron.

"I know that for certain" replied Michel.

"And who's this person?" asked Madame Veron in a stern voice.

"She's a lesbian gendarme called Evette" replied Michel.

"Monsieur, I suggest you go up to your room immediately" said Madame Veron.

"Oui, I certainly will, are you coming too?" he asked. Madame Veron ignored the remark.

"Whilst you were out this evening, you had two phone calls, the first was from your fiancé, Josette, asking you to call her as soon as possible and the other was from your wife, Monique, who said that her mother has taken a turn for the worse." Michel shrugged his shoulders and looked at Evette who on hearing what Madame Veron said, released herself from the inebriated Michel.

"Bon nuit, mon ami, I'll see you in the morning" said Evette with a long face as she turned and made for the front door. At that moment the numerous glasses of double scotch mixed with champagne took their inevitable toll and Michel's balance finally gave in. He staggered back and began to sink towards the floor with his arms outstretched. Both Monsieur Veron and his wife leapt forward to save him, unfortunately Monsieur Veron missed Michel's outstretched arm but his wife caught the other one and as Michel descended to the worn carpet he dragged the full bodied blonde with him. She landed squarely on top of him in the missionary position, forcing all the air from his lungs, but he managed to gasp "kiss me now…" Monsieur Veron then stumbled to his right and fell over the bodies of his wife and the guest from room 12, twisting his ankle as he landed.

"Mon Dieu! Mon Dieu!" he exclaimed as the pain shot through his body. Evette rushed back from the door and began to pull the injured hotelier from the other bodies. She grabbed Monsieur Veron under his arms and dragged him clear as his wife attempted to kneel up from Michel. Unfortunately her right knee came up too far, rammed into Michel's private parts and he let out a scream of tortured agony.

"Oh, I'm so sorry, Monsieur" said Madame Veron before she struggled to her feet. Michel curled up into a ball and rolled to his side, whispering "oh, mon Dieu, mon Dieu…" By now the injured hotelier was sitting up and nursing his twisted ankle.

"You look after your husband, Madame, and I'll get Monsieur Ronay to his room" said Evette.

"Bon, merci, he's in number 12" replied Madame Veron now standing and surveying the two men on the floor. Evette struggled with Michel up the stairs and into his room where he collapsed onto the bed. She started to undress him but he kept trying to put his arms around her, eventually he stopped and laid down before falling asleep, wearing only his red underpants and black socks. Evette looked down at him and whispered "Monsieur Ronay, what a day you've had, an accident that closed the autoroute, causing chaos, an unbelievable win at the club, phone calls from your fiancé and wife, and all this whilst you were returning from a catastrophe in Le Touquet! It seems your whole life is a moving catastrophe and I'm not sure I'm emotionally ready for you." At that moment Michel opened his eyes and mumbled "get undressed and come to bed, cherie."

"Bon nuit, mon ami, I'll call for you in the morning" said Evette coldly before she left the room. Downstairs she wished Madame Veron and her injured husband 'bon nuit' on her way out of the hotel and drove to her apartment confused by the events of the evening. Gerrard had warned her to expect the un-expected from Michel, but she was not prepared for this level of un-expectedness!

It was mid morning when Evette arrived at the Hotel Arnaux and found Michel in the small dining room, sitting at a corner table, holding his head with one hand whilst drinking a cup of black coffee.

"Bonjour, Monsieur, how are you?" she asked as she sat at the table.

"Shh, just shh, will you, I'm still trying to recover from last night" he mumbled.

"I'm sure you'll survive, now the plans for today are…"

"I'm not going anywhere, Mademoiselle lesbian until I'm fully recovered" he interrupted.

"But, Monsieur, you're on police business, and as all the expenses are being met by the police, I must insist that you give good value for the tax payers money" she replied in a serious tone.

"You may think what you like, but I'm not going anywhere or doing anything until the room stops spinning and I've found out where they've taken my taxi" said Michel firmly.

"Right, drink up and I'll drive you to the Gendarmerie and we'll find out" she replied.

"Bon, now you must wait whilst I drink this slowly" he said.

"Of course, mon ami, you take your time" she replied in a sympathetic tone, which alarmed Michel.

"Hmm" he mumbled suspiciously. They sat quietly whilst Michel had two more cups of hot coffee, brought to the table in quick succession by Madame Veron, who informed them that her husband's ankle was much better this morning and that the swelling had gone down.

"Bon" said Evette.

"Personally, I think the whole thing could have been avoided" said Madame Veron before she left the dining room.

"Fancy being married to her" mumbled Michel.

"That reminds me, mon ami, have you phoned your wife and fiancé yet?" asked Evette with a grin as she saw Michel wince.

"Non, not yet" he mumbled.

"I suggest you do so before we leave here" she said. Michel looked up at her and said "I think you're enjoying this."

"Oh, I am, I am" she smiled and he groaned before taking another sip of coffee.

It was almost midday before Evette drove Michel to the

Gendarmerie and despite her attempts to get him to make his two phone calls, he insisted that he would leave the unpleasant chore until later, much later. At the Gendarmerie, the officer in charge of the crash investigation, consulted all his paperwork before he announced that Michel's Mercedes had been taken to Auto Peintures, S.A., on the Rue du Commerce in the zone industrie. Michel thanked him and then Evette drove them slowly to the repair shop as Michel was feeling distinctly queasy.

"You do realise, mon ami, that we've got to go back to the Jardine Bleu tonight" she said.

"Oh, non, I can't manage another night there, I'll be dead by morning" he wailed.

"Just drink sparkling water, you'll be alright" she replied.

"And what if I win again?" he asked.

"I'm sure you won't."

"You never know, so I think we'll give the Roulette a miss and just have dinner there."

"As you wish, but I think you'll arouse Montreau's suspicions if you don't play a little, remember, mon ami, he wants to see you lose all that money" she said as they pulled up outside the imposing entrance of Auto Peintures, S.A.

The receptionist was as helpful as she could be but Michel's demands to examine his taxi were met with stubborn refusals. The manager was sent for and within moments, Monsieur Jean Trouville arrived and invited them to go to his office.

"Of course, Monsieur Ronay, we can't start work on your Mercedes until your insurance company has seen the vehicle and approved our estimate for the repairs, I trust you have contacted them?" asked Monsieur Trouville with a smile. In all the excitement, Michel had forgotten to do that and he said so.

"Once you have informed them, they will send an engineer assessor and we'll agree a price for the job" said the manager.

"How long will that take?" asked Michel.

"I don't know, but as time is money, I suggest you phone them from here, who is your insurer?"

"Auto and Marine, S.A. they're in Marseille."

"Have you their number?"

"Oui."

"Please feel free to call them now" smiled Monsieur Trouville thinking of the large profit the repair bill would yield. Michel found the insurance 'help card' in his wallet and telephoned the insurers office. He told them that the repairs were very urgent as he had to get back to Marseille as soon as possible, because his mother-in-law was seriously ill and he needed to be at work as he was totally broke, stranded in Lyon. The young woman in the office was very sympathetic and promised that an engineer would call at Auto Peintures, S.A. as soon as possible. Monsieur Trouville was pleased at the news as his business had been a little slow recently.

"As soon as we get the 'go ahead', Monsieur, we'll have your taxi repaired in a couple of days at the most" said the manager.

"Bon, I'm pleased to hear it" smiled Michel.

"Your Mercedes is a popular model and I think we'll have most of the new parts in stock" beamed Monsieur Trouville.

"Merci, you've been very helpful, Monsieur" smiled Michel.

"My pleasure."

"Now, I just want to go to the car and…"

"I'm afraid that's not possible, Monsieur" interrupted the manager.

"Why not?"

"We've been instructed by the Gendarmes to hold the vehicle and that the driver at the time of the accident, that's you, Monsieur, is denied access to it until the criminal investigation is complete." Michel was stunned and he just looked blankly at the manager, before he asked "you will repair it quickly, won't you?"

"Oui, Monsieur, as I said, time is money" smiled the manager.

When they were outside the repair shop, Michel looked at Evette with a glum expression and said "another catastrophe."

"Oui, but never mind, let's go and have a bite to eat" she smiled and Michel nodded. She drove to the Café des Americain in the Rue du Plat and parked outside. The fresh coffee helped revive Michel and Evette tempted him to have a cheese baguette. After he had eaten, he began to feel a lot better and they lingered for some while in the pleasant little café, talking and laughing whilst enjoying several more cups of coffee.

"I think we'd better go somewhere in the car, park up and make plans for tonight" she said in a serious tone. Michel shrugged his shoulders and replied "okay." Evette drove her Renault out of Lyon and parked in a picnic area overlooking the river Rhone.

"You know all the little places, don't you?" asked Michel.

"Oui, I do."

"Is this where you bring your girlfriends?" he smiled.

"Mon ami, we're on serious police business and I never mix business with pleasure…"

"Alright, Mademoiselle" he interrupted.

"So, this is my plan for tonight" she began and Michel listened carefully to what Evette had to say and made up his mind that he wouldn't follow any plan but his own. He decided that, as he was the one who would be rewarded by a grateful Police Chief at the Palace du Justice in Marseille, it was going to be his show and not Evette's. When she had finished speaking she looked at him and asked "are you happy with my plan?"

"Oui, it's perfect" he replied.

"Bon."

"I just hope it works, that's all."

"Of course it'll work" she said angrily.

"Then we've nothing to worry about" he replied and she pulled a face before looking out over the river. They sat in silence for a while before Evette suggested that they return to their respective places to rest before going to the Jardine Bleu at about eight for dinner. Michel readily agreed, because although he was feeling much better, he knew that a shower and a sleep would improve his ability to remain alert during the long night ahead.

Back in his room at the Hotel Arnaux, he relaxed and was just about to get into the shower when there was a knock at the door. He called "entre" and Madame Veron came into the room, smiling.

"Madame…" he began.

"How are you feeling this afternoon, Monsieur?" she interrupted.

"Much better than this morning, merci" he replied.

"Bon, you were well past it last night" she smiled.

"Oui, I was…"

"You said that you were celebrating a win, a rather large one…" she said trying to keep the curiosity out of her voice.

"Oui, Lady luck was certainly with me at the Roulette table."
"Fortune favours the brave, Monsieur."
"Oui."
"And just how fortunate were you, may I ask?" she beamed and moved closer to Michel as he tightened his grip on the towel wrapped around his waist.

"Over forty six million Francs" he replied as he watched her blue eyes widen.

"Mon Dieu!" she whispered and Michel knew that the statuesque blonde was going to seduce him there and then.

"It was a shock for me too" he said with a smile.
"Let me give you a kiss for being…"
"So rich?" he interrupted.
"Oui, but I don't really need an excuse" she replied and lunged at him, planting her big red lips on his. He put his arms around her and the towel fell to the floor. He felt her body pushing against his nakedness before her hands drifted down over his back to his bare bottom. She squeezed his firm buttocks and said in a whisper "I'm very hot and sweaty with all the excitement, I think I'd better join you in the shower, don't you?"

"Oui, a very good idea." He stood back, watching her undress at a remarkable speed until she was down to her bra and pants, and then he went into the shower. She joined him, after dropping her underwear on the bed, and pushed her naked body against his as he turned the taps on.

"How do you like it?" he asked.
"Long and hot." They kissed as the water cascaded down upon them before she reached for the soap and began to wash his chest, then after moving downwards over his stomach, she fondled his rigid penis.

"This is très bon" she whispered.
"It certainly is, Madame."
"Call me Gabrielle" she said.
"Your husband is a very lucky man" said Michel as he soaped her breasts, squeezing the nipples gently.
"So is your fiancé and your wife" replied Gabrielle.
"True, but they don't really appreciate me" he replied.
"I know the feeling, Jacques doesn't appreciate me."
"What are we to do?" mused Michel.

"Make love and then leave them all behind and start a new life somewhere, ma cherie" she whispered.

"If only I could, Gabrielle."

"Why can't you, ma cherie?" she whispered.

"Because I've no money."

"What about you winnings?"

"I gave it all back" he replied and she looked stunned for the moment.

"You mean you lost it all?"

"Non, I gave it back to the club…"

"You fucking idiot!" she screamed as she realised that her dreams of escaping from her husband and hum drum life were disappearing down the plug hole.

"I think I've just spoilt the magic of the moment" he said with a grin.

"Oui, Monsieur, you certainly have!"

"Does this mean that we're not going to make love?"

"I've only one question for you, Monsieur."

"And what's that?"

"Are you in for dinner tonight?"

"Non, merci, I'm out…"

"With your lesbian gendarme, no doubt!"

"Oui, Gabrielle…"

"Call me 'Madame' from now on" she said as she stepped out of the shower and began drying her body. She dressed hurriedly and then stormed out of the room slamming the door. Michel smiled to himself and continued with his shower.

Evette arrived just after eight, looking fabulous in a low cut, white dress with black shoes and evening bag. Her hair and makeup were just so and her sparkling pendant ear rings added an air of sophistication to the ensemble.

"Are you ready, mon ami?"

"Oui, and may I say that you look very nice."

"One has to do one's best when on duty" she replied.

"Of course."

"Now, whilst we are talking about duty, have you called your wife and fiancé?"

'Why do some women always have to spoil everything?' thought

Michel as he shook his head and replied "non."

"They'll be worried about you" she smiled.

"Possibly."

"Then call them, I'll wait downstairs in the car, so don't be long." With that she left the room and Michel picked up the phone and dialled Josette's number, unsure of what to say to her.

"Hello."

"Josette, c'est moi."

"Oh, Michel, I've been worried about you, ma cherie, are you alright?"

"Oui, I am, and I've got good news…"

"Tell me, cherie."

"I've been to the garage today and spoken to the manager, and he said that the car can be repaired and ready for my collection in a couple of days…"

"Oh, bon."

"He said that they've got all the parts in stock and he's just waiting for the insurance 'okay' to start work."

"Oh, bon, ma cherie."

"So, I should be back home soon" he said confidently.

"That's wonderful news, ma cherie, phone me tomorrow and let me know if everything is still alright" she said.

"I will, ma petite."

"What are you going to do this evening?" she asked.

"Just have dinner and rest here in my room."

"Bon, I don't want you gallivanting around Lyon on your own, you're bound to end up in trouble!"

"Non, don't worry, after the accident, I need a lot of rest."

"Oui, as long as your resting alone, that's okay."

"I will be, ma petite."

"Call me tomorrow, ma cherie."

"I will."

"I love you, Michel."

"I love you too, Josette."

"I can't wait for us to be married" she whispered.

"Neither can I" he replied. They wished each other sweet dreams and Michel eventually put the phone down and deliberated whether to call Monique. He decided that he should, after Evette's firm instruction, and he quite liked being told what to do by a beautiful woman. This was a role reversal that he had not really experienced before and he found it quite appealing. He smiled as he dialled the number of his flat in Montelivet. Monique took some time before she answered.

"Hello."

"Monique, c'est moi."

"Oh, Michel, I've been so worried about you, what's happening?"

"Everything is alright, you've nothing to worry about."

"Really?"

"Oui, I've been to the garage today and the manager told me that the car will be repaired in a couple of days."

"Bon, that's good news."

"Oui, now, how's Mama?"

"She's still in hospital, but she seems a little better."

"Do they know what's wrong with her?"

"Non, she remains a mystery."

"Nothing new there then."

"I go in every afternoon to visit and Aunt Helene has come with me most days" said Monique in a resigned tone.

"Bon, well I'll be back in a day or two and then we can try and sort Mama out."

"Oui, I hope so, cherie."

"Don't worry, I'm sure everything will be okay."

"Oui." Then with words of love and understanding, Michel said good bye to his wife.

Evette drove through the busy streets and parked near the Club Jardine Bleu. They ascended the steps and the door was opened by the smiling man in an evening dress, who nodded his recognition of the couple.

"Another lucky night for you, Monsieur Ronay?" he asked, and Michel realised that his fame as a winner had obviously permeated to all the staff.

"Possibly" he replied with a smile as the receptionist took Evette's coat. They then went through and were greeted once again by another smiling member of staff, who informed them that a table had been reserved in the restaurant, should they wish to dine, and their places at the Roulette table were awaiting them.

"Mon Dieu, they are making a fuss" whispered Michel.

"Let's have a drink before we go into eat" said Evette and the attentive man stood to one side, gave a little bow and said "Monsieur Montreau has arranged everything for you, Monsieur Ronay, so, please make yourselves comfortable at the bar and just let me know when you wish to see the menus." Michel nodded and whispered "merci" before they made their way across to the crowded bar. As soon as they reached the two stools at the end of the bar, the very attentive young man was waiting with an eager expression on his face.

"Bonsoir, Mademoiselle and Monsieur Ronay" he said and Michel was impressed once again.

Evette ordered a white wine and Michel had a sparkling water. They sipped their drinks and Michel relaxed, knowing that he was safe in the very centre of Montreau's crooked empire. He wondered what was going to happen next as he had planned to lose a substantial amount at the Roulette table, which would undoubtedly please Conrad Montreau.

Half an hour later, after perusing the menus, they were shown to an intimate, candlelit table in the corner of the luxurious restaurant. They were positioned quite close to the stage where a four piece band played subdued and gentle music whilst a number of diners danced smoochily around a small dance floor.

"This is very nice" said Michel as he looked into Evette's eyes.

"Oui, but remember, we're on duty, mon ami" she whispered back.

"Does that mean we can't enjoy all this?"

"Only a little, our mission is the most important thing, must I remind you, that's why we're here?" Michel smiled and nodded as the waiter arrived to take their order. Evette started with melon followed by Coq au Vin and Michel had crevettes followed by Boeuf Bourguignon. He ordered a rich Burgundy and determined to drink it steadily as he did not wish to suffer another grotesque hangover. The meal was delicious and Michel watched Evette unwind, as the meal coupled with the wine, relaxed the undercover gendarme. She smiled a lot and laughed at his silly, but amusing stories about his life as a taxi driver. Her body language told him that she was quite attracted by his charm and he hoped that by the end of the evening he could convert her away from being a lesbian. Then, before the sweet trolley arrived, Michel asked her to dance and she readily accepted his invitation. The band played a lilting, slow, Gershwin tune and Michel held her close as he guided her around the floor. He felt her melting into his body and when the dance finished he kissed her on her cheek.

"You shouldn't have done that" she whispered.

"There's lots of things I shouldn't have done in my life, but I have and look where it's got me, dancing with a beautiful woman in an expensive night club!"

"You are too much, mon ami, I'm not prepared..." she whispered as the band started another slow melody and Michel held her close once again. They danced two more dances before returning to their table where, along with the impressive sweet trolley, was a bottle of Champagne in an ice bucket.

"Compliments of the management, Monsieur Ronay" smiled the waiter as he popped the cork of the Môet Chandon.

"Merci" smiled Michel as he sat down and thought 'this undercover work can be quite enjoyable'. They sipped the Champagne and then chose their sweets. Evette had a rich, chocolate gateaux covered in thick cream whilst Michel decided that a mixed fruit salad was the least fattening thing that he could see on the trolley. After coffee, Michel signed the substantial l'addition, before they left the restaurant and made their way to the Roulette tables upstairs. Monsieur Gabon was in attendance and welcomed them with smiles and bon homie. They sat at the table that gave the spectacular win the previous night and Michel requested chips to the value of a hundred thousand Francs. The croupier nodded, smiled and said "certainly, Monsieur Ronay" which surprised all the players seated at the table. Michel was enjoying his power and he realised that the other gamblers must have thought him a very wealthy man.

"Madams and Messieurs, place your bets, s'il vous plait." Michel placed chips to the value of ten thousand Francs on red twenty. The wheel was spun, the ball clattered and landed.

"Rouge, dix-huit" called the croupier and Michel smiled as his chips were gathered up. He looked at Evette, who smiled at him sympathetically at his loss, then at the blonde woman sitting opposite, who was amazed that Michel was smiling after losing so much.

"Madams and Messieurs, place your bets, s'il vous plait." Michel placed another ten thousand on black thirty. He smiled when the ball clattered into red seven, much to the surprise of the blonde opposite whose bosom began to heave as her eyes widened at his losses. Michel then lost each bet until the last one, when luck deserted him. He placed the chips on red twenty three, the ball clattered and finally stopped.

"Rouge, vingt et trois" said the croupier and Michel pretended to be happy as chips to the value of three hundred and thirty six thousand Francs were placed in front of him.

"Mon Dieu, why do I always win" he whispered as he looked at Evette, who shook her head in disbelief. The blonde opposite could hardly contain herself and said "congratulations, Monsieur."

"Merci, Madame" he replied as suddenly, Monsieur Gabon was at his side.

"Monsieur Ronay, Monsieur Montreau would like to see you for a moment, s'il vous plait" smiled the elegant manger.

"Oui, certainly, Evette, ma cherie, see if you can lose this lot before I come back" whispered Michel and Evette nodded "oui, ma petite, I'll try."

Michel was ushered into the spacious office as Montreau looked up from his desk.

"Ah, Monsieur Ronay, bonsoir, I see that you are enjoying another run of good luck this evening."

"Oui, it seems so."

"I like a man who's lucky, it inspires such confidence, don't you agree?"

"Oui."

"Please sit down, and Maurice, some Champagne, s'il vous plait." The manager nodded and left the office.

"Now, I won't keep you too long, Michel, may I call you Michel?"

"Oui, by all means."

"Bon, now, Michel, I have a little business proposition for you…"

"Really?"

"Oui, as your car is being repaired, I presume that you are free for a few days?" asked the Snake with a crooked grin. "So…. I have a close associate, a Monsieur Guy Descoyne, he's an old family friend of mine who is about to help me with some business development in Marseille…"

"That's interesting."

"Oui, and tomorrow he's coming to Lyon from Paris to see me, then he will be going down to Marseille to visit various people to discuss new opportunities."

"Bon, so what have you in mind for me?" asked Michel as Maurice returned with the blonde and bottles of Champagne.

"Something well within your capabilities, Michel" smiled Montreau as he waved to Maurice to pop the corks. The sparkling nectar of the Gods was poured into large glasses and the blonde handed the first to Michel. After 'cheers' there followed a moment of savouring the Champagne and reflection before Montreau said "I'd like you to take my spare Mercedes and drive Guy down to Marseille, with all expenses paid of course."

"Oui, I can do that" replied Michel with a smile.

"Bon, then that's arranged" nodded Montreau.

"Is there anything else you'd like me to do whilst I'm in Marseille?"

"Non, merci, Michel, just take Guy wherever he wants to go, show him some of the night life if you wish" Montreau replied airily as he waved his hand.

"I'd be pleased to" said Michel.

"I expect you'll be down there for a day or two, is that alright, Michel?"

"Oui, perfectly alright."

"Excellent, well, if you and Maurice would like to get together sometime tomorrow morning to sort out the arrangements and then I'll introduce to Guy."

"I look forward to it."

"Bon, now, I suggest you return to the Mademoiselle that you left at the table, I believe she's winning at the moment!"

CHAPTER 3

Michel returned to the Roulette table and was surprised to see Evette with an even larger pile of chips in front of her. She looked at him, shrugged her shoulders and said "beginners luck, I'm afraid, mon ami."

"Never mind, it can't be helped."

"You try now, perhaps you'll have better luck at getting rid of this lot" she whispered and the blonde opposite was shaking her head in disbelief. She turned to her partner, a white haired man with a moustache and said in a loud whisper "I think they must be so wealthy they've become mentally unbalanced, don't you, Papa?" He nodded and looked hard at Michel.

"Madams and Messieurs, place your bets, s'il vous plait." Michel put fifty thousand Francs on black thirteen and the ball landed in red twenty.

"Thank God" said Michel and then pushing the remainder of his substantial pile of chips towards the croupier, said "Monsieur, I'm not going to play anymore tonight, please credit my account with these."

"Certainly, Monsieur." They left the table and the other gamblers watched them go whilst remaining in stunned silence.

Once outside the club, Michel said to Evette "take us someplace where we can talk." She drove them to the picnic spot overlooking the Rhone without saying a word. When they were parked, she said "well?" Michel told her everything and she became more excited as he expanded on the conversation that he had had with Montreau.

"You are really something, mon ami."

"I know" he replied.

"Gerrard said you were good, but I didn't think you'd be this good!"

"Oh, I knew I would be" he replied modestly.

"You'll know all the movements and contacts that this Descoyne crook makes in Marseille, it couldn't be better!"

"True, I expect you'll tell me it's all heaven sent in a moment."

"Well, it is!"

"You're so predictable" he replied.
"That's what you think, mon ami" she whispered.
"Really?"
"Oui, I'm going to take you home for a reward session you will always remember, then if you're very good, I'll make you a coffee!"
"I do like this undercover work, it's so different somehow from the usual run of the mill" said Michel with a grin.
"Oui, it is."
"And the rewards are exceptional" he smiled as he wondered for a moment whether Evette was bi-sexual, but he dismissed the thought because he did not really care.

Her flat was quite close to Toni's Bar in the Rue Napoleon and she parked her Renault almost outside. The apartment was quite spacious but cosy and warm.
"You live here all on your own?" Michel asked as he slumped down on the sofa.
"Oui."
"Why?"
"I like it that way, I've got no-one asking me what I'm doing or where I'm going or if I'm going to be in for dinner, it suits me and I can get on with my job" she said firmly.
"Makes sense."
"And I can entertain anyone I like" she said with a smile.
"You certainly can."
"Now, what would you like to drink?"
"A scotch, Mademoiselle" he replied with a grin.
"Trés bien, I'll join you" she replied. After she had poured the scotch, they sat looking at each other from either ends of the sofa, sipping their drinks and as Michel finished his, Evette said "I'll go and get changed now."
"Into what?"
"I think you're a man who likes to see a woman in uniform" she replied with a mischievous grin.
"Oh, you know me so well."
She kissed him lightly on his cheek and left the room, returning ten minutes later in her Gendarme's uniform. She paraded up and down whilst Michel gazed at her neat, full figure.

"What do you think?" she asked.

"Very smart" he replied.

"Bon." Then she turned her back on him and dropped her skirt to the floor before stepping out of it.

"Is that better?" she asked as Michel looked at her firm bottom contained in frilly white knickers.

"Oui, much better" he replied.

"Bon, now then, mon ami, it's time for action" she said as she stepped backwards to the sofa and then bent over. Her bottom was within his reach.

"Mon Dieu" he whispered as she pulled her knickers down and said "kiss my bum and do it now, otherwise I shall arrest you under City Ordinance 213."

"And what is that?"

"Failure to obey an instruction from an officer in uniform!"

"Mon Dieu" he said as he kissed each of her soft, round cheeks.

"You are very predictable, mon ami" she said.

"Really?" he asked between kisses.

"Oui, I knew that you were going to do that when I told you to" she laughed as Michel put his hands on her hips and drew her closer. Evette then pulled away and wriggled out of her knickers before parading once again. Wearing just her buttoned up tunic and black boots she looked very desirable.

"Mon Dieu, you're gorgeous" whispered Michel.

"So I've been told" she smiled.

"Take your tunic off."

"You want me out of uniform?"

"Oui."

"Then how will I control you?"

"Easily."

"If you promise to obey me, I'll think about it."

"I promise, oh, oui, I promise!"

She stopped walking and stood in front of him whilst slowly un buttoning her tunic. Her slow, deliberate actions made him sweat. When she had undone all the buttons, she half pulled it open so he could catch a glimpse of her pert breasts. He reached up under the tunic and grabbed each breast and gently squeezed.

"Mon Dieu" she whispered.

"I've never done this to a Gendarme before" he whispered just before she opened her tunic and pulled his head to her breasts.

"And I've never done this to a taxi driver" she replied.

"There's a first time for everything" he said as he kissed her nipples. Suddenly she pulled away and pushed him backwards before straddling him on the sofa. He struggled to undo his trousers and eventually freed his rigid penis, which she guided into her moist body.

"Mon Dieu, that's so good" she said with a smile.

"It certainly is" said Michel in a whisper before kissing her.

"Now then, mon ami, push hard but slowly to begin with and wait 'til I tell you to go faster…"

"Oui, Mademoiselle Gendarme."

"Trés bien, you're getting the idea now" she giggled. Michel did as he was told and his deliberate movements into Evette brought her ever closer to the orgasm she desired. Being ordered to perform was a real turn on for Michel and he struggled to control himself. Fortunately, raw nature took over and Evette soon commanded him to go faster, which he did, until he could no longer hold back that un-stoppable release. She tightened on him and shouted "mon Dieu!" several times as he pushed himself up into her with all the force he could muster. Then, flushed and gasping, he asked "so you're not a lesbian, Mademoiselle?"

"Only sometimes" she smiled and he nodded. They disentangled themselves and were revived by several scotches before she eventually got dressed and drove him back to the hotel. They kissed in the car and then made arrangements to meet in the morning. He was glad that the hotel was still open and he did not have to ring the doorbell to get in. He collected his key from the board behind the deserted reception desk and made his way up to room 12 where Madame Veron was in his bed waiting for him.

"Oh, non" he whispered as he gazed at her, propped up against the headboard.

"Forgive me, Michel, I think I was a little too hasty in the shower" she smiled cutely.

"Nothing to forgive, Madame…"

"Call me Gabrielle, ma cherie, then I'll know that you've really forgiven me…"

"Forget all about it, Gabrielle" he smiled as he wondered how to get her out of his bed.

"A woman in love says foolish things, cherie" she purred.

"That's understandable" he nodded as he sat on the bed.

"Have you been to the Club tonight?" she mused.

"Oui, I have."

"And did you win?"

"Oui, I did" he smiled.

"Bon, then you're not broke any more" she smiled.

"Apparently not."

"That's very good news, cherie, now I think it's way past your bedtime, don't you?"

"Oui."

"So, come to bed, cherie, it's nice and warm, just like me."

"That's a very good idea" he replied, hoping for a miracle. She watched him slowly undress until he was completely naked and her eyes just widened at the prospect of having him at last, then he was saved.

"Gabrielle... Gabrielle, where are you?" called Jacques from downstairs.

"Mon Dieu! What does the silly bastard want now!" she exclaimed as she hurried out of bed, pulled on her dressing gown and made for the door.

"I'll be back later, cherie" she said as she left the room and as Michel went to close it, an elderly lady guest passed by in the corridor and turned to gaze at his naked body.

"You men are all the same, you disgust me" she said before she went on her way. Michel smiled, locked his door and went to bed. Thankfully, Madame Veron never returned and he slept soundly until the morning. As he handed his key into reception, he informed Monsieur Veron that he would be away for two nights in Marseille, but would require his room for several days after he returned. The hotelier nodded, said that his room would be reserved and he looked forward to seeing him again. Evette was waiting for him in the Renault and he gave her a quick kiss before they set off for the Jardine Bleu.

"I will stay here and keep a close eye on Montreau whilst you're in Marseille" she said.

"Bon, and let Monsieur Gerrard know that I'm bringing Descoyne on business..."

"He already knows" she interrupted.

"How?"

"I called him first thing this morning and told him everything…"

"Not everything, I hope?" interrupted Michel.

"Non, I left out last night's movements in police uniform" she giggled.

"Bon" he smiled.

"I'll make contact with you when you get back, mon ami" she said as she stopped the car outside the Club.

"Trés bien."

"Bon chance, mon brave" she said before she kissed him

Michel was shown up to Monsieur Maurice Gabon's office as soon as he arrived. The elegant manager was all smiles and arranged for coffee immediately Michel sat down opposite him.

"Monsieur Montreau will see you shortly and introduce you to Monsieur Descoyne" said Gabon.

"I look forward to meeting him" replied Michel, trying not show his concern about being in the company of a mobster for a couple of days.

"Oui, he's a very nice young man, from a good family, Monsieur Montreau has been friends with his father, Jean Descoyne for many years" smiled Gabon as the blonde arrived with the coffee. It was not long after they had finished drinking that the telephone rang and after several "Oui's", Gabon nodded and said "Monsieur Montreau will see us now." Michel followed the manager along the corridor and past the heavily built men into Montreau's office, where a tall, good looking young man, about thirty five years old, in a light grey suit stood up to greet him.

"Bonjour, Michel, let me introduce you to Monsieur Guy Descoyne, the son of a very good friend" smiled Montreau.

"Bonjour, Monsieur Descoyne" said Michel as he shook the young man's hand.

"Bonjour, Michel, I'm pleased to meet you, I've heard a lot about you from Monsieur Montreau…"

"Well, I'll try and live it down" said Michel and Guy laughed.

"Not at all, I hear that you are a very lucky man, and I like that" said Guy. Michel smiled and was impressed by the young man, it seemed that the face of organised crime was a lot more congenial than he had first supposed. Compared with the Salvator's, Guy was almost angelic.

"Now Guy, as I've told you, Michel knows Marseille like the back of his hand and he will take you to all the meetings that I've arranged" said Montreau.

"Bon."

"Michel, you'll drive my spare Mercedes and take Guy to the addresses on this list" said Montreau as he held up a piece of paper.

"Oui, Monsieur" replied Michel as he took the list.

"You've been booked into the Hotel de Paris for two nights and I expect you back after that" said Montreau.

"Oui, Monsieur."

"Everything is either on account or has been paid for in advance, and any other expenses you have, I'll reimburse you when you get back, okay?"

"Oui, Monsieur" smiled Michel.

"I'll also arrange for a reasonable sum to be credited to your account for your valuable services, Michel."

"Merci, Monsieur Montreau" smiled Michel.

The spare Mercedes was a long wheelbase limousine in gleaming black, with black leather interior and heavily tinted windows. After putting their cases in the cavernous boot, Michel slid behind the wheel and Guy sat next to him.

"Wouldn't you prefer to sit in the back, Monsieur?"

"Non, Michel, and please call me Guy, although I'm new to all this, I don't like formality."

"Trés bien, Guy, I'm sure we're going to get along just fine" smiled Michel as he slipped the automatic car into 'drive' and accelerated away towards the autoroute, his mind racing with the possibilities ahead. They chatted amiably as they sped, effortlessly, down towards Marseille, stopping at Valence for coffee and cheese baguettes at lunch time. He felt relaxed with Guy and when he asked him about the women in Marseille, Michel elaborated in great detail to the wide eyed amazement of Guy.

"Monsieur Montreau did say, when he first asked me to do this little trip, that I was to show you a good time after your business was finished."

"I'd look forward to that, Michel."

"Oui, I know a place, it's owned by my very good friend, Pierre, the girls are really lovely and they cater for all tastes" said Michel with a smile.

"How nice."

"You'll enjoy yourself at Pierre's."

"Take me there tonight after dinner" said Guy.

"My pleasure." said Michel.

It was not long before they passed the sign for Orange then Avignon and finally, Salon. Then Marseille lay before them and Michel could smell the glorious sea air as he at last drove towards his home.

"We'll book into the hotel and then I'll take you to your first appointment" said Michel.

"Bon."

Attentive porters from the Hotel de Paris rushed to take the cases from the boot of the limousine and after booking in, they were shown to splendid adjacent rooms on the first floor. Michel made himself very comfortable and planned to take full advantage of the situation over the next two days. In his room he carefully copied all the addresses from Montreau's note on to the hotel headed paper before slipping it into his wallet. He then met Guy in the afternoon café, close to the reception, where they had coffee, cream cakes and chocolate biscuits.

"My first meeting is at five" said Guy.

"That's at number 38, Rue du Aviateur" said Michel consulting the list.

"Oui, I'm meeting several people there and I expect I'll be at least a couple of hours" said Guy.

"Right, after I've dropped you, I've got to see a friend of mine, so when you're ready to be picked up, ring this number and ask for Jacques and he will know where I am" said Michel as he wrote the number of Ricky's Bar on the bottom of Guy's list.

It was just ten to five when Michel pulled up outside number 38, Rue du Aviateur and Guy slipped out of the Mercedes carrying his black leather attaché case. Michel watched him go into the house before accelerating the limousine away and into the busy traffic. He drove to the Vieux Port, then turned into Rue Bonneterie and parked on the pavement right outside Ricky's Bar.

When he entered, all the familiar sounds and smells engulfed his senses then he relaxed, feeling happy to be there. Jacques looked up and smiled broadly when he saw him, his eyes wide open with delight.

"Michel, Michel, mon ami, ça va?"
"Bonsoir, Jacques."
"Oh, you've come back to us…"
"It's only a fleeting visit" Michel interrupted.
"Mon Dieu! You're not going back to Le Touquet, are you?"
"Non, only to Lyon."
"Lyon?"
"Oui, I've got to collect my taxi when it's repaired."
"What's wrong with it?"
"I had an accident on the autoroute…"
"Mon Dieu! Are you alright, mon ami?"
"Oui, but I could with a drink…" Michel smiled.
"Oh, pardon, pardon, a brandy?"
"Oui."
"I'm so glad your home, tell me about Le Touquet" said Jacques as he poured the golden liquid for his friend.
"It was a catastrophe…"
"Mon Dieu, in that case you'd better have this drink on the house" said the barman sympathetically.
"Merci, Jacques, now before I tell you about my catastrophe, I need to make a phone call."
"Oui, bien sur, in the corridor" Jacques nodded and Michel took a sip of the brandy and left the bar. He went into the narrow corridor behind the bar and telephoned the Gendarmerie.

"Hello, Gerrard, c'est moi."
"Who?"
"It's me, Cyril."
"Who's 'me'?"
"Michel Ronay."
"Is this police business, Michel?"

"Oui."

"You must call me Monsieur Gerrard, you never know who is listening" said Gerrard.

"Of course, now, Monsieur Gerrard, can you meet me in Ricky's as soon as possible?"

"What for?"

"Why do you ask so many questions?"

"I'm a Gendarme, that's my job."

"Bon, can you come now?"

"Not really."

"I have an important document for you."

"In that case, I'll be there soon."

"Bon." Michel hung up and returned to the bar where he was greeted by Antone. The corpulent, warm hearted gay held out his arms and embraced Michel, before kissing him on both cheeks.

"Michel, mon ami, you've returned, I knew you would, I just knew it!"

"Oui, Antone, but I'm only here for a couple of days then I have to return to Lyon to pick up my car…"

"Why?"

"He's had an accident" said Jacques from behind the bar.

"Mon Dieu! Are you alright?" asked Antone.

"Oui."

"Here, let me get you a drink to steady your nerves" said Antone.

"I've already got one, merci."

"I gave it to him on the house" said Jacques.

"Bon, but I'm sure that you could do with another one" said Antone.

"Merci, Antone."

"Another brandy?" asked Jacques and Michel nodded.

"Your usual, ma petite?" asked Jacques, glancing at Antone before he poured more brandy into Michel's glass.

"Oui, of course" replied Antone and Jacques nodded.

"Now, I'm meeting Gerrard here soon…"

"You're not involved with him again, are you?" asked Antone with alarm.

"Oui, I'm undercover in Lyon…"

"Mon Dieu! After the Salvator debacle, I should have thought you'd had enough" interrupted Antone.

"True, but another crook, called Montreau is trying to take over Salvator's rackets and Gerrard saw my accident on the autoroute as an ideal opportunity to infiltrate his gang."

"I know all about Monsieur Montreau, he's a nasty bit of work and Gerrard asks too much of you dear boy" said Antone as he raised his glass of brandy and then said "cheers." Michel smiled and responded.

"Tell us about Le Touquet before Gerrard arrives" said Antone.

"It was a catastrophe from the start…"

"I knew it would be" interrupted Antone.

"Oui, you were right" nodded Michel.

"It's too far north to begin with" said Antone with authority.

"Oui, it was cold and grey."

"And the people are the same, that's because it's too near England" added Antone helpfully. Michel then told of his misadventures, exaggerating where necessary for effect, to the cries of 'mon Dieu', oh, la, la' and 'formidable' from Antone, whilst Jacques shook his head in disbelief.

"You've had a very lucky escape, mon brave" said Antone in a grave tone when Michel had finished his grim account of life in the north.

"Oui, I have."

"Is your fiancé safely back in Marseille?" asked Antone as he gestured to Jacques to pour some more brandy.

"Oui, she is."

"Bon, and is your wife pleased that you're home?"

"I haven't told her yet, but I expect she will be" replied Michel with a smile as he sipped his refreshed brandy.

"I'm sure" nodded Antone as Gerrard entered the bar.

"Ah, Monsieur Gerrard, what will you have to drink?" asked Antone.

"Bonjour, Antone, nothing thank you, I'm on duty" replied Gerrard.

"That doesn't usually stop you" replied Antone with a grin. Gerrard half smiled as he knew that he had to be careful when talking to Antone, as the corpulent man was an intimate friend of the Chief of Police, both having a shared interest in young men.

"It's serious business today, so no thank you" smiled Gerrard.

"Oh, oui, the Montreau undercover infiltration plan" said Antone in a whisper.

"Mon Dieu! That's secret!" exclaimed Gerrard.

"Quite right, and it will remain so, as only Michel, Jacques and I know about it" nodded Antone.

"Bon, I feel confident that it will remain secure as only a gay barman, his overweight lover and a Marseille taxi driver know anything that could compromise my plan" said Gerrard, with a touch of sarcasm.

"A nice cup of coffee, Monsieur Gerrard?" asked Jacques as he tried to diffuse the situation.

"Merci, Jacques" nodded the Gendarme.

"Let's sit down so we can talk" said Michel and Gerrard nodded.

"I'll bring your coffee, Monsieur" said Jacques as Gerrard followed Michel to the back of the bar where they sat in creaking wicker chairs by a small glass topped table.

"So, what have you got for me?" asked Gerrard and Michel produced the list of addresses.

"In the next two days, I've to take Guy Descoyne to these places for meetings."

"Well done, Michel, this is excellent information!" exclaimed Gerrard his eyes lighting up with delight as he perused the list.

"I haven't any names, I'm afraid…"

"It doesn't matter, I can put a tail on everyone who comes and goes as well as finding out who lives there" interrupted Gerrard.

"Bon."

"Is there anything else, Michel?"

"Non, not at the moment."

"Bon, now mind how you go with Montreau, he's very dangerous."

"Oui, so you say, but I think I've made friends with him."

"I should think so, after handing back all your winnings" grinned Gerrard.

"You know about that?"

"Oui, Evette Ricard told me this morning, a very clever move, Michel."

"I'm glad you think so, now as we're talking about money, how much is the reward for turning Montreau in?" asked Michel as Jacques arrived with the coffee.

"I can't discuss that at the moment" blustered Gerrard.

"It's my life on the line" said Michel.

"It will be substantial, I assure you."

"I hope so."

"Where are you staying?"

"The Hotel du Paris."

"Bon, I will have someone keep an eye on you."

"That's comforting."

"Oui, it's part of the service, now, another thing, I want you to bring Montreau's car into the Gendarmerie so we can search it for traces of drugs…"

"That could be difficult" interrupted Michel.

"Never mind about the difficulties, I'm relying on you, Michel."

"Oui, I know."

"We need evidence to bring a case against Montreau" said Gerrard.

"Oui."

"Remember, your reward hinges on that."

"Don't remind me."

"You've got help from Ricard, she's a very effective undercover Gendarme" smiled Gerrard.

"Oui, she is a great help" replied Michel.

"And she's quite attractive."

"I hadn't noticed" replied Michel as he sipped his brandy and Gerrard smiled.

"Are my friends the Veron's treating you well?"

"Oui, they're both very attentive, especially Madame Veron" replied Michel.

"Bon, they're good people and so content with each other."

"Oui, I'm sure." They then talked for a while before Jacques came over and told Michel that Guy had called and was ready to be collected.

"Of I go" said Michel and Gerrard nodded.

"Bring the car in tomorrow for our forensic people to check" said Gerrard as Michel stood up.

"I'll try" he replied. As he passed Antone on the way out he said "I'll be in sometime and I'll see you then."

"Oui, and bon chance, mon ami" he smiled as Jacques gave a little wave from behind the bar.

Guy was standing outside the house in Rue du Aviateur when Michel glided the limousine to a halt.
"I hope you've not been waiting too long" said Michel as Guy slipped in beside him.
"Non, only a few minutes."
"Bon, how did your meeting go?"
"Well enough for a first time" replied Guy a little anxiously.
"Bon, now back to the hotel?"
"Oui, then dinner and out for the evening" replied Guy.
"Ending up at Pierre's?"
"Oui, that's for certain!" exclaimed Guy.

In the hotel, Michel took his time and had a relaxing bath, using up most of the soaps, foams and gels placed there for guests, before getting dressed for the evening. He looked at himself in the full length mirror and thought that in his blue jacket, with white shirt, red tie and black trousers he looked like a man of substance. He reminded himself that he had won a huge sum of money at Roulette and was in line for a substantial reward, provided he could live long enough to collect it.

He met Guy in the lavish bar at eight and after a few drinks the two men went into dinner. Michel determined to spend as much of Montreau's money as he could and perused the menu for the most expensive dishes.

"I'll start with Foie Gras truffle, then Sole Meuniere and as my main course, I'll have the Tournedos Rossini" said Michel to the attentive waiter.

"Oui, Monsieur."

"That sounds very good, so I'll have the same, s'il vous plait" said Guy and the waiter nodded. From the wine list, Michel chose Cassis Rosé to start, then a full Burgundy for the main course before settling back and engaging Guy in conversation.

"Well, I hope this business trip is a great success for you" said Michel.

"Oui, so do I, but it seems that the people I've met this afternoon are a little suspicious of me and Monsieur Montreau."

"Surely not" said Michel in a comforting tone.

"I'm afraid so, Michel, not everyone is as trusting and open as you" replied Guy and Michel knew that whatever the business operations that Guy had proposed at his meeting were probably dead in the water. The Marseille mindset is peculiar to those who live there and any outsider is met with suspicion, reinforced with hostility. Michel guessed that the remnants of Claude Salvator's gang would do everything they could to keep the rackets going for themselves whilst he was in prison and Montreau would have great difficulty in taking over Salvator's business. He thought that violent confrontations as well as underhand operations were certain between the rival factions. Michel talked in a relaxed fashion and he learned a great deal about Guy and his connections with Montreau. It appeared that the Descoyne family were more than afraid of Conrad Montreau and Michel determined to do all he could to help bring the Snake to justice.

The pate with truffles was unbelievably good, the sole, with its gentle flavours, melted in the mouth and the fillet steak fell before the knife. The wine complemented the food perfectly and Michel could only manage a sorbet for sweet, whilst Guy struggled to finish an ice cream. After a glass of brandy, Guy said "I think it's time you took me to Pierre's for a little female company."

"My pleasure" Michel smiled.

"That will round the day off nicely" said Guy.

Michel parked the limousine almost outside Pierre's brothel in the Rue Charbonniere and Guy followed him in to the warm, plush interior.

"Michel, ça va?" smiled Pierre.

"Pierre, ça va?" and they put their arms around each other.

"I thought you'd gone to Le Touquet for good" said Pierre.

"Change of plan, I'm afraid."

"Oh?"

"Oui, it was a catastrophe from the start…"

"Mon Dieu! Tell me all about it…"

"Later, Pierre, first let me introduce Monsieur Guy Descoyne, a very important business man, here for a little relaxation" said Michel and Pierre shook hands with Guy.

"It will be our pleasure to see that you have a night to

remember, Monsieur" smiled Pierre.

"Merci" replied Guy.

"Now if you would like to go with Michel into the bar and order something to drink, I'll get all the available girls to parade for you" said Pierre.

"Merci" said Guy as he followed Michel into the ornate lounge with its glass topped bar, subtly lit from below. Tania, the full bosomed bar maid with a magnificent cleavage, leaned forward in anticipation and smiled. Michel ordered two brandies and Guy settled himself on a vacant bar stool.

"This is very nice" said Guy.

"Wait 'til you see the girls" whispered Michel They did not have to wait long before five scantily dressed beauties filed into the lounge and smiled at them. Christine and Nicole came over to Michel, smiled, kissed him and Christine said "I've missed seeing you so much lately, make a fuss of me first, Michel."

"Non, have me…" began Nicole.

"I'm sorry, ma petites, not tonight, I have business to attend to but take good care of Monsieur Guy, he's a very important man and a good friend" interrupted Michel. The girls looked disappointed for the moment but then turned their attentions to Guy, who was mesmerised by all the lovely young women. Michel noticed two new girls and asked Pierre in a whisper "who are they?"

"Elaine and Jacqueline, they were with Salvator, but got out and came to me after he was arrested" replied Pierre.

"You're taking a bit of a risk with Salvator's girls" said Michel.

"Possibly, but they're good and have brought quite a lot of clients with them."

"Really."

"Oui, they cater for the sado masochistic lot, you know, all leather, chains and whips" said Pierre.

"Oh, nice."

"Oui, it's amazing what some men want" said Pierre and Michel smiled. Whilst they were having their quiet conversation, Guy had made his choice.

"I think I'll spend the night here with Nicole and Christine, so you can go Michel and collect me in the morning" smiled Guy.

"Oui, of course, about ten o'clock?"

"Oui, I should be awake by then" he grinned as he put his arms around the two girls. Michel smiled and with a nod to all the girls he left the bar. Pierre followed him out into the hallway and asked "can he pay alright?"

"Oui, no problem, he's a close friend of Conrad Montreau…"

"Mon Dieu! What are you doing with him?" asked Pierre anxiously.

"I'm just driving him around for a couple of days, don't worry" replied Michel.

"I hope you know what you're doing, mon ami."

"Oui, I do."

"I hope it's not another catastrophe like Le Touquet" said Pierre.

"You worry too much…"

"And you don't worry enough!"

Michel drove straight to the flat in the Rue du Camas and after parking the limousine, rang the sonnet.

"Oui?" asked Josette.

"C'est moi, ma cherie" he whispered.

"Oh, Michel! Michel!" she exclaimed and the door clicked open. Within moments they were in each other's arms, holding tight and exchanging kisses.

"I'm so glad your back, cherie" she whispered.

"So am I."

"Have you eaten?"

"Oui."

"What did you have?" she asked and Michel wondered why women want all the details.

"Steak and a sorbet" he replied, he thought it best to minimise the meal.

"Where?"

"At the Hotel du Paris" he replied truthfully and then regretted it.

"Who with?"

"A friend…"

"What sort of friend?" she interrupted.

"A very nice gentleman."

"What's his name?"

"Guy Descoyne and he's a business associate of a friend in Lyon."

"Who's that?"

"He's someone that Gerrard knows…"

"I might have guessed!"

"Listen, whilst the car is being repaired, Gerrard asked me to just do him a little favour…"

"Michel, you're mixed up in something that's bound to go wrong, you know that!"

"Non, it's not."

"We'll wait and see, now, I suppose you're off back to Lyon?"

"The day after tomorrow, then my taxi should be ready for me to collect and I'll drive straight back here, I promise" he smiled.

"You promise?"

"I promise."

"Bon, let's have a drink before we go to bed" she smiled. They sat and drank several brandy's before they snuggled up close and made gentle love until Michel released himself into his lovely fiancé and fell into a deep sleep.

It was just after ten when Michel arrived at Pierre's place in the Rue Charbonnerie. He parked the Mercedes and rang the sonette. A woman's voice answered and he was admitted into the plush brothel, where Pierre met him in the hallway.

"Bonjour, Pierre."

"Bonjour, Michel, I'm afraid that Guy isn't here."

"What?"

"He's gone off with two of my girls…"

"Who?"

"Elaine and Jacqueline…"

"Where have they gone?"

"No idea, apparently after he had been with Christine and Nicole, the other two came into the bedroom, woke him up and persuaded him to go with them, Christine thought they were taking him downstairs into the cellar for a bit of whipping…"

"And didn't they?"

"No, they all went out somewhere."

"Mon Dieu! He's been kidnapped!" exclaimed Michel.

"That's nonsense, Michel, I expect he'll be back any minute."
"I hope so."
"I heard him tell you to be here at ten…"
"Oui."
"Come and have a coffee whilst you're waiting."
"Merci, Pierre."
"And you can tell me all about Le Touquet."
"It will be another catastrophe if Guy has gone missing… Montreau will kill me!"

CHAPTER 4

Michel sat at the bar with Pierre and told him everything about the failed business in Le Touquet. Pierre nodded sympathetically in all the right places and it was almost eleven o'clock when Michel eventually finished his tale of woe.

"You've had a lucky escape, mon ami" said Pierre.

"Oui, and I need another one now" Michel replied as he glanced at his watch.

"Guy will turn up any minute, you'll see" said Pierre reassuringly.

"I don't think so."

"Oui, he will."

"I think I'd better start looking for him, any idea where the girls might have taken him?"

"Non, not really, let's ask Christine, she may know" replied Pierre. Although anxious to help, the pretty prostitute was unable to give any helpful information to Michel, except that Elaine had told her that she had a small flat near Saint Victor's, on the hill. He then decided that he would have to enlist the help of Gerrard.

"What's Elaine's surname?" he asked Pierre.

"Duvaux, Elaine Duvaux" replied Pierre and Michel made a note on a bar pad.

"If Guy shows up, ask him to wait here, I'll give you a call in an hour or so" said Michel.

"Right" replied Pierre.

"Now I feel a bit like a mouse looking for the cat" said Michel.

He drove to the Hotel du Paris and when he collected his key from the reception, the young woman behind the desk said "Oh, Monsieur Ronay, you've had two calls this morning from Monsieur Montreau, he asked for you to call back urgently, here's his number." Michel felt his blood run cold.

"Merci, Mademoiselle, tell me, have you seen Monsieur Descoyne this morning?"

"Non, Monsieur."

"Merci" he said before he hurried to his room to collect his thoughts. He decided not to call Montreau until he had definite

67

news of Guy, he then picked up the phone and dialled Gerrard's number.

"Cyril, c'est moi."

"Is that you, Ronay?"

"Oui, you know it is."

"What do you want?"

"I need help."

"What sort of help?"

"The helpful kind."

"Ronay, are you in trouble again?"

"Just a little."

"Better tell me then" said Gerrard with a sigh.

"Descoyne has gone missing…"

"What! You've let him slip away from you?" interrupted Gerrard.

"He didn't 'slip away', he went off with two girls from Pierre Montard's in the middle of the night!"

"Where you when this was happening?"

"Home and in bed!"

"I hope for your sake this doesn't get out of hand."

"Look, I've got the name of one of the girls he disappeared with, she's Elaine Duvaux and she has a flat on the hill near Saint Victor's…"

"And you want me to waste valuable police time looking for her?"

"Oui, I do, because she'll know where Descoyne is…"

"I can't justify that" interrupted Gerrard.

"Can you give me her full address from the City records then I'll go and look for her?"

"Oh, very well, where are you now?"

"At the hotel."

"I'll call you as soon as I've got it, mon Dieu, what a mess!" said Gerrard as he hung up.

Michel waited patiently whilst he tried to gather his thoughts before the phone rang.

"Hello."

"It's Evette, mon ami."

"Oh, Evette, I would love to talk to you but I'm waiting for Monsieur Gerrard to call me back with some vital information" said Michel.

"What is it? Are you in trouble?"

"Oui, terrible trouble…"

"What's gone wrong?" she interrupted.

"I've lost Descoyne…"

"Mon Dieu! How did you manage that?"

"He disappeared with a couple of girls…"

"Men! You're all the same!" she interrupted.

"It wasn't my fault…"

"Well, if you don't find him soon, I'd better come down to Marseille and help you look."

"Non, ma petite, I'm in enough trouble already, now please go and I'll call you when I have some news."

"Alright, mon ami, phone me as soon as you can."

"Oui, I will."

"And stay away from women whilst you're on police business!" with that she hung up. Moments later Gerrard called and gave him the last known address of Elaine Duvaux. Michel then hurried to 28, Rue du Olivier, near Saint Victor's, and parked on the pavement outside the old block of flats. He glanced at the names listed on the sonette and felt elated when he saw Elaine's. He rang the sonette and waited but there was no reply so he tried three more times before he rang the sonette to Madame Defure in the flat below.

"Oui?"

"Madame Defure?"

"Oui."

"I wonder if you could help me, I'm looking for Elaine Duvaux, she lives upstairs…"

"I know where she lives, Monsieur" interrupted Madame Defure.

"Do you know where she is now?"

"Non, Monsieur, and I don't care either, au revoir…"

"Have you seen her recently?" asked Michel in desperation.

"Non, not for several weeks and neither has the landlord, so au revoir, Monsieur" with that she was gone. Michel slipped back into the Mercedes and drove to Ricky's for sustenance.

"Mon Dieu, you look awful" said Jacques.

"I feel awful."

"You need a brandy" said Jacques and Michel nodded.

"Merci."

"What's wrong?"

"I'm trying to find two women…"

"Oh, you boys, you're insatiable" interrupted Jacques with a knowing smile.

"…who have disappeared with Guy Descoyne, the friend of Conrad Montreau, who I am supposed to be looking after!" added Michel after the interruption.

"Mon Dieu! You are in trouble."

"This is true" said Michel as he sipped the brandy.

"What are you going to do now?"

"Pray for a miracle." Just then Antone walked into the crowded bar, he smiled when he saw Michel and nodded to Jacques for his usual.

"Ça va, Michel?"

"Ça va, Antone."

"You look a little downcast, why is that, mon ami?"

"He's looking for two women" said Jacques.

"Ah, not a problem that I am acquainted with, thank heaven" smiled Antone as Jacques placed his double brandy on the bar.

"Guy Descoyne has disappeared with them" said Michel.

"Mon Dieu! That is serious."

"That's what I told him" added Jacques helpfully.

"Have you started to look for them?"

"Oui, Gerrard gave me the address of one of them, Elaine Devaux, and I went to her apartment but she's not there."

"Her name rings a bell" said Antone thoughtfully.

"She was one of Salvator's girls…"

"Mon Dieu, it gets worse!" exclaimed Antone.

"It does, Montreau called the hotel twice this morning and wants to talk to me urgently" said Michel.

"Whatever you do, don't call him until you've found Descoyne" said Antone.

"I'm not going to, but Montreau wants us back in Lyon tomorrow…"

"If you've not found Descoyne by then…"

"Don't say that!" interrupted Michel.

"Then return without him and tell Montreau the truth" said

Antone.

"I can't do that."

"Listen, Michel, you're not your brother's keeper."

"I know."

"All's not lost, have you tried the hospitals?"

"Non."

"Well start with the Hospital Timone, then the others, you never know…" said Antone as Michel shook his head. He finished his brandy deep in thought and then went into the corridor behind the bar and telephoned the Hospital Timone. Guy Descoyne was not there, neither were the two girls. He tried the two smaller hospitals but all to no avail, so he returned to the smoke filled bar and ordered another brandy.

"No luck then?" asked Antone.

"Non."

"What now?"

"I'll finish this and then take Montreau's car to the Gendarmerie" replied Michel.

"What for?"

"Gerrard wants his people to search it for traces of drugs."

Michel parked the limousine in the only space available and went into the Gendarmerie. The woman seated at the reception desk phoned through to Gerrard and he appeared minutes later.

"Bonjour, Monsieur Ronay."

"Bonjour Monsieur Gerrard."

"Any sign of Descoyne yet?"

"Non, I went to Elaine Duvaux's flat be she wasn't there and her neighbour said she'd not seen her for weeks, so no luck I'm afraid."

"I expect someone connected to Salvator has got him now…"

"Oh, don't say that" interrupted Michel.

"You can be sure that the women were used to lure him away somewhere."

"Mon Dieu!"

"Face the facts, Salvator's people will try anything to stop Montreau moving in."

"Do you think they'll murder him?"

"Anything is possible, they're a ruthless bunch, so who

knows?" Michel paled at that.

"Please help me find him or I'm dead!"

"I'll do what I can, now is the car outside?"

"Oui."

"Bon, bring it round to the side entrance and I'll meet you there."

"Right" said Michel and he nodded. As he approached the Mercedes he saw that something had been placed on the windscreen and his worse fears were confirmed as he reached the driver's door. The parking ticket, under the windscreen wiper, fluttered faintly in the breeze.

"Merdre" he whispered as he slipped behind the wheel and drove the car around to the side entrance where Gerrard was waiting by the gate. The barrier was raised and he parked, at Gerrard's, direction in front of a large green door.

"Leave the keys in it and come with me" said Gerrard.

"I've got a parking ticket!"

"You've got to be very careful where you park round here" replied Gerrard.

"Well get it cancelled, will you?"

"Non, that's impossible…"

"What?"

"Impossible, no one can interfere with the parking Gendarmes, you'll have to pay the fine…"

"But I'm here on police business!" interrupted Michel.

"Oui, I know."

Michel followed Gerrard to his office, from where he phoned Pierre who told him that there was no sign of Guy Descoyne. He thanked his friend, hung up and looked at Gerrard.

"Mon Dieu, I've got to go back to Lyon tomorrow and if I don't have Descoyne with me, Montreau will kill me!"

"Non, he won't, he needs you for the moment, so you're quite safe, it's only later, when he's got what he wants, that'll he'll kill you" replied Gerrard in a matter of fact tone.

"Oh, thanks a lot!"

"Don't worry, we'll arrest him before that happens" replied Gerrard.

"I'm beginning to wish I'd stayed in Le Touquet."

"Nonsense, you're wanted here, besides, I'm sure that with all this going on you feel at home already" Gerrard smiled. Michel gave him a hard stare and asked "how long are you going to keep the Mercedes?"

"An hour or two."

"I'll come back later then" said Michel.

"As you wish."

Michel left Gerrard's office and went in search of a taxi. He decided to go home to Montelivet and confront Monique with all his news. He arrived at his flat and when he opened the door he was greeted by a wide eyed Monique.

"Ma cherie!"

"Monique, ma petite" he said as he embraced her before they kissed.

"I didn't expect to see you home so soon!"

"Non, it's a surprise."

"Oh, it is, cherie."

"I've got things to tell you…"

"Is the car repaired?"

"Oui, but it's still in Lyon, I'm going back tonight and then I'll collect it first thing tomorrow and have an early start…"

"Then you'll be home for good?"

"Oui."

"Bon, now have you eaten, cherie?"

"Non…"

"I'll get you something, now sit down, you look tired…"

"Oui, I am."

"Pour us a celebration drink" she beamed before she hurried away to the kitchen. Michel poured two scotches and slumped down on the settee and glanced around his comfortable lounge. Sometimes he wondered why he had ever left this, then he thought of Josette and knew that his life with her would be so much happier. Then, on the other hand he knew that he would have to forgo all his affairs with his obliging mistresses when he married Josette, after he got divorced from Monique, which was not going to be easy. Perhaps it would be better to stay married and just keep Josette as his very best mistress, but, he reasoned, that would not be fair, however, all's fair in love and war. He dismissed further thoughts from his mind as he concentrated on the realities of his present situation. As usual, he was up to his neck in trouble and he felt sure that it was not all his fault. Monique arrived back with two cheese and tomato baguettes.

"Here, cherie" she smiled as she handed him the plate and sat down beside him.

"Merci, ma petite."

"Cheers" she said and they touched glasses.

"Cheers."

"It's good to have you back, cherie."

"It's good to be here at last."

"Tell me about the accident" she said as he started on his baguette.

"In a minute, let me eat first" he replied through a mouthful of food.

"Oui, of course, cherie, when you've finished you can tell me all about Le Touquet and then the accident…" said Monique with a cruel smile as Michel nodded, grateful for some time to gather his thoughts to embroider the truth. After he had eaten the baguettes and had a second large scotch, he began his tale of woe. Monique listened intently, only interrupting on occasions to clarify some point or other. Michel attempted to skirt round Josette, although Monique found it difficult to believe a word he said and realising that, he amplified the dreadful experiences with Sophia Christiane when she attempted to take over their new business. Monique believed everything about Sophia, as Michel highlighted the anger that both he and Henri felt towards this over bearing woman. With her cries of 'mon Dieu, oh, la, la,' and 'catastrophe' at suitable points along the way, Michel believed that he had convinced his long suffering wife that he had made a dreadful mistake and had her sympathy. He then apologised to her before launching into his latest predicament which, although he left out some of the more lurid facts, horrified Monique.

"Mon Dieu! What will you do if you can't find this man?" she asked.

"Just tell Montreau the truth" replied Michel.

"Then what?"

"I've no idea, ma petite."

"Oh, Michel, why do you get so involved?"

"Things happen to me, that's life, ma petite."
"But it always seems to happen to you…"
"Look, was it my fault that the stupid Englishman caused an accident?"
"Non, I suppose not."
"Exactly, then when Gerrard found out about it, he took advantage of me and my situation…"
"He always does" she interrupted.
"Oui, that's true."
"Well, what are you going to do now?"
"Collect the Mercedes from the Gendarmerie and then drive back to Lyon, I suppose" he replied.
"Oh, cherie, please be careful."
"I will be, don't worry."
"I do worry and so does Frederik, Mama too…"
"Oh, oui, how is she?"
"Still the same, but if they can't find anything wrong with her today, the Doctor said they'll send her home" replied Monique.
"Bon, that's good news."
"I'm glad you think so" replied Monique firmly.
"I'll be back some time tomorrow and then we can sort things out" he smiled.

Michel phoned for a taxi then, after promises with kisses, he left his wife and returned to the Gendarmerie where the receptionist called Monsieur Gerrard.
"Did you find anything?" Michel asked.
"Non, nothing at all."
"He's a clever, devious crook then" said Michel.
"Oui, he is, but we'll get him, or rather you will" said Gerrard.
"Oui, and speaking of my imminent disaster, any news of Descoyne?"
"Non, but what do you expect? I am not looking for him… you are!"
"Why do I have to do everything?"
"Think of the reward, Monsieur Ronay" and Michel shrugged his shoulders as Gerrard handed him the keys of the limousine.
"It's where you left it" said Gerrard.
"Merci."

"What are you going to do now?"

"Kill myself before Montreau does." Gerrard laughed at that and gave him a little wave before he turned away and headed back to his office.

Michel drove round to his flat in the Rue du Camas where Josette welcomed him with kisses.

"What a day, and it's not over yet" he said as he slumped down onto the settee.

"You look tired, cherie, why don't you have a shower and lie down for a while?" she asked.

"Good idea."

"Then I'll cook something nice for dinner tonight…"

"Don't bother, ma petite, I've had enough of it today, so I'm taking you out for a very expensive meal at the Hotel du Paris" he interrupted and she just smiled.

"Bon, I'll get all dressed up then!"

They arrived at the hotel just after eight and Michel inquired if Monsieur Descoyne had put in an appearance. The receptionist shook her head and checked just to make sure, but the answer was still 'non'. The maitre d' ushered them to a romantic candlelit table in an alcove before placing the extensive menus before them. Michel gazed at his lovely fiancé and felt his love for her well up inside as he put all his fears behind him. Her dark hair was swept up in an elegant French roll and her pendant ear rings enhanced her olive skin. Her eyes glistened with her love for him and her beautiful lips pouted just a little. Her red satin dress shimmered in the candlelight as her breast heaved gently and Michel knew deep in his heart that he would have to marry her.

"What are you going to have, cherie?" she asked.

"You forever" he replied and she smiled.

"Bon, but before that, I'll start with Moules Marinières then Chateaubriand…" she said brightly.

"Perfect, ma petite, I'll join you." The waiter came and took their order before Michel perused the wine list. He chose a light rosé and then a heavy burgundy to complement the fillet steaks. They relaxed and talked of their future together and it seemed to Michel as if he was in another world of dreams and make believe.

They had Crepes Suzette to finish the meal followed by a bottle of Môet Chandon, after which, Michel could not have cared less about his return to Lyon. They drove back to their flat where Michel made love gently to his fiancé before he fell into the deepest sleep.

In the morning he felt hung over and a little nervous, but after a hot shower followed by several cups of coffee, he thought that he could face the day. He telephoned Pierre in the hope that he might have some news.

"Non, Michel, I've not seen Monsieur Descoyne."

"What about the girls?"

"They've completely disappeared too..."

"You must be concerned about them" interrupted Michel.

"Oui, I am, mon ami, I'm losing money and customers..."

"Really?"

"Oui, I've had loads of clients wanting to be chained up and whipped..."

"Mon Dieu!"

"What sort of business is it that can't satisfy its customers?" asked Pierre.

"That's not good, Pierre."

"It's ruining my reputation."

"Oui."

"I've always said that we cater for all tastes here, but at the moment, I'm failing!"

"Well, don't worry, I'm sure everything will work out in the end, au revoir, mon ami."

"Au revoir, Michel, and bon chance!"

Michel kissed and promised Josette that he would return sometime that night then he set off to the Hotel du Paris to collect his belongings. He asked at reception for Guy Descoyne but the two young women behind the desk shook their heads and Michel knew that all his hopes of finding him were disappearing fast. He went to his room and packed his clothes before returning to the reception to sign the bill. The two nights in luxury rooms plus the two meals had come to a staggering sum and Michel shivered slightly as he quickly scribbled his signature.

He accelerated the powerful car up La Canebiere and headed out of Marseille towards Lyon. The Mercedes was a delight to drive and he relaxed as the car built up speed on the autoroute. He put the dreaded confrontation with Montreau out of his mind and decided to call at Evette's before going onto the Jardine Bleu. He hoped that she would be able to give him some advice on what to do next. The autoroute flashed by and he made good time up to Lyon, glancing at the dashboard clock as he left the peage. It was just after two o'clock, and hopefully, Evette would be at home. He was delighted when she answered her sonette and he was quickly admitted to her cosy apartment.

"What news, mon ami?" she asked.

"He's completely disappeared…"

"Mon Dieu!"

"Gerrard thinks that someone in Salvator's mob has got him" said Michel in a serious tone.

"Well let's not panic for the moment" she replied.

"Non, but I'm worried when 'the moment' has passed."

"Look, I don't think Montreau will do anything to you… yet."

"Mon Dieu" he mumbled as he sat down on the settee.

"Let me get you a coffee."

"Merci, Evette" he said as the phone rang. She answered it and after several "oui's" she handed it to Michel, saying "it's Monsieur Gerrard for you." He took the phone and looked anxious.

"Hello, Cyril."

"We're on police business, Ronay…"

"Pardon, Monsieur Gerrard."

"That's better, now, we've found Guy Descoyne…"

"Oh, bravo Monsieur! bravo…"

"And we've arrested him…"

"Why, Monsieur Gerrard?"

"Listen carefully…"

"Oui" nodded Michel.

"This morning we received an anonymous phone call saying that Descoyne was at an address just off Le Vieux Port, so I went down there with two Gendarmes…"

"Trés bien!"

"Don't interrupt, Ronay!"

"Pardon."

"My men had to force their way into the locked apartment and we found Descoyne…" Gerrard paused for a moment.

"Oui, go on, Monsieur"

"He was naked and strapped into a leather harness which was suspended by a chain from the ceiling…" said Gerrard without emotion and Michel began to giggle.

"He was hanging, face down and gagged, about one metre above a double bed, where apparently two women, had been performing lewd and un-natural acts…" on hearing this Michel tried to suppress his laughter but failed.

"I'm glad that you find it amusing, Ronay."

"Pardon, Monsieur…"

"We believe that one of the women was Elaine Duvaux…"

"That explains everything" said Michel.

"Not quite, it seems Monsieur Descoyne was a willing party to all this un-natural behaviour as his clothes were neatly folded and had been placed on his attaché case, which contained two kilo's of heroin and a hundred thousand Francs."

"Mon Dieu!"

"So he was arrested for possession of drugs" said Gerrard firmly.

"Bon."

"But he denies the charge, insisting that he has been framed by the women, who planted the heroin and the money whilst he was chained to the ceiling."

"Why would they want to do that?" asked Michel with another giggle.

"Someone paid them to do it, Ronay."

"Why?"

"As a warning to Montreau to keep away from Marseille."

"Was he hanging there for long?" asked Michel, anxious to have all the details.

"Oui, ever since he was lured there by the women."

"Mon Dieu!"

"The neighbour, down stairs, heard a muffled noise every so often when he tried to shout for help, but she thought it was the plumbing…"

"That's understandable" said Michel sympathetically.

"Now you can face Montreau with confidence and tell him that his friend is in police custody and will remain there until the examining judge has heard the case against him."

"Bon, it seems I've been saved" said Michel with relief.

"Only for the moment, Ronay, now put Gendarme Ricard back on the line, I need to speak with her."

"Certainly, Monsieur." Michel handed the phone to Evette before he sank back into the settee, relieved and happy.

Evette spent some time talking to Gerrard but Michel was unable to get the gist of the conversation, anyway, he was so relieved that he did not care, as long as Gerrard's plans no longer involved him. He decided to return the limousine immediately, inform Montreau of Descoyne's arrest, then hopefully collect his taxi from the repairers and drive back to Marseille.

He looked at Evette and thought that an 'au revoir' dinner date with her would be nice before he returned to the comparative tranquillity of life in Marseille. She finished the call and smiled as she hung up.

"Well, it's all good news, mon ami."

"Oui, it certainly is" he smiled.

"Descoyne has been found, bon, now, the next part of the plan to incriminate Montreau is…"

"I don't think you should tell me" he interrupted.

"Why?"

"Because I've done my part, I'm finished…"

"Nonsense, mon ami, we're relying on you to…"

"Non, ma petite, I'm going back home as fast as possible!" he interrupted.

"We think that Montreau will want to use you to…"

"Never mind what you think or what he wants, I'm finished playing this dangerous game…"

"Monsieur, you're on police business…"

"Not anymore! Gerrard can keep the reward and Montreau, my winnings!"

"You're in too deep to leave now" she said firmly.

"I'm likely to end up dead soon and I'd rather stay alive."

"Why don't you just wait and see what Montreau says when you tell him about Descoyne?"

"I know what he'll say…"

"Non, you don't, you might be pleasantly surprised." Michel thought for a moment and reasoned that as he had to face the Snake, it might be to his advantage to keep his options open, at least for the time being. Evette made coffee for them and they sat and talked until it was almost four o'clock when Michel felt he was ready to face Montreau. With a promise of dinner with Evette at the Bistro Romaine, he set off to the Jardin Bleu in a confident mood.

Conrad Montreau fixed his black eyes and said "Guy is now in police custody?"

"Oui, Monsieur" replied Michel.

"How did that happen?"

"He was set up by two women who used to work for Salvator."

"Mon Dieu! We must do something quickly."

"Oui, Monsieur."

"Now, Michel…"

"I'm so sorry that this has happened, Monsieur" interrupted Michel.

"It's not your fault, if Guy had stayed with you then all this could have been avoided" said Montreau and on hearing that Michel felt very relieved.

"Tell me everything that you know" said the Snake and Michel went into great detail with enthusiasm, embellishing his never ending search for Guy, giving it his absolute dedication, so much so, that he failed to return Montreau's telephone calls. When he had finished, the Snake nodded and remained silent for a few moments.

"This is what we'll do" he said in a menacing tone and Michel waited anxiously as he did not care for the 'we'll do' part.

"You will return to Marseille tomorrow with my notaire, Monsieur Raphael and two of my staff…"

"But, Monsieur, I'm sure that you don't need me to…" interrupted Michel.

"I certainly do need you!"

"Bon."

"I'll make plans for Raphael to get Guy released and my staff will pay visits to certain people to find out who is responsible for what has happened."

"Right."

"Now, as you were instrumental in the arrest of Salvator, you must be well known to the police" said Montreau with a curious smile.

"Oui" Michel nodded.

"I'd like you to try and get close to them, infiltrate if you will, find out what you can about what's been going on since Salvator's arrest" said Montreau and Michel smiled at the thought of being a double agent.

"Oui, I'll try, Monsieur."

"Bon, now come back tomorrow at mid day and I'll introduce you to Monsieur Raphael, give you a list of addresses as well as fifty thousand Francs for your service" beamed Montreau.

"Merci, Monsieur, you're very generous."

"So my friends tell me."

"I'll see you tomorrow then."

"Au revoir, Michel."

Evette was all smiles when Michel told her what had transpired.

"You see, mon ami, I was right!"

"Oui, but you don't know what's going to happen next" he said.

"Oui, I do."

"What then?"

"We can start the next part of the plan…"

"Oh, non!"

"Oh, oui" she smiled and began to outline the action that Gerrard had decided would bring the Snake to justice. Michel half listened whilst wishing he was on the beach at Le Touquet with Sophia Christiane. When Evette had finished, he half nodded and suggested that they drive to Auto Peintures, S.A., to see if his taxi had been repaired, as he was anxious to have his Mercedes back, in case things went wrong.

After they arrived at the body repairers and the receptionist was unable to give any information regarding the taxi, so Monsieur Trouville was summoned.

"Ah, Monsieur Ronay…"

"Oui."

"I'm afraid there's been a slight delay" beamed the manager.

"Why?"

"We've started the repairs of course, stripped all the damaged panels off your taxi…"

"Go on, s'il vous plait" said Michel as the manager hesitated.

"I'm afraid that we're now in the hands of others, Monsieur."

"What others?"

"Well for a start, the Mercedes dealer in Lyon hasn't got all the parts we require and has had to order them from Germany…"

"Mon Dieu!"

"Secondly, the Gendarmes are still examining your taxi, now and then."

"What do you mean 'now and then'?"

"As we stripped the vehicle down they came and examined some parts and told me to call them when I had stripped some more, it seems that your taxi has been repaired many times by somewhat unorthodox methods…" Michel sighed and shook his head when he remembered all the scrapes he had that were repaired by Jean Gambetta in his dusty garage.

"So this could be a long job?"

"I'm afraid so, Monsieur Ronay."

"I'll call you in a day or so, Monsieur Trouville."

"Very good, Monsieur, and I hope by then I have some more positive news for you."

Michel drove Evette back to her flat and arranged to collect her for dinner at eight. He then went to the Hotel Arnaux, where Madame Veron was delighted to see him and gave him the key to his room. He slumped onto the bed and promptly fell asleep until he was wakened by the telephone.

"Hello."

"Michel, c'est moi, cherie" said Monique.

"Ah, ma petite, I was asleep…"

"Oh, pardon, cherie…"

"It's alright, I've got to get up now" he replied.

"Bon, are you coming home tonight?"

"Non, ma petite…"

"Oh" she sighed with disappointment.

"The car's not finished yet, but I will be in Marseille tomorrow with some business people and I'll see you sometime…"
"Bon, make it in the afternoon as Mama is coming home from the hospital in the morning."
"Right, I will."
"I'll see you tomorrow, cherie."
"You will, au revoir, ma petite."
"Au revoir."

Michel showered and dressed slowly, all the while thinking and planning what to do next. He decided eventually, to let the situation develop as it may and he would just go with the flow whilst trusting that everything would come right in the end. He was a survivor, he had to be on the dusty streets of Marseille, so he felt confident that he would come out on top. On his way out of the hotel, he told Madame Veron that he would not be back that night as he had to return to Marseille on business for a few days. She looked disappointed but promised to keep his room for him.

Evette looked beautiful in a tight fitting black dress with a deep cleavage. Her makeup and hair were perfect, and as Michel kissed her, the perfume she was wearing invaded his senses.
"I wish all the Gendarmes in Marseille looked like you."
"I expect you do" she laughed.
"But unfortunately they all look like Gerrard!" he said and she laughed some more before giving him a quick kiss.
"Take me to dinner, I'm starving" she smiled.

The Bistro Romaine in the Boulevard Chavre was very busy but the maitre d' managed to find them a candle lit table for two in an alcove between the busts of Caesar and Augustus.
"I feel very relaxed tonight" said Michel as they perused the menus.
"Bon, I'll see if I can relax you some more later, now what are you going to have to eat?" she replied with a smile and Michel knew that he would be sleeping at her flat tonight.
"I think the crevettes followed by Coq au Vin, and you?"
"Crevettes and then Carre d'Agneau, mon ami…"
"I wish you'd call me 'Michel'" he said firmly.

"It's best that we don't get too friendly" she replied in a serious tone and Michel laughed.

"In case you hadn't noticed, we're having an affair and I'd call that very friendly!" he said.

"That's different" she replied and Michel raised his eyes towards the ceiling sure in his own mind that he would never understand women.

"Are you ready to order, Monsieur?" asked the waiter, which put a stop to further conversation.

"Oui" Michel nodded.

The meal was delicious and fulsome, the red wine complemented the meal satisfying them both. A sweet of sorbet for Evette and ice cream for Michel were the perfect end to a good dinner.

"Now it's time for bed" smiled Michel and she nodded coyly. It was outside the restaurant that the evening turned sour. Underneath the windscreen wiper of the limousine was an envelope, which made him apprehensive. Michel slipped behind the wheel clutching it and with the interior light he saw that it was addressed to 'Monsieur Conrad Montreau'.

"What shall I do?" he asked Evette.

"Open it…"

"But it's addressed to Montreau" he replied.

"Never mind, just open it, you can make up some story when you give it to him tomorrow" she said firmly.

"Mon Dieu! I'm going to end up dead!"

"We all will eventually, mon ami" she said as he opened the letter and read it out aloud.

"Monsieur Montreau, the little escapade with your man, Descoyne, is a warning that you disregard at your peril, keep away from Marseille and concentrate on your business in Lyon and leave well alone, we know every move you make and have friends in high places who can destroy you, we have eyes on you every hour of the day and night, You have been warned."

"Mon Dieu" whispered Evette.

"This is going to get very serious" said Michel as he started the car.

When they arrived at Evette's flat they sat drinking brandy in a melancholy mood. A threatening letter found on your parked car, even if not directed at you, had a sobering influence on one's joi de vivre and certainly reduced a man's ardour. So, after a lengthy discussion on what might happen next, they went to bed where neither of them was inclined to be amorous.

It was exactly mid-day when Michel was shown into Montreau's office and a grey haired, middle aged man in a dark suit stood up as Montreau smiled.

"Bonjour, Michel."
"Bonjour, Monsieur."
"I'd like you to meet Monsieur Raphael, my notaire."
"Monsieur" smiled Michel and shook hands with the nervous looking man.
"Monsieur Raphael will go to Marseille with you to sort out the little local difficulty over Monsieur Descoyne and the Gendarmerie" Montreau smiled.
"Oui, of course" nodded Michel.
"And Pierre along with George, will accompany you" said Montreau as he pushed a button on his elaborate phone. Moments later two men entered the office and nodded to Montreau, who then introduced them to Michel. Pierre had a feminine tone of voice which reminded him somewhat of Jacques, whilst George just grunted.
"I have a list of addresses for you, Michel, and I want you to take Pierre and George to each one in order" said the Snake as he handed Michel the list.
"Oui, Monsieur."
"You've all been booked into the Hotel du Paris, where you will stay until I decide that everything I want done has been accomplished satisfactorily, is that understood?" asked Montreau firmly. They all nodded whilst Michel felt horribly trapped and decided then to give Montreau the warning letter found on the limousine.
"This is for you, as promised, Michel" and the Snake handed him a white envelope.
"Merci, Monsieur, and this is for you" he replied as he handed the opened letter to the Snake.
"What's this, Michel?"
"I found it last night under the windscreen wiper of your

Mercedes, Monsieur."

"It's been opened…"

"My mistake, Monsieur." Montreau read it, then smiled and whispered "we shall see." Michel felt relieved and half smiled back at Montreau.

"Nothing too serious then, Monsieur…"

"Non, Michel, nothing I can't handle… so off you go, mes amis, and bon chance!" said Montreau.

As Michel slipped behind the wheel of the limousine, Pierre joined him in the front and as he moved to fasten his safety belt, Michel saw a gun in his shoulder holster. After he had fastened the belt he looked at Michel and smiled.

"There, I'm all strapped in and ready for anything" Pierre said in his feminine voice. Michel smiled, nodded and thought 'just what I need now, a gay gunman!' He looked in the rear view mirror and observed the anxious looking notaire, clutching his brief case.

"Ready, Monsieur Raphael?"

"Oui."

"George?"

"Oui."

"Bon" said Michel as he started the engine and accelerated away from the Jardine Bleu. He wondered if he would ever actually return safely to Marseille for good.

CHAPTER 5

The limousine glided effortlessly down the A6 autoroute to Marseille and it was just before five o'clock that Michel stopped outside the Palace du Justice.

"I hope that I will not be too long, Monsieur Ronay" said Raphael.

"Very good, Monsieur, do you want us to wait for you?" asked Michel.

"Non, merci, I suggest you go to the hotel and book in, I'll phone you there as soon as I've arranged for Monsieur Descoyne to be released" replied the notaire.

"Oui, Monsieur" nodded Michel as Raphael slipped out of the Mercedes and made his way up the steps to the grand entrance. Michel then drove to the Hotel du Paris where they booked in and Michel was horrified to find that he was sharing his room with Pierre, who smiled coyly at the news.

"There, Michel, isn't that nice?" Pierre said in a whisper that sent a shudder down Michel's spine.

"Certainly is" he replied. Monsieur Raphael would also be unpleasantly surprised to discover that he was sharing with George, 'a clash of intellects there', thought Michel. Apparently, Guy Descoyne had been booked a room to himself, so obviously Conrad Montreau was certain that he would be released from police custody immediately. Michel waited in the hotel lounge for the call from the notaire whilst the other two wandered about aimlessly. He was anxious to let Gerrard know that Montreau had sent two of his 'staff' to make inquiries around Marseille as well as giving him the list of addresses. His chance came when the receptionist called him to the desk to take a call.

"Oui, Monsieur Ronay speaking…"

"Monsieur, it's me and I'm ready to be picked up from the Palace du Justice" said Raphael.

"Bon, I'll be there in ten minutes, Monsieur" he replied and hung up. He then dialled Gerrard's number.

"Oui?"

"Cyril, it's moi…"

"Monsieur Gerrard s'il vous plait, we're on police business…"

"Oui, Monsieur."

"What is it, Ronay?"

"I'm at the Hotel du Paris with two of Montreau's men and a list of addresses, I think there's going to be trouble…"

"Nothing new there then" interrupted Gerrard.

"Do you want this list?"

"Oui, make a copy and leave it with Jacques at Ricky's, I'll pick it up later" replied Gerrard.

"Right, and tell me, have you released Descoyne?"

"Non, despite Monsieur Raphael's protests, he's staying in custody until the examining judge has reviewed his case."

"When will that be?"

"No idea, but if I have my way, as long as possible" replied Gerrard.

"Bon."

"Keep in touch, Ronay, au revoir" said Gerrard and he was gone. Michel, with smiles and charm, got the receptionist to photo copy the list and give him an envelope upon which he wrote Gerrard's name. He then drove to the Palace du Justice where Raphael was waiting at the top of the steps. As he got into the back seat of the Mercedes, Michel asked, in a surprised tone "where is Monsieur Descoyne?"

"They won't release him yet" replied the notaire anxiously.

"Why not?" asked Michel as he accelerated away into the evening traffic.

"Oh, just legal formalities that you wouldn't understand" replied Raphael in an offhand tone.

"Well I hope Monsieur Montreau will understand when he phones tonight to speak to Monsieur Descoyne…"

"What?" asked the notaire anxiously.

"A room has been booked for Monsieur Descoyne tonight…"

"Mon Dieu!" whispered the notaire.

"And by the way, I'm sharing a room with Pierre and you're sharing with George" smiled Michel, then he added "isn't that nice?" as he glanced in the rear view mirror at the unhappy man in the back seat.

"Oui" mumbled Raphael. They drove on in silence for a while and then Raphael asked "how did you come to be involved with Monsieur Montreau?"

"It was an accident on the autoroute" replied Michel.

"An accident?"

"Oui, it wasn't my fault, a stupid Englishman lost control of his caravan and swerved out in front of me…"

"Mon Dieu."

"Then as a result of me crashing into the back of that, the whole autoroute had to be closed and Paris was cut off…"

"So how did you meet Monsieur Montreau?"

"As I was stuck in Lyon until my car was repaired, I went to the Jardine Bleu and won a lot of money at the Roulette table" replied Michel.

"May I ask how much?" asked Raphael and when Michel told him, he let out a gasp before whispering "mon Dieu."

"So, Monsieur Montreau told me that I was very lucky and when I said that I didn't want to take my winnings…"

"What?" interrupted the notaire.

"I asked him to keep my winnings as credit so I could play the tables whenever I wanted" said Michel.

"A very wise decision, Monsieur" said Raphael.

"Oui, I thought so at the time."

"It probably saved you from a horrible fate."

"Oui, I understand that Monsieur Montreau is not a good loser…"

"That is correct, Monsieur, and believe me he can change his mood very quickly if things don't suit him."

"Oui, I'm sure" said Michel as they arrived at the hotel. Raphael sat silently for a few moments and then asked "do you think that Pierre or George would mind if one of them changed rooms and we shared?"

"No harm in asking" replied Michel, who was relieved at the suggestion. However, when it was put to Pierre, he would not agree and his reason was that it would be going against Monsieur Montreau's orders. He had a sly smile when he was saying that and Michel suspected the real reason was that he wanted to be with him. He shuddered once again at the thought of it but as he planned to stay with Josette, on the pretext of some urgent family crisis, he relaxed and smiled when he imagined Pierre's later disappointment. Michel telephoned Monique and told her that he would be along later to see her and Mama. She was happy to hear him but was a little annoyed when he said he would be having dinner with the business men at the hotel. Michel was determined to spend as much of Montreau's money as possible and expensive dinners at the hotel were one of the most satisfactory ways of doing that. They enjoyed a very substantial dinner and afterwards Pierre asked Michel to show them around Marseille for a little taste of the night life.

"I'd like to, but I've had a message from my wife that her mother has just arrived back from hospital and I really must go home tonight" replied Michel. Pierre was disappointed, George could not have cared less and Raphael looked relieved.

"But I'll tell you what I can do…" Michel began.

"What?" asked Pierre.

"On my way home, I'll drop you off at Ricky's Bar, where my friend, Jacques is the bar man and his close friend, Antone, is always there and I know that they are just the people to tell you all the right places to go to in Marseille" said Michel with a smile.

"Bon" smiled Pierre. George said he would watch television in the lounge whilst Raphael informed them that he had a lot of paperwork to do and would be in his room if anybody wanted him. Michel reminded the notaire to expect a phone call from Monsieur Montreau, at which Raphael paled visibly.

Michel drove to Ricky's and introduced Pierre to Jacques in the busy, smoke filled bar. After ordering drinks, Michel spotted Antone at a table, reading a paper, and wandered over to him, leaving Pierre at the bar engrossed in conversation with Jacques.

"Bonsoir, Antone." On hearing that the great man lowered his paper and smiled when he saw Michel.

"Bonsoir, mon ami, ça va?"

"Oui, ça va, merci."

"Are you finally back from Lyon now?" asked Antone.

"Non, not yet."

"In good time then."

"Oui."

"Sit down and let me get you another drink" said Antone.

"Non, merci, I can't stop…"

"Why?" asked Antone.

"Have to get home to see the mother-in-law, she's just out of hospital."

"Oh, dear, nothing serious I hope?"

"Non, I think it was trapped wind" replied Michel.

"Ah, always a problem."

"Now, I've brought two of Montreau's men and a notaire down from Lyon, I've told Gerrard…"

"That's one of them at the bar, I take it?" interrupted Antone as he gazed in that direction.

"Oui, his name is Pierre and he's carrying a gun…"

"How un-necessary" said Antone.

"Exactly, now, Gerrard is coming in later to collect this list from Jacques, I don't want Pierre to see me giving it to Jacques, so will you give it to him after I'm gone?" said Michel as he handed the letter to Antone.

"Oiu, bien sur" smiled Antone.

"And keep an eye on Pierre if you will" said Michel.

"Oui."

"He shouldn't go far."

"Why?"

"Because he's gay and by the look of him, he fancies Jacques!"

"Mon Dieu! I'll have to go over and break that up!" exclaimed Antone and Michel nodded.

"Oui, you do that."

"Are you coming back later to pick him up?"

"Oui, in a couple of hours" replied Michel as he glanced at his watch.

"Bon, and don't leave it any longer."

"I promise" smiled Michel. On his way out of Ricky's he told Pierre that he would be back for him about eleven o'clock and the gay gunman replied that he need not hurry as he was very happy to spend time with his new friend. Michel smiled and left the bar.

Arriving at his flat in Montelivet Michel was kissed and hugged by Monique, then by his step son, Frederik and finally, Mama.

"It's so good to see you, Michel, I've been worried about you" said Mama as she waved her handkerchief in front of her face for air.

"No need to worry any more, Mama, I'm back in Marseille for good" Michel replied as he sat down on the settee next to her.

"What would you like to drink, cherie?" asked Monique.

"A scotch, ma petite."

"Bon, and Mama?"

"I'm too ill to drink, I'm afraid" Mama replied.

"Not even a little celebration one?" persisted Monique.

"Well, just a little brandy then."

"Bon."

"I've been in hospital, you know, Michel."

"Oui."

"They couldn't find anything wrong with me, the Doctors said that I was a medical mystery…"

"You've always been a mystery to me, Mama" interrupted Michel and the old woman smiled as Monique handed them their drinks before they toasted Michel's return.

"What's Le Touquet like?" asked Frederik.

"It's a terrible place and my going there was a catastrophe!"

"That bad?"

"Oui, it's cold, the people are un-friendly and it's too near England for my liking" said Michel.

"What about the business with Henri?" asked Mama.

"A complete failure…"

"Mon Dieu" she whispered.

"Oui, I'm just glad I'm out of it" said Michel.

"Did you lose much money?" asked Mama.

"Non, luckily, Henri managed to cover all the start up costs from his shoe shop business and said he could put the losses against tax."

"A lucky escape then, Michel."

"Oui, Mama."

They sat drinking and talking until Michel looked at his watch and informed them that he had to return to the hotel where he would be staying for a few days until he returned to Lyon with the businessmen. He promised to see them every day, then with kisses he said 'au revoir' and left the flat. He hurried round to his other flat in the Rue du Camas and was greeted by Josette with kisses and relief.

"I have to collect a business man from Ricky's and take him to the hotel and then I'll be back, ma petite" he said.

"Why can't he take a taxi?" she asked.

"Listen, he's one of Montreau's men and I'm supposed to be looking after him…"

"Mon Dieu!"

"I'm going against his instructions by not staying at the hotel tonight, ma petite" said Michel as he kissed her quickly.

"You promise that you're coming home later?"

"I promise" he smiled.

"Bon, what d'you want to drink before you go, cherie?"

"Pour me a large scotch, ma petite, it's been a bit of a day" he sighed as he slumped down on the settee.

It was a quarter past eleven when he swung the limousine into the Rue Bonneterie and saw the crowd outside Ricky's Bar. He stopped the Mercedes, double parking it before hurrying in to Ricky's, where he pushed his way through to the bar. A white faced Jacques looked at him and said "oh, Michel, I'm glad you're here at last…"

"What's happened, Jacques?"

"The ambulance has just taken him away…"

"Who?"

"Pierre…"

"Mon Dieu!"

"We're all shocked…" said Jacques.

"What happened to him?"

"He fell into the harbour…"

"What?"

"He isn't drowned…"

"Thank God…" whispered Michel.

"Unfortunately he fell onto a boat…"

"Is he badly hurt?" asked Michel.

"Oui, apparently he screamed loudly…"

"Mon Dieu!"

"You see, Roger said that he fell about four metres onto a little speed boat…"

"Mon Dieu!"

"And he landed on the outboard motor…"

"How did he manage to fall into the harbour?"

"Well, he drank quite a few scotches and then went out for a breath of air to wait for you, Roger, one of the taxi drivers waiting by Le Vieux Port saw him stagger about and then fall in…"

"Mon Dieu! Where have they taken him?"

"To the Hospital de Timone."

"Merci, Jacques…"

"Antone is with him" said Jacques as Michel raced out of the bar and slipped behind the wheel of the limousine. He drove quickly to the hospital and parked close to the Accident and Emergency entrance. When he hurried into the reception he saw Antone sitting there, pale faced.

"I'm afraid it's serious, Michel" said the great man as he stood to meet him.

"Mon Dieu! How serious?"

"He fell onto a little boat and has done some terrible damage to his leg…"

"Mon Dieu, what do the Doctors say?"

"Nothing yet, they've only just taken him in and stopped him screaming…"

"Why does everything happen to me?" asked Michel in a whisper.

"You! Pierre's the one in agony in there!" exclaimed Antone.

"Oui, I know, but the problems this is going to cause for me, you can't imagine" said Michel.

"Anything to do with Montreau is going to cause problems."

"True."

"There's nothing we can do now except wait to find out how serious his injuries are" said Antone.

"Oui."

"Then you'll have to let Montreau know what has happened to his man."

"Mon Dieu" whispered Michel. They sat quietly for some time before a Doctor came out and spoke to them.

"Are you relatives of this man?" asked the Doctor.

"Non, I'm a business acquaintance and this Monsieur was at the scene of the accident" said Michel.

"Can you inform his next of kin?"

"Oui, through the office in Lyon" replied Michel.

"Please do it as soon as possible" said the Doctor.

"Is he going to be alright?" asked Michel in a worried tone.

"Oui, I'm sure he'll make a full recovery… eventually."

"Eventually?"

"Oui, it appears that he's sustained a compound fracture to his femur but we won't know the extent of the damage until we've x-rayed him…"

"Mon Dieu."

"And possibly he's injured his pelvis, in any event, we'll have to operate and pin his leg…"

"Is this going to take long?" interrupted Michel.

"Normally a person with this type of injury is in hospital for about three weeks before they can go home" replied the Doctor.

"So he'll be off work for a while then" said Michel.

"Oui, possibly three or four months, depending on what his job is, of course" replied the Doctor.

"Of course" nodded Michel.

"Contact his next of kin then I suggest that you both go home, there is no point in you staying here" said the Doctor.

"Right" replied Michel.

"If you call tomorrow about mid morning, I'll be able to give you some more information on how he is progressing."

"Merci, Doctor."

They drove back to Ricky's in silence but once in the crowded bar they were inundated with questions. Jacques poured them both a large brandy and after a reviving sip, Antone made an announcement for all to hear.

"Tonight, as some of you may know, Pierre, a business associate of Michel's had an accident and fell into the harbour after leaving the bar to take in a breath of fresh air, unfortunately, his fall into the water was abruptly stopped by a small boat, luckily Roger Manton, saw him fall and immediately summoned help. Michel and I have been to the hospital where the Doctor has told us that Pierre has a broken leg, with multiple fractures" at which point there was a collective gasp and murmurs of 'mon Dieu' from those assembled "and he will be operated on tonight, then Michel will find out tomorrow how he is and we'll let you know of course." On hearing that there were murmurs of 'bravo'.

"Merci, Antone" said Michel before he finished his brandy and ordered another for them both.

"I suggest you go home, Michel, you look worn out" said

Antone.

"Oui, I will."

When he left Ricky's he drove to the hotel to inform Raphael and George what had happened to Pierre. He went up to their room and knocked at the door. Eventually it was opened by George who looked both sleepy and annoyed.

"What d'you want?"

"Can I come in?"

"Why?"

"Stop asking so many questions will you?"

"Who is it, George?" asked Raphael from his bed.

"Michel…"

"What's happened?" asked the notaire with alarm.

"It's Pierre, he's had an accident" said Michel as he pushed past George.

"Mon Dieu!" exclaimed Raphael.

"What's happened to him?" demanded George in a menacing tone.

"He's fallen into the harbour…"

"Is he hurt?" asked the notaire, now sitting up in bed.

"Oui, he's broken his leg" replied Michel.

"Mon Dieu" whispered Raphael.

"This is your fault, Michel…" said George.

"Non, it isn't, I wasn't even there, he'd been drinking, had too much and went outside Ricky's, lost his balance and fell over…"

"How did he break his leg?" asked Raphael.

"He landed on a small boat…"

"This is all your fault, Michel, just wait 'til I tell Monsieur Montreau!" said George.

"Oui, you can do that first thing in the morning whilst I'm at the hospital" replied Michel.

"What do the Doctors say?" asked Raphael.

"He'll be alright, it's just going to take a little while for him to recover" replied Michel.

"How long?" demanded George.

"About three weeks in hospital…"

"Three weeks! Monsieur Montreau won't like that!" exclaimed George.

"Then several months off work…" On hearing that, George looked stunned and Raphael said, in a worried tone "well, this changes everything."

"Non, we'll carry on without Pierre, and when Monsieur Montreau hears about this, he'll send someone to replace him" said George firmly.

"Bon" said Michel.

"I knew this trip down here would be a catastrophe" mumbled Raphael.

"It is for Pierre" said Michel.

"You'd better go to the hospital first thing and then come back here, I need to go to the Palace du Justice again" said Raphael in a resigned tone and Michel nodded.

"I'll leave you to get some sleep then" said Michel.

Josette was relieved to see him at last and when Michel told her about the accident, she was horrified.

"Mon Dieu, will you be in trouble, cherie?" she asked.

"Oui, I expect so…"

"Oh, non."

"Pour me a large scotch, ma petite, then take me to bed and let me sleep" he smiled.

The Hospital de Timone in Marseille is a busy, modern facility, serving the population well with care and consideration. Michel arrived the next morning and finding nowhere to park the limousine, left it close to the Accident and Emergency entrance, where the ambulances frequently arrive. After making inquiries at the reception he waited until the Doctor appeared with news of Pierre.

"It's more serious than we thought" said the Doctor.

"How serious?"

"We've operated on him and pinned his leg but we found further injury to his pelvis and have had to fix a plate there" replied the tired looking Doctor.

"What does that mean?"

"He'll be here for more than three weeks and eventually, if all goes well, he'll have to come back for further operations to remove all the metalwork that we've pinned in."

"Mon Dieu" whispered Michel.
"I'm afraid it's going to be a long job" said the Doctor.
"I see."
"Have you informed his next of kin?"
"That's being done this morning" replied Michel.
"Bon, thank you for coming in" said the Doctor and with a nod he left Michel and hurried away.

It was just as Michel was getting into the limousine that the speeding ambulance came up the access road with its siren blaring and failed to negotiate around the parked Mercedes, striking it from behind with a shattering blow.

"Mon Dieu!" shouted Michel as he heard the tinkling of glass cascading over the tarmac. The driver of the ambulance switched off the siren before leaping from the cab.

"You shouldn't have parked there, mon ami" he said as Michel stared at the rear of the damaged Mercedes. He noticed that the ambulance had hardly a scratch on its sturdy front bumper.

"Well never mind that, you hit me!" he exclaimed as the driver shrugged his shoulders and disappeared to the back of his vehicle to assist in carrying the stretcher with the new arrival into the entrance. Michel did not know what to do as he surveyed the broken rear light, the damaged bumper and the dented rear wing of the immaculate limousine. His only hope of a quick repair was with Jean Gambetta in his dusty garage in the Rue de Verdun, just off the Rue du Camas. Jean was a dear old friend of Michel's late father and ran his small garage in a slightly haphazard way, carrying out all repairs in his own time to his own satisfaction. His customers were understandably few, but loyal, and mostly late payers. It was rumoured that he was one of the richest men in Marseille, but no one knew why.

"Jean… Jean!" called Michel as he entered the dark and dusty garage.

"Oui, hello" replied Jean from under an old Renault parked in the corner.

"Jean, c'est moi, Michel."

"I thought it was you" replied Jean as he slid out from beneath the Renault. He sat up, wiped his grease covered hands on a cloth, tipped back his Breton beret and smiled.

"Oui, c'est moi" said Michel.

"I heard a whisper that you were almost back from Le Touquet" said Jean.

"Oui, almost, I've had a slight accident…"

"Another one?"

"Oui, and it's not my car or my fault" said Michel.

"Ah, let me guess, the car belongs to a woman who reversed into you whilst you were parked somewhere…"

"Non, an ambulance hit me whilst I was parked and the limousine belongs to Conrad Montreau!"

"Do I know him?" asked Jean.

"Non, but I do, and if he finds out I've damaged his car, he'll probably kill me!"

"You do exaggerate, Michel."

"Come and look at it will you?" Jean nodded and after struggling to his feet, followed Michel out to examine the Mercedes. Jean scratched his head, put his beret to the back of his head and let out a low whistle before muttering "mon Dieu" several times as he sighted along the damaged rear wing. At this, Michel began to feel deeply uneasy.

"Well?" he asked

"Could be a long job."

"Merdre."

"I don't know how you do it, but you're always in trouble with women and cars" said Jean.

"Oui, possibly, but you're here to get me out of trouble and you get paid for it…"

"Only sometimes" interrupted Jean.

"So, what can you do quickly?"

"I can order a new rear light, that should be here this afternoon, and I can fill the bumper, beat the wing and fill that, then spray some primer and a few coats of black paint, it won't be the best job in the world, but no one will know it's been damaged if you don't tell them" said Jean.

"Oh, merci, Jean, I'll bring the car back this evening…"

"This evening?"

"Oui, you can have it all night to repair…"

"That will cost you…"

"I don't care how much it costs, just do it, please!"

"Okay."

"Merci."

"By the way, where's your Mercedes?"

"It's being repaired in Lyon…"

"You know, single handedly you're keeping the auto repair industry in France ticking over nicely" Jean smirked.

"Very funny, but if you knew the trouble I was in you'd have some sympathy" said Michel.

"You're always in trouble and you always will be!"

"I'll see you later" said Michel as he slipped behind the wheel and then drove off to the hotel. He hoped that Raphael would not notice the damage at the rear of the car, but he did not have to worry as the notaire was pre-occupied with Pierre's accident and wanted the latest information to update an angry Monsieur Montreau.

"He's very annoyed at the police keeping Monsieur Descoyne in custody and upset over Pierre's accident" said Raphael from the back seat as they hurried in the traffic towards the Palace du Justice.

"Oh, dear."

"Oui, and he wants to speak to you about the accident as soon as we get back to the hotel" said Raphael.

"Right, Monsieur."

"I can tell you, Monsieur Montreau is not a happy man at the moment" said Raphael as he glanced out of the side window of the limousine.

"I'm sure."

"George has told him that we haven't visited anybody on his list yet…"

"You can rely on George to stir things up..."

"Apparently we'll have to stay here until that's been done."

"Could be a long stay then" murmured Michel as they stopped outside the Palace du Justice.

"Do you want me to wait, Monsieur?"

"Non, go back to the hotel and I'll call you when I'm ready to be picked up…"

"With Monsieur Descoyne, I trust."

"Mon Dieu, oui, I do hope so" replied the notaire as he left the car and made his way, once more, up the steps.

Michel then drove straight to Ricky's for a reviving drink.

"You look awful, mon ami" said Jacques as he poured a large scotch for him.

"I feel awful, Jacques."

"Any news of Pierre?" Michel told him the latest and just finished when Antone entered the bar. He had to repeat it all over again, with Jacques adding little points of interest. Michel asked if Gerrard had been in to collect the list and Jacques confirmed that he had done so last night, just before Pierre fell into the harbour.

"Bon" said Michel.

"And the owner of the boat, a Monsieur Cousteau, has been in here this morning hoping to find out from you where he should send his claim for the damage to his outboard motor" said Jacques.

"Oh, non" muttered Michel.

"Oh, oui, and he left this for you" said Jacques as he produced an envelope from behind the bar. Michel opened it and read the short note with Monsieur Cousteau's contact details.

"Come and sit down for a while" said Antone and Michel nodded and followed him to the back of the bar where they sat down on the creaking wicker chairs.

"I'm glad I'm back in Marseille, Antone."

"Oui, you may be back, but not out of trouble" replied Antone.

"That's true" said Michel as he sipped his scotch.

"You know, Michel, you're like a juggler with half a dozen balls in the air…"

"Really?"

"Oui, and you keep accepting more balls to juggle with…"

"Go on."

"Soon, you'll drop one or two, then you'll really be in trouble" said Antone as he sipped his brandy.

"I'm always in trouble, it seems to follow me around like a bad smell!" said Michel as a woman dressed in a cream raincoat, buttoned and belted, entered the bar followed by two young men, she spoke to Jacques before heading straight for Michel. As they got closer one of the men produced a camera and pointed it at him and then Antone, the flashes illuminated the bar.

"Monsieur Ronay?" asked the attractive woman in her thirties.

"Oui."

"We're Press reporters from the 'Marseille Citizen'…"

"What's this about?"

"We're covering the story about the failed suicide" she replied.

"What suicide?"

"Your business partner from Lyon, can you tell us, is the business in financial trouble?" she asked as the young man produced a notebook and started writing whilst the camera man positioned himself for more shots.

"You see what I mean about trouble?" asked Michel as he looked hard at Antone.

"Oui, mon ami…"

"So, your business is in trouble, Monsieur Ronay" persisted the woman as the photographer flashed away.

"Non, not at all…"

"What kind of business are you in, Monsieur?"

"I'm a taxi driver here in Marseille…"

"What about your business in Le Touquet?"

"That was a catastrophe and has now closed" replied Michel firmly.

"Did your partner follow you down here after that?"

"Non, he has nothing to do with my business in Le Touquet…"

"He's from Lyon, is that where your new business is?" she asked.

"Non, Madame…"

"Mademoiselle" she corrected.

"Pardon, Mademoiselle, er, who are you exactly?" asked Michel, anxious to gain time to gather his thoughts.

"Mademoiselle Cressant, chief reporter at the 'Marseille Citizen', Monsieur…"

"Pleased to meet you" Michel smiled and he thought 'she's more than a handful to cope with'.

"Now tell me about this business partner of yours" she said.

"Look, he's not my partner, we're not in business together, the Monsieur who had the unfortunate accident is employed by Monsieur Montreau who has a night club in Lyon…"

"What was he doing here?" she asked.

"I drove him down to Marseille because Monsieur Montreau asked me to…"

"So you work for Monsieur Montreau?"

"Just for the moment, whilst my taxi is being repaired in

Lyon…"

"You've had an accident?"

"Oui, on the autoroute, it had to be closed, you must have seen it on the television…"

"Oui, you caused that, Monsieur?" she asked, wide eyed.

"Non, a stupid Englishman caused it…"

"Is that what the police say?"

"I've no idea…"

"Now, tell me, why did this man, Pierre Chandon, want to commit suicide?"

"He didn't! He had too much to drink, went outside and fell into the harbour" replied Michel firmly.

"We have spoken to an eye witness who said that Monsieur Chandon threw himself into the harbour…"

"Who said that?" asked Michel.

"I cannot reveal my sources, Monsieur" she replied.

"I shouldn't say anymore if I were you, Michel" said Antone.

"And who are you, Monsieur?" she asked fixing her gaze on Antone..

"A person of no importance, I assure you, Mademoiselle Cressant" he replied with a smile.

"Let me be the judge of that, Monsieur" she said with a grin.

"Ah, a woman judge, how interesting" said Antone and she was not amused.

"Your name, Monsieur, just for the record…"

"Whose record, Mademoiselle?" and she blushed slightly at Antone's reply.

"I shall find out who you are" she said.

"Oui, possibly you will, and I suggest you start with your 'unrevealed sources', they are sure to know" said Antone and she realised that it was a waste of time pursuing him further so she returned her gaze to Michel.

"We understand from the hospital that his injuries are quite serious" she stated.

"Oui, that's what the Doctor told me" nodded Michel.

"What does his employer, Monsieur Montreau say about the accident?"

"I've no idea, but his notaire, Monsieur Raphael will probably know" replied Michel.

"Is he here in Marseille?"

"Oui."

"Where's he staying?" she asked and at that point Michel wished he had kept Raphael's whereabouts to himself.

"At the Hotel du Paris" he said lamely.

"Bon, we'll contact him, thank you for your help Monsieur Ronay, now if you'll just let us take a few last shots of you, we'll be on our way" she smiled as the photographer flashed away.

"Merci" nodded Michel. The Press pack were gone moments later and Michel breathed a sigh of relief as Jacques came over.

"What was all that about?" he asked.

"The silly Press asking silly questions" replied Antone.

"About the accident?"

"Oui, may we have something to eat and more drinks?" asked Antone.

"D'you know what I think…" began Jacques.

"Oh, do stop thinking, you know how it upsets you" interrupted Antone and Jacques just stared at him for a moment.

"You know, you can be quite cruel sometimes" said Jacques.

"I know, ma petite, so that's two cheese baguettes, a brandy and a scotch, s'il vous plait!"

Michel arrived back at the Hotel du Paris and waited in the lounge for the call from Raphael. He had only just sat down and began to read the paper when the receptionist called him to the phone.

"Hello, Michel Ronay here…"

"Ronay, can you tell me what the devil is going on in Marseille?" demanded Montreau as Michel's blood ran cold at the sound of the Snake's voice.

"Oh, bonjour, Monsieur Montreau, I thought the call was from…"

"Never mind that, what's happening?"

"Well, I'm waiting in the hotel for Monsieur Raphael to call…"

"Listen, Ronay, Pierre is in hospital with a broken leg, Guy Descoyne is still in custody, you've not been staying at the hotel and I've just received a ticket for parking illegally outside the Palace du Justice!"

"Oui, Monsieur…"

"So, what's going on?"

"I can explain everything, Monsieur…"

"It had better be good, Ronay, otherwise I shall come down there with some more of my staff, who are not known for their kindness, and personally sort things out!" Michel then did his best to pour oil on troubled waters but he did not manage to convince the Snake that all was well.

"Get Raphael to call me as soon as he gets back to the hotel, and he'd better have Guy with him!"

"Oui, Monsieur" replied Michel in an anxious tone.

"And stay at the hotel!"

"Oui, Monsieur."

"Your meals and accommodation are costing me a fortune and I don't want to pay for empty rooms!"

"Non, Monsieur."

"Now, is everything else alright?"

"Oui, Monsieur" replied Michel as he swallowed hard and prayed that Jean could repair the damaged limousine over night. As Antone said, he was juggling with too many balls at the moment, and Michel knew that that was uncomfortably close to the truth. As soon as Montreau had finished the call, Raphael phoned and Michel hurried off to collect him. The notaire stood alone by the kerbside as the limousine drew up.

"No luck then, Monsieur?" asked Michel as the pale faced notaire sat in the back of the Mercedes.

"Non, the Marseille police are so bloody provincial and pedantic!" he replied as Michel pulled away into the traffic.

"Now you know what I have to put up with" said Michel as he glanced in the rear view mirror at the unhappy notaire.

"Oui" he mumbled.

"Monsieur Montreau just called before I left the hotel, and he wants you to call him as soon as you get back" said Michel and he heard Raphael groan with despair.

"I think I'll leave that until after lunch" said Raphael.

"A very good idea, Monsieur" nodded Michel.

They arrived back at the hotel and had just reached reception when Mademoiselle Cressant and her men followed them in.

"Monsieur Ronay" she called and Michel, recognising the voice, turned to face her.

"Mademoiselle…"

"Is this Monsieur Raphael?" she asked with a determined smile.

"Oui, I'm Raphael, who wants to know?" demanded the angry notaire as the photographer flashed one off.

"Mademoiselle Cressant, chief reporter on the 'Marseille Citizen'" she replied.

"I've nothing to say to the Press" said Raphael as he turned away and asked for the key to his room.

"Monsieur Ronay has already given an interview about the attempted suicide of Pierre Chandon…"

"What?" demanded Raphael as he whirled round to face the smiling reporter.

"My Editor would like to have your version of events, Monsieur Raphael…"

"What have you telling these people, Ronay?" asked the notaire angrily as he glared at Michel.

"Nothing…"

"It doesn't sound like it!" exclaimed Raphael.

"Monsieur, can you tell me if Guy Descoyne will be released soon?" asked Mademoiselle Cressant with a knowing smile. Raphael looked as if he had just been hit by a Marseille tram and opened his mouth to speak as the photographer flashed off another.

"I, er, er…" he struggled for a reply.

"Does Guy Descoyne work for Monsieur Montreau?" she asked as Raphael went pale and shook his head.

"Non, he's, he's a business associate" stammered Raphael and Michel realised that there were moles at the Palace du Justice as well as those in Lyon.

"Is he innocent of the drugs charge, Monsieur?" she persisted.

"Oui, my client is totally innocent, it's all a dreadful mistake" said Raphael firmly.

"Why do you think Pierre Chandon tried to commit suicide?" she asked.

"I can assure you he didn't!"

"Were you there, Monsieur?"

"Non."

"We have an eye witness who saw everything, Monsieur."

"So?"

"Our witness states that Monsieur Chandon threw himself into the harbour and if he hadn't landed on the boat, he would have drowned."

"That's nonsense!"

"With Monsieur Descoyne and Pierre Chandon in Marseille, along with yourself and Michel Ronay, our readers will want to know if Monsieur Montreau intends to extend his business interests from Lyon to here" she said and Raphael went a light shade of green whilst Michel sweated a little. 'Bulls eye' thought Michel and wondered what ever was going to happen next as George appeared from the street outside carrying a shopping bag..

"What's going on here?" he demanded.

"It's alright, George" said Raphael.

"These people bothering you, Monsieur?" asked George.

"Non, everything is okay" said the notaire.

"Who are you, Monsieur?" asked Mademoiselle Cressant.

"None of your business!" he replied as the photographer flashed him.

"Here, give me that!" shouted George as he lunged at the man. The photographer leapt back, out of George's reach as Mademoiselle Cressant shouted "don't let him get the camera, run, Henri, run!" The man nodded and set off towards the revolving door of the hotel. He managed to get into it but before he could escape into the street, George stopped the door and trapped the unfortunate man. Cressant and her other reporter rushed to the assistance of the photographer, she grabbed George around the neck whilst her note taker held onto his legs. They both pulled as Michel joined the fray, attempting to pull Cressant off George. The photographer shouted for help from passers by outside who genuinely thought that the door had become stuck and two men and a stout lady rushed to his aid and began pushing at the revolving door to free it but George hung on grimly whilst Raphael shouted for assistance from reception. The duty manager arrived along with the two female receptionists, and whilst he shouted for everybody to remain calm, as he was uncertain of the situation, they all grabbed at someone and began pulling. Michel could see a small crowd gathering outside and more onlookers added their strength to the original threesome. The door began to creak horribly as more weight was put upon its strained mechanism.

"Call the Gendarmes!" shouted the manager to one of the receptionists, who let go of Michel's leg and hurried off.

"You'll pay for this, Monsieur!" hissed Cressant in George's ear.

"You wish" he replied. At that moment a Gendarme on normal street patrol arrived outside and quickly summed up the situation. He called for the brave rescuers to push harder as he added his weight and when they did so, George could no longer hold on. The door spun round, depositing the photographer into the crowded street whereupon the Gendarme hit him sharply over the head with his truncheon. As the disorientated man fell to the pavement, the Gendarme relieved him of his camera and held it up as the onlookers shouted 'bravo'. The brave rescuers, pushing at the door, had been catapulted into the foyer of the hotel when George let go, allowing it to spin round, and they had tumbled headlong into the struggling mass on the marble floor. Mademoiselle Cressant screamed as the fat lady fell on her and the receptionist fainted as she realised that she was about to be crushed by two men.

"Send for an ambulance!" shouted the manager as Michel tried to untangle himself from Cressant, the fat lady and George.

"I bet this is all your fault, Ronay" said George in a menacing tone.

"Non, you're wrong as usual, mon ami" replied Michel as the fat lady struggled to get up.

"Are you alright, Madame?" asked Michel as he held her hand.

"Oui, Monsieur, I think so" she replied as Cressant groaned and her note taker tried to lift her.

"Leave me, just leave me, I think I've broken my ankle" she said, her face contorted with pain.

"Mon Dieu!" said her note taker.

"Did Henri get away?" she asked.

"Non, the Gendarme knocked him down and took his camera…"

"Mon Dieu! You wait 'til I see the Chief!" she exclaimed as Michel gently extricated his leg from under her body. George got up and Raphael stepped forward.

"Don't either of you two say a word to anybody, to you

understand?" said the notaire forcefully.

"Oui, Monsieur" replied Michel as George nodded. The wailing police sirens heralded the arrival of more Gendarmes and soon everyone was being interviewed by the sergeant to establish exactly what had happened. Whilst this was taking place the ambulance arrived and the medics quickly examined Mademoiselle Cressant as well as the receptionist, before declaring that both women required hospital treatment. Willing hands lifted the two women onto stretchers and they were whisked away at lightning speed. Having listened to what the witnesses had to say, the sergeant decided to arrest George, Michel, Raphael, the note taker and the photographer. They were taken out to the large blue Renault police van and driven to the Palace du Justice.

CHAPTER 6

Once inside the Palace du Justice the miscreants were separated and taken to interview rooms where they waited for the arresting officer. When it was his turn, Michel explained exactly what had happened in the hotel lobby and left nothing out. The sergeant, after making copious notes, appeared satisfied and when the interview was over, he told Michel to wait. Within five minutes of his leaving, the door opened and Gerrard stepped into the room.

"Bonjour, Ronay" he smiled as he sat down opposite Michel.

"Is it?" asked Michel.

"Oui, it certainly is, the plan to get Montreau down here is working perfectly, I congratulate you" he smiled.

"Congratulate me?" asked Michel in a puzzled tone.

"Oui, you and Gendarme Ricard have followed instructions to the letter."

"We have?"

"Oui, and as soon as Montreau leaves Lyon with his men, Gendarme Ricard will follow on and make contact with you" said Gerrard.

"Really?" asked Michel as he realised that he was sinking deeper into the mire.

"When she arrives, you'll carry on as before and I want you to be seen around Marseille with her, introduce her as your new girlfriend…"

"But I already have a fiancé and a wife!" interrupted Michel.

"This is serious police business, Ronay, and sacrifices have to be made…"

"Mon Dieu!"

"Now, we're holding Montreau's man, George Dupres, for a while…"

"Why?"

"When he was searched just now, he was found to be carrying a gun, he hasn't got a licence for it, so, it will be tested by ballistics to see if it has been used in any criminal activity."

"Right, so how long will that take?" asked Michel lamely.

"Days, if I have my way" replied Gerrard with a smile.

"What about Monsieur Raphael?"

"We'll hold him overnight and he can talk his way out of custody tomorrow, in front of the examining judge" said Gerrard.

"And Monsieur Descoyne?"

"He's facing serious drug charges and will be held until his trial."

"Mon Dieu" whispered Michel.

"So he's not going anywhere" said Gerrard in a firm tone.

"Bon, can I go now?"

"Oui, bien sur."

"Thank heavens."

"Now, Montreau is bound to come down here once he finds out what has happened, so, be on your guard and keep to the plan, bon chance, Ronay" smiled Gerrard and he left the room.

Michel left the Palace du Justice and took a taxi back to the hotel. He decided to have a leisurely lunch in the restaurant to make up for his catastrophic morning and was just passing the reception when the young woman called out to him.

"Monsieur Ronay!" Michel turned towards the desk.

"Oui?"

"There's a call for you…"

"Merci."

"You can take it here if you wish" she smiled.

"Merci" he said and picked up the phone.

"Hello, this is Michel Ronay."

"Ronay! At last I've got one of you!" exclaimed Montreau as Michel's heart sank at the sound of his voice.

"Oui, Monsieur, I'm here."

"Where's Raphael?"

"At the Palace du Justice, Monsieur…"

"I suppose he's still trying to get Guy released" said Montreau and at this point Michel decided to tell the Snake everything that had happened, with a touch of exaggeration here and there to emphasise the predicaments of the men from Lyon.

"Non, Monsieur, he's helping the police with their inquiries…"

"What!"

"Monsieur Raphael is being questioned about George's arrest…"

"Mon Dieu! What has happened?"

"Unfortunately George was unpleasant in the hotel lobby…"
"Why?"
"He had his photograph taken and he didn't like it…"
"Mon Dieu!"
"So he trapped the photographer in the revolving door…"
"I'm surrounded by idiots!" exclaimed Montreau.
"Then Monsieur Raphael got involved and then a fight started, that's when Mademoiselle Cressant was hurt…"
"Who's Mademoiselle Cressant?"
"She's the reporter from the 'Marseille Citizen'…"
"Oh, Mon Dieu! Mon Dieu!" exclaimed Montreau and Michel thought he heard the Snake give a little sob.
"So after the Gendarmes arrived and arrested Monsieur Raphael along with George, the ambulance came to take Mademoiselle Cressant and the other injured lady to hospital…"
"What other lady?"
"The receptionist…"
"I'm frightened to ask, but what happened to her?"
"She was injured when the men, from outside in the street, forced the door open and fell on her as she was trying to stop the fight between Mademoiselle Cressant and George…"
"I don't believe this" said Montreau lamely.
"Well, I'm sure all the details will be in the 'Marseille Citizen' tomorrow, Monsieur, shall I send you a copy?" replied Michel in a helpful tone.
"Non! I'm coming down there tomorrow to sort this nonsense out!"
"Oui, Monsieur…"
"I will be at the hotel by lunchtime, see that you are there, Ronay, and be ready to drive me around!"
"Oui, Monsieur."
"And stay in the hotel until then, in case I need to speak to you!"
"Oui, Monsieur."
"Get Raphael to call me as soon as he gets back…"
"He won't be coming back today, Monsieur, he's under arrest as well…"
"What?"
"But I'm sure whenever he's released from custody, he'll call

me to pick him up and I'll give him your message." said Michel.

"What's he been arrested for?"

"Fighting, Monsieur."

"What, Raphael?"

"Oui, Monsieur, believe me it all got quite violent, even the photographer was knocked out by the Gendarmes once the door gave way…"

"Oh, Mon Dieu! Mon Dieu! Mon Dieu!"

"Was there anything else, Monsieur?" asked Michel.

"Non…"

"Then I'll see you tomorrow Monsieur, au revoir" said Michel brightly before hanging up. He then went into the restaurant and enjoyed a delicious lunch of onion soup, followed by chicken salad finishing with a sorbet, which he happily charged to his room.

After lunch, he drove the limousine round to Jean's dusty garage and after parking outside, wandered in to find his friend.

"Hello, Jean, are you there?"

"Oui, I'm over here" replied Jean and Michel made his way towards the flickering light emanating from under a large Citroen DS. He bent down as Jean's head appeared from under the car.

"I've come earlier than expected, Jean."

"So I see."

"That's because I must have the car back first thing in the morning…"

"Why?"

"Montreau is coming down from Lyon and will be here by lunchtime, that's why" replied Michel.

"I'll see what I can do…"

"Has the rear light arrived yet?" asked Michel.

"Non, but it will be here later this afternoon."

"I hope so."

"I suppose you'll want another car to drive around in whilst I'm sorting the Mercedes out?"

"Oui."

"You can borrow the rusty, but trusty, Renault as usual" said Jean.

"Merci."

"But I must warn you that something is wrong with the starter motor…"

"Can't you fix it?" asked Michel in an anxious tone.

"Non, I don't know what's wrong with it…"

"Well if you don't know, shouldn't you take it to a proper garage?"

"It's an intermittent fault and I am a proper garage!"

"If you say so" Michel smiled.

"Just make sure that when you switch off there's some people about to give you a push start if necessary" said Jean with a grin.

"Very funny."

"Come about nine in the morning" said Jean.

"Right."

"And see if you can stay away from accidents and women until then!"

"I'll try" replied Michel with a smile.

He parked the rusty Renault outside Ricky's and said a little prayer as he switched the engine off. The interior of the bar was crowded and smoke filled, several regulars nodded at him as he made his way to the counter as Jacques looked up and smiled.

"Michel, ça va?"

"Jacques, ça va?"

"Oui, the usual, mon ami?"

"Oui" nodded Michel and Jacques poured him a scotch. As he was about to drink a hand tapped him on the shoulder and he turned to see the smiling face of Rene, his best friend who lived just opposite his flat in the Rue du Camas with his statuesque wife, Yvonne.

"Rene! Ça va?"

"Oui, Michel, ça va?" and they embraced and held on to each other for a few moments.

"I heard you were back from Le Touquet…"

"Oui, I was almost home but an accident on the autoroute near Lyon…"

"Mon Dieu! Are you alright?" interrupted Rene with concern.

"Oui, but my car isn't."

"Oh, non."

"But it's being repaired, so it's okay."

"Bon."

"Oui, it was quite an accident, it closed the autoroute on both sides and Paris was cut off…"

"Mon Dieu!"

"An Englishman was the cause of it all.."

"Ah, the stupid English!"

"Oui."

"They are always a problem."

"What are you drinking, Rene?"

"A Pernod, s'il vous plait" he replied and Jacques nodded.

"So, what are you doing now?"

"Well, it's a bit complicated but I'm doing a little fill in job for Conrad Montreau" replied Michel.

"Who's he?"

"A businessman in Lyon."

"But you are back for good from Le Touquet?" asked Rene as he sipped his Pernod.

"Oui."

"Bon, I'm so pleased and so is Yvonne, she told me to say, when I met you, that she sends her love and looks forward to one of our special dinner parties" and Rene smiled as he winked at Michel.

"Give her my love and tell her that I'm really looking forward to the next one" Michel smiled as he remembered the unbridled sexual performances that he enjoyed with Rene and his wife.

"Do you remember the great time we had on the boat last August?" asked Rene with a smile.

"How could I ever forget" sighed Michel as his thoughts drifted back to their naked love making on Rene's yacht as it drifted lazily in the blazing sun.

"It seems a long time ago" said Rene.

"But a wonderful memory never fades" replied Michel.

"True, but tell me about Le Touquet" said Rene.

"It was a catastrophe and that episode is something I really want to forget!"

"Mon Dieu" whispered Rene.

"It's a long story and I'd rather tell you all about it another time, if that's okay."

"Oui, certainly."

"Perhaps I could drop by…"

"Anytime, Michel, just pop in and have a drink with us" replied Rene.

"Bon, now, I just want to call Monique and find out how her mother is…"

"She's not well?"

"Non, she's been in hospital."

"Oh, dear, nothing serious?"

"They couldn't find anything wrong with her, I think she just had trapped wind" replied Michel and Rene raised his eyebrows and murmured "ah." Michel asked Jacques if he could use the phone in the narrow passage way behind the bar and Jacques nodded his approval.

Frederik answered the phone.

"Hello…"

"Frederik, it's Papa here.."

"Oh, Papa, thank heavens you've called…"

"What's wrong?" asked Michel anxiously.

"Mama has gone with Gran Mama to hospital again…"

"When?"

"At lunchtime" replied Frederik.

"Is she ill?"

"I don't know, she just came over all peculiar."

"Right, I'll go to the hospital straight away, don't you worry now, I'm sure everything will be alright."

"Bon, Papa."

"I'll see you later, Frederik."

Michel said 'au revoir' to Rene and Jacques then prayed as he slipped behind the wheel of the rusty Renault. As it started immediately, he gave a sigh of relief and with a puff of black smoke from its exhaust, it accelerated away from Ricky's towards the Hospital de Timone.

The receptionist gave him Mama's details and he hurried through the vast hospital to her bedside. Monique and Mama were overjoyed to see him and he kissed them both before sitting by the bed.

"Thank heavens you've come, Michel, I wanted to see you one last time before I died…" said Mama.

"That's nonsense, Mama, you're not going to die" he said firmly.

"We're all going to die, it's just a matter of when and my time is now" Mama replied.

"I don't believe that" said Michel.

"I do."

"Why do you think that, Mama?"

"Because I feel all 'fuzzy' inside…"

"That's trapped wind, I often get that" he interrupted and she smiled.

"If only that was true" replied Mama.

"Now, what do the Doctor's say?" asked Michel.

"They don't know, but they're all too young to know much about anything" said Mama with disdain.

"I'm sure that's not true."

"I know that the end is near…"

"It's being so cheerful that keeps you going" interrupted Michel and Mama had to laugh as a Doctor suddenly appeared.

"How are you feeling now, Madame?" he asked.

"Not good, I think I'll be dead soon" she replied.

"I don't think so, Madame…"

"How do you know?" she demanded.

"Because I'm a Doctor, Madame, and all the tests we've done show that you are physically well…"

"Am I mad then?"

"Oui, and you always have been!" said Michel and they all laughed.

"Non, Madame, we think that you may have an anxiety neurosis that's affecting you…"

"So what's the cure?"

"Just rest and don't worry" replied the Doctor with a smile.

"Don't worry? With my family, that's impossible!" she exclaimed.

"Nevertheless…" began the Doctor.

"Can my mother come home now?" asked Monique anxiously.

"I think we'll keep her in overnight and see how she is in the morning, then all being well, she can go home" smiled the Doctor, he then nodded and went on his way. Michel sat for a while talking and making them smile before he told Monique that he had to make a phone call and he would be back soon to take her home. Then he returned to the reception and made inquiries about Mademoiselle Cressant and the hotel receptionist. He was told that the reporter had a broken ankle and was in the Madame Curie ward whilst the hotel receptionist had gone home after treatment. He entered the ward and Mademoiselle Cressant looked up at him as he approached her bed.

"What are you doing here, Monsieur?" she asked in an angry tone.

"I've come to see how you are, Mademoiselle" he replied.

"Well, I've got a broken ankle, thanks to you and that other thug!"

"I'm very sorry that you've been hurt."

"Oh, really?" she asked in a sarcastic tone.

"Oui, I really am sorry."

"But believe me, Monsieur, I can still write!"

"I'm sure."

"And that escapade in the hotel will be splashed across the front page in tomorrow's edition!"

"I'm pleased to hear it" smiled Michel.

"You're pleased?" she asked with a puzzled look.

"Oui."

"Why?"

"Because, as you say, the man's a thug."

"Isn't he your friend?"

"Non, he certainly isn't and neither is Pierre Chandon or Monsieur Raphael…"

"You amaze me" she interrupted.

"I frequently amaze people, in fact, I sometimes amaze myself" he replied.

"Well, you are a puzzle…"

"Oui, I am."

"I've been wondering who you are, and it's coming back to me now, you're the Monsieur Ronay who helped the Gendarmes arrest Claude Salvator at his father's funeral, aren't you?"

"Oui, I am that man" he beamed.

"Mon Dieu! You're the undercover agent!"

"Shh, Mademoiselle, the walls have ears."

"Oh, mon brave, what can I say?"

"Nothing Mademoiselle, just tell me how you are, as that is the most important thing to me right now and all I wish to know" he replied with a smile as she became hopelessly disarmed.

"Oh, Monsieur Ronay…"

"I'm still here…"

"You're so brave…"

"So I've been told, Mademoiselle…"

"Call me Helene…"

"So, how are you, Helene?"

"Much better now…"

"Bon, I'll come and see you again, if I may?"

"Oui, and when your under cover mission is finished, perhaps you'd give me an exclusive interview?" she asked.

"Certainly, over dinner one evening would be nice" he murmured.

"Oui, very" she smiled.

"So, au revoir, until we meet again" he whispered as he left her bedside. He returned to the reception and made a phone call to Josette telling her to get dressed up for dinner at the hotel before he made his way back to find Monique. The rusty Renault started easily and he drove his wife home to their flat in Montelivet. On the way, Michel told Monique everything about the unseemly brawl in the hotel, which amused her, as well as Montreau's instructions about tomorrow. She was not happy that he had to stay in the hotel but accepted it with her usual reserve. He kept the engine running as he said 'au revoir' to Monique outside the flat, then after kisses as well as promises to see her the next day, he drove away and headed back to his flat in the Rue du Camas.

Josette looked stunning in a blue satin dress with a plunging neckline and gathered waist. Her hair and makeup were exquisite, complemented by her diamond stud ear rings and matching necklace. Her perfume wafted around Michel's senses as he kissed her passionately.

"Mon Dieu, you're beautiful" he murmured.

"I'm glad you've noticed" she whispered as they kissed again.

"I always notice" he murmured in her ear.

"Bon, now I'm hungry, so take me to dinner!"

"My pleasure, Mademoiselle" he smiled.

"Not 'Mademoiselle' for much longer, ma cherie" she said firmly.

"Non" he replied as he raised his eyebrows.

"I think we'll get married in May, it's such a lovely month" she said with a smile.

"Oui, I agree…"

"That we'll get married then?" she asked.

"Non, I was just agreeing that May is a lovely month" he replied.

"You'd better be joking…"

"Let's go and eat" he replied.

The Renault started instantly and Michel drove to the hotel in a relaxed mood. He checked with reception for any messages and was relieved when told that there were none. The maitre d' showed them to a candlelit table for two in the restaurant and then with a bow presented the menus. They sat for some while perusing the extensive number of dishes on offer before Michel announced "I'm having Anchois followed by Chateaubriand, what do you fancy, ma petite?"

"I'll have Crudités and then Tournedos Rossini, cherie."

"Bon, now let's have a look at the wine list." Michel chose Cassis Rosé to start and then Saint Emillion to accompany the main courses.

"I hope you will be able to drive home after all this" smiled Josette.

"We're not going home, ma petite" he replied.

"Why not?"

"Orders from Monsieur Montreau, we have to stay here tonight" he replied with a smile.

"Oh, bon…"

"So, we can relax, eat and drink before wandering upstairs to bed…"

"I hope you won't be too tired to see to me" she whispered.

"Never fear, ma petite, when I've finished with you tonight, you'll be breathless!"

"Roll on bedtime" she smiled. They talked quietly and

intimately throughout the delicious meal, Michel finishing with pear belle Helene while Josette enjoyed a sorbet. After coffee and brandy, Michel glanced at his watch and said "time for bed, ma petite." They were soon naked and under the bedclothes in one of the single beds and made love for some while before Michel could no longer hold on. He released his passions into his fiancé gently and with deep love, before falling fast asleep on top of her.

The morning came far too quickly and the ringing of the bedside telephone woke them both up with a start.
"Oui?" mumbled Michel.
"Bonjour, Monsieur, this is you morning call" said a sweet female voice.
"What time is it?"
"Eight o'clock, Monsieur."
"Mon Dieu" he whispered before he hung up and struggled out of bed.
"Come back, cherie, there's no hurry to get up" said Josette
"There is, I've got to get the limousine back from Jean's at nine and be all ready for Montreau when he arrives…"
"Oh" she said before she slipped out of bed and joined him in the shower.

Josette felt a little self conscious eating croissants and drinking coffee in the restaurant dressed in her blue satin dress, but she just smiled at everyone who gave her a quizzical glance. It was just after nine when they left the hotel and climbed into the Renault, which then stubbornly refused to start.
"Merdre!" exclaimed Michel
"What's wrong, cherie?"
"The bloody thing won't start!"
"I realise that, cherie, but why won't it?"
"Because Jean can't fix it because he doesn't know what's wrong with it!"
"Mon Dieu!"
"I'll have to get some help to push it."
"Can't I do that?"
"Non."
"You push then and I'll start it" she said brightly.

"But you can't drive" he replied.

"Tell me what to do, it'll be alright."

"Okay, sit here and push that pedal in and put your other foot on the accelerator and when the car begins to move, take your foot of that clutch pedal and push the accelerator gently, then when the engine starts, push the clutch pedal in and take your foot of the accelerator, got that?"

"I think so" she replied. Michel then engaged second gear, released the handbrake and switched on the ignition before he got out. Josette sat behind the wheel and pushed the clutch pedal to the floor as he went to the back of the car.

"Ready, ma petite?"

"Oui."

Michel pushed and the Renault gathered speed towards the exit to the car park where a white pole on either side, marked the way out.

"Now, ma petite, now!" shouted Michel between gasps of breath. Josette stepped off the clutch and the engaged gear spun the engine over which burst into life immediately. Unfortunately, Josette was not paying much attention to where she was going, being far too occupied with trying to push the clutch pedal back to the floor whilst attempting to take her foot off the accelerator. It was a giddy kaleidoscope of roaring engine and lurching car until she finally hit a white pole. The Renault came to an abrupt halt with a crunching sound as Michel caught up with the runaway car.

"Mon Dieu! What have you done?" he yelled through the open window.

"What you told me to do!" she shouted back.

"You stupid woman, why didn't you put your foot on the brake?"

"I don't know where the bloody brake is!" she shouted

"It's the pedal in the middle!"

"You didn't tell me that!"

"Well everybody knows where the brake pedal is!"

"I don't and I'm not stupid!"

"Mon Dieu!"

"You're the stupid one, if you'd have let me push the car, this wouldn't have happened!" Just then a hotel guest in a large BMW, wishing to leave the car park, pulled up behind and tooted his horn. Michel turned, glared at the man and said "alright, alright, just wait a minute, can't you see this woman's had an accident?"

"Me?" queried Josette loudly.

"Oui."

"You're the cause of it!" she exclaimed.

"Alright, alright, just move over and let's get out of here!" Josette slipped across to the passenger seat and Michel reversed the Renault back a few metres, waved to the BMW driver, then set off towards the Rue du Camas. Michel and his fiancé did not speak until he pulled up outside the flat.

"I don't suppose you're coming in?" she asked.

"Non, I'm late already and God knows what Jean will say when he sees the state of his car."

"Oh, I expect you'll find some excuse and talk your way out of it as usual" she replied as she gave him a quick kiss on his cheek.

"I'll see you later, ma petite" he smiled.

"Okay" she nodded and slipped out of the Renault.

The limousine was parked outside Jean's garage and Michel was delighted to see that it had been repaired perfectly. He stood admiring it in the bright sunlight as Jean came out of the gloomy interior.

"Bonjour, Michel."

"Bonjour, Jean."

"Well?" asked the old man as he tipped his Breton beret back and scratched his head.

"A wonderful job as usual" replied Michel.

"I'm glad you're satisfied."

"I am, now see if you can fix that one" said Michel as he nodded at the rusty Renault.

"Oh, Mon Dieu! Mon Dieu!" exclaimed Jean as he looked at the Renault with its bent bumper, badly distorted front grill and damaged bonnet.

"Sorry..." began Michel.

"How did you manage that? Non, don't tell me, I'm sure that a woman was involved!"

"She was driving" said Michel.

"Didn't I tell you to stay away from accidents and women?"

"You did..."

"Why can't you stay out of trouble?"
"I try, but it just seems to follow me about" replied Michel.
"Well, it's going to cost you" said Jean.
"That's okay, and whilst your repairing it, fit a new starter motor, I'll pay for it…"
"Really?" asked Jean in surprise.
"Oui, I don't want to have to push it again!"
"That's how it happened?"
"Oui, in the hotel car park, I was pushing and Josette was steering…"
"Oh" said Jean, slightly embarrassed at the failure of the starter motor being the cause of the accident.
"Such is life" said Michel.
"I'll go halves on the motor" said Jean.
"Okay, now how much do I owe you for the Mercedes?"
"I haven't done the bill yet, it's too early in the day for me to write out all those big numbers and noughts then add them all up" he grinned.
"I'll see you later then" smiled Michel as he patted his friend on the shoulder.
"Oui, bon chance" replied Jean as Michel sat in the driving seat and started the limousine.

He arrived at the hotel, parked the limousine and was sitting in the lounge, drinking coffee, when the receptionist came over to him.
"Monsieur Ronay."
"Oui."
"There's a phone call for you, Monsieur."
"Merci."
"You can take it at the desk" she said, Michel nodded and followed her.
"Hello, Michel Ronay speaking."
"Michel, c'est moi" said Evette.
"Ah, bonjour, Mademoiselle."
"Listen very carefully as I haven't got much time" she whispered and he smiled.
"I'm listening."
"Montreau has just left the club with three of his men and they are on their way to Marseille."

"Right…"
"I'm going to follow them now…"
"Bon."
"Where shall I meet you when I get down there?" Michel was caught off guard for the moment and then decided that Ricky's would be the best place for Evette to wait for him.

"Go to Ricky's bar in the Rue Bonneterie, just by Le Vieux Port, and tell Jacques the bar man who you are, he'll look after you until I can get there."

"Trés bien."
"You'll get on well with him and his partner, Antone."
"Why is that?" she asked.
"They're gay, like you" he replied.
"Only sometimes" she said firmly.
"I'll see you at Ricky's later."
"Right."
"Au revoir, my lesbian Gendarme" he whispered.
"Au revoir, mon ami." The receptionist, who had overheard the conversation gave him a quizzical look.

"Tell me Mademoiselle, is a Mademoiselle Evette Ricard booked in as a guest tonight?" Michel asked.

"I'll check for you, Monsieur." The young woman consulted her computer screen and then announced "non, Monsieur, we have no one of that name booked in."

"Merci."
Michel then called Gerrard.

"Monsieur, c'est moi, Ronay."
"Oui?"
"You know who is on the move, our Mademoiselle has just called and is following on…"
"Bon."
"We're meeting at Ricky's later…"
"Bon."
"Tell me, where is she staying?"
"With you, Ronay."
"With me?"
"Oui, she's your new girl friend, don't you remember?"
"But, but, Monsieur, I can't have her stay with me, I've already got a wife and a fiancé!" On hearing that, the receptionist gave

him a very old fashioned look.

"Serious Police business, Ronay, I've already told you that you'll have to make sacrifices like the rest of us" replied Gerrard.

"I'll have to book her into a hotel…"

"Non, you can't do that…"

"Why?"

"That's not been included in the overall budget" interrupted Gerrard.

"But, I can't…"

"Sorry, Ronay, I have to go now and put the next stage of the plan into operation…"

"Listen…"

"You are keeping to the plan, aren't you, Ronay?"

"Oui, bien sure" replied Michel hopelessly as he made a mental note to ask Evette what the plan was.

"Bon chance, Ronay" said Gerrard before he hung up.

"Mon Dieu" whispered Michel as he put the phone down.

"Did you want to make a reservation, Monsieur?" asked the receptionist. Michel thought for a moment and replied "oui, for a Mademoiselle Evette Ricard, s'il vous plait."

"Oui, Monsieur, a single room?"

"Oui."

"How long will Mademoiselle Ricard be staying for?"

"Several days, at least."

"Merci, Monsieur, and will she be settling her account?"

"Non, I will" replied Michel, thinking that he would take the cost out of the reward for the arrest of Montreau.

"Bon, Monsieur, Mademoiselle Ricard is now booked in."

"Merci"

Michel returned to the comfortable seat in the lounge and ordered another coffee, knowing he had a few hours grace before Montreau and his men arrived. He glanced at his watch and then calculated that the men from Lyon would arrive at about two in the afternoon. That gave him time to call in at Ricky's, warn Jacques of Evette's arrival and enjoy a leisurely lunch of scotch and baguettes. He felt in a confident mood and he reasoned that, with the net closing around the Snake, nothing could seriously go wrong. He picked up a copy of the 'Marseille Citizen' which he noticed was on a table close by and read the front page with horror. The first thing that caught his attention on the front page was the photo of Raphael and George with the caption 'notaire and gunman arrested at the Hotel du Paris'. From then on it became steadily worse, the headline read 'Police arrest suspects in drug plot' and as he read on he felt distinctly uneasy. Mademoiselle Cressant's literary talents were greatly enhanced by her imagination and her report made Michel wonder if he was actually in the lobby when the fight took place.

The report started with the arrest of Guy Descoyne, stating that 'Police were called to an apartment near Saint Victor's where Monsieur Descoyne was found naked, strapped in leather hanging from the ceiling in the possession of several kilos of heroine. He had been part of a wild, drug crazed, sex orgy with an undisclosed number of women and had been hanging there for a number of days when the Police forced their way into the apartment. After the arrest of Descoyne, Pierre Chandon, a business associate, based in Lyon, was seen attempting to commit suicide by drowning in the harbour, but survived after inadvertently falling onto a luxury speedboat owned by a Monsieur Cousteau. Chandon was taken to the Hospital de Timone where he was operated on by a team of surgeons all through the night in a desperate attempt to save his life. He is now under Police guard in intensive care and is not expected to live.

A prominent notaire from Lyon, Monsieur Raphael and his armed bodyguard, George Dupres, both men are associates of Descoyne and Chandon, attacked our ace reporter, Mademoiselle Cressant, and seriously injured her in the lobby of the Hotel du Paris, when she requested an interview. Our photographer, Henri Dalmas, who took these photos of the men, was also injured when he was trapped in the revolving door of the Hotel du Paris by Dupres before being knocked unconscious. Passersby, who rushed to help, were also injured and some were taken to hospital but released after treatment.

A Police statement is expected later today on the high level investigation, meanwhile all the arrested gang will remain in custody.' Michel put the paper down and whispered "Mon Dieu" just as the receptionist came over once again.

"Another call for you, Monsieur Ronay" she smiled.

"Merci" he replied and followed her to the desk.

"Hello."

"Ronay, c'est moi, I'm free and ready to be picked up" said Raphael.

"Right, Monsieur, I'll be there straight away."

"Merci."

When Michel pulled up outside the Palace du Justice and glanced at the notaire, he was surprised to see how pale he looked. Once inside the Mercedes he said "get me away from here, Ronay" and Michel nodded as he pulled out into the mid morning traffic.

"Monsieur Descoyne is still being held then?" he asked as he glanced up at his rear view mirror.

"Oui, he's not coming out for a while" replied Raphael.

"Monsieur Montreau will be annoyed when he hears about that when he arrives after lunch" said Michel. The notaire looked like a frightened rabbit, cowering in the back seat.

"Mon Dieu, he's coming here today?" Raphael whimpered.

"Oui, Monsieur, he told me on the phone yesterday" replied Michel with a grin.

"Oh, mon Dieu" whispered the notaire.

"And what's happened to George?" asked Michel, enjoying the moment.

"The Police are holding him, just for the moment on a technicality" replied the notaire.

"What would that be, Monsieur?"

"You wouldn't understand, Ronay."

"The paper says he was carrying a gun, Monsieur…"

"What?" interrupted Raphael.

"You've both made the front page of the 'Marseille Citizen' and the photos of you are very good" said Michel cheerfully.

"This gets worse" whispered Raphael.

"And according to the paper, Pierre is under Police guard in intensive care and not expected to live."

"Mon Dieu! Can it be true?"

"That's what the paper says..."

"This is a nightmare" whispered Raphael.

"I'll drop you at the hotel, I'm sure you'll want to have an early lunch and get ready before Monsieur Montreau arrives."

"Oui" mumbled Raphael.

"I've got to pop home and see my wife, her mother has just come out of hospital this morning, I won't be long" said Michel as the limousine glided to a halt outside the hotel. Raphael nodded, slipped out of the Mercedes and made his way unsteadily towards the revolving door. Michel felt relaxed as he headed towards Montelivet in the busy traffic, confident that everything was working out nicely.

CHAPTER 7

Michel sat drinking coffee and commiserating with Mama whilst Monique 'tut tutted' and busied herself in the kitchen, half listening to their conversation. Mama was intent on making all the arrangements for her funeral and Michel waited patiently until she had finished, before asking "when is it?"

"What?" demanded Mama.

"Your funeral, I need to check to see if I'm free that day" replied Michel with a grin.

"It's not funny!" exclaimed Mama.

"Indeed it isn't!" said Monique as she came into the lounge.

"I don't know why you are so unkind to me…" said Mama as she began to cry.

"We're not unkind, Mama, but you're being stupid!" exclaimed Monique.

"I'm not…"

"The Doctor has told you, there's nothing wrong with you" Monique said firmly.

"I know I'm going to die" she wailed.

"As you said before, Mama, we're all going to die one day" said Michel.

"Oui, we are."

"But it's not your time yet" said Michel firmly.

"Exactly" said Monique.

"And if I'm not at the hotel when Montreau arrives from Lyon, you might all be coming to my funeral!" exclaimed Michel and on hearing that Mama began to cry again whilst Monique looked glum.

"I suppose that means you won't be home tonight?" she asked.

"Non, I'm afraid not, ma petite, but I'll ring you tomorrow and let you know what's happening."

"I'll be glad when this is all over" said Monique.

"Me too" replied Michel. He finished his coffee, kissed them both and left for Ricky's Bar.

After the usual greetings and the first scotch, Michel said "Jacques, sometime today a friend of mine will be arriving from

Lyon and I've asked her to meet me here…"

"Not another woman, Michel?"

"Oui, but she's just a friend…"

"There's no such thing where you're concerned" he interrupted.

"Look, I promise you…"

"Does Josette know about this 'friend'?"

"Non, but…"

"And your wife, does she know about her?"

"Non, but…"

"You will be dead soon with sexual exhaustion, it happened to a friend of Antone's, the poor boy was only nineteen" said Jacques as he wiped a tear from his eye with his cloth before wiping the bar with it.

"Possibly, but please look after this friend of mine, her name's Evette and she's helping me…"

"To do what?" interrupted Jacques as Antone came in and joined them at the bar,

"Bonjour, mes amis, I hope I'm just in time for Michel to buy me lunch" said Antone as Jacques poured a brandy and nodded to his lover.

"Oui" said Michel.

"Bon, so, Michel what have you been up to since the fracas in the Hotel du Paris?" beamed Antone as he took a sip of brandy.

"He's got involved with another woman" said Jacques.

"Mon Dieu, is this true?"

"Non, Antone, she's just a friend and I'm…"

"I find that hard to believe, Michel" interrupted Antone.

"That's what I told him" said Jacques.

"Ah, oui, we both know you too well, Michel" smiled Antone.

"Listen…"

"Why don't we order more drinks and baguettes, then you can tell me all about your latest conquest before it is a feature in the 'Marseille Citizen'."

"Antone, sometimes you…"

"Michel, as your friend, I can promise you, you're the most entertaining person I know, that's why Jacques and I are devoted to you" interrupted Antone and Michel smiled.

"Ham and cheese alright?" asked Jacques.

"Oui, and make sure the baguettes are fresh, ma petite" replied Antone as he finished his brandy.

"Oui, Monsieur" replied Jacques sarcastically before he nodded.

"Let's sit" said Antone as he headed off towards the back of the bar. When they were seated and Jacques had brought their lunch, Michel whispered to Antone "this friend is meeting me here later today…"

"Is that wise?"

"She's working for Gerrard, undercover…"

"Mon Dieu" whispered Antone in surprise.

"She's involved with the Montreau investigation" said Michel.

"In that case, we'll give her all the help she needs" said Antone.

"Merci, I don't know what time I'll be free to meet her, so keep an eye on her and don't let her know that you know who she is."

"Right" nodded Antone.

"Montreau is coming to Marseille this afternoon and I've got to drive him around" said Michel.

"Rather you than me, mon ami."

"I'm not looking forward to it" said Michel as a stranger approached them.

"Monsieur Ronay?" the man asked.

"Oui, Monsieur."

"Bon, I'm Marcel Cousteau, the boat owner, I left my details for you with the barman, but you haven't contacted me about the damage caused by your friend, who according to the paper, is not expected to live."

"I assure you, Monsieur, that he will live and I'm meeting his employer, Monsieur Montreau when he arrives from Lyon this afternoon" Michel smiled.

"Ah, bon, I'm pleased to hear it" smiled Cousteau.

"And I will give your details to Monsieur Montreau and I'm sure he will pay for all the damage that has been caused to your boat."

"Merci, Monsieur, I look forward to that."

"Bonjour, Monsieur" smiled Michel and Cousteau nodded and wandered off.

"See what I mean, Antone? Trouble just follows me about!"

"Oui, it certainly does, but it makes all your misadventures so much fun for us!"

"I'm glad you think so" said Michel glumly.

It was exactly two o'clock when Michel parked the limousine in the car park, casually glanced at the bent marker pole at the exit and strolled into the hotel. He found Raphael sitting in the lounge surrounded by paperwork, looking pensive as he made copious notes on a pad.

"Monsieur Montreau should be here soon, Monsieur Raphael" said Michel brightly as he sat in a comfortable arm chair opposite the harassed notaire. Raphael glanced up at him over his glasses and replied sarcastically "oui, won't that be good?"

"Oui, I look forward to driving him around the town."

"Bon, I'm glad that you will enjoy it, simple things, simple minds…" said Raphael unkindly as he returned to his writing.

"Oui, but then the advantage of me being simple is that I'm not in deep trouble, Monsieur" replied Michel and the notaire glared at him as he grinned annoyingly.

"I don't know what to make of you, Ronay, you're either very smart or incredibly stupid."

"Stupid, I assure you, Monsieur, because if I was a clever person I would not be involved with Monsieur Montreau" replied Michel and he watched as the notaire's shoulders droop as he sank into despair. The man was trapped and frightened by the Snake, he knew that there was little chance of escape until Montreau faced justice. The notaire shook his head slowly and returned to his note pad, writing furiously. Michel sat quietly and watched until he suddenly heard Montreau's unmistakable voice, so he glanced up and saw him approaching accompanied by three men in dark suits, all of whom were nodding.

"Raphael, Michel, ça va?" grinned the Snake as the notaire sprang to his feet to shake hands with him and Michel followed.

"A good journey down, Monsieur?" asked Raphael nervously.

"Oui, not too much traffic this time of day, and Nick here is a good driver." At that the youngest of the men nodded and gave a crooked smile.

"Bon, have you had lunch, Monsieur?" asked Raphael.

"Oui, just a quick stop on the way."

"Bon."

"Now, how have you been getting on?" asked the Snake in a menacing tone.

"Ah, we've had a few little problems…" began Raphael.

"So I understand" glared Montreau.

"It's all here in the paper, Monsieur" said Michel helpfully as he picked up a copy of the 'Marseille Citizen' from a nearby table. They all just stared at him with stern, fixed expressions for a few moments and made no comment.

"Nick, take the spare car back to Lyon, there's a good boy" said Montreau.

"Oui, Monsieur."

"Give him the keys, Ronay" and Michel took the keys from his pocket and handed them to Nick.

"The limousine is in the car park, near the exit" said Michel in a helpful tone.

"Bon, now off you go, Nick" said Montreau.

"Oui, Monsieur" nodded the driver and he left immediately. When he was out of ear shot, Montreau glared at Raphael and said " Nick's a good boy and I wish everybody who worked for me was as reliable."

"Oui, Monsieur."

"Now then, Ronay, are you ready to drive us around?"

"Oui, Monsieur, my pleasure" smiled Michel.

"Bon, we'll start at the Palace du Justice and find out what's been going on there, then to the hospital to see Pierre."

"Oui, Monsieur" said Michel.

"You'll brief me on the way, Raphael."

"Oui, Monsieur."

"Vincent, you'll ride in front with Michel" said Montreau and the big man nodded and glanced at Michel.

"You'll stay here Marcel, get us booked in and take care of everything."

"Oui, Monsieur" replied Marcel.

"Then when we get back from the hospital, you'll stay here Raphael, then Marcel, you'll come with us on our little trip around Marseille when we call on some of our friends, who may be pleased to see us, or not, as the case may be" said Montreau grimly.

"Oui, Monsieur" Marcel nodded as the Snake turned away and headed for the revolving door with Raphael, Vincent and Michel following on. The limousine parked outside was almost brand new and its jet black paintwork gleamed in the afternoon sun. The tinted windows were even darker than those in the spare Mercedes and the alloy wheels were deep set, making the car look very special indeed. Michel was very impressed and he looked forward to driving it around Marseille. Vincent raced ahead of Montreau and grabbed the rear passenger door handle but the door would not open. He pulled again before announcing that the car was locked.

"Give Michel the keys then" commanded Montreau.

"I haven't got them, Monsieur" replied Vincent lamely.

"Then go and get them from Marcel, and hurry up!"

"Oui, Monsieur" Vincent replied as he rushed off to find Marcel. Montreau raised his eyes to the heavens and tut tutted whilst walking around in small circles as the minutes passed, waiting for the return of Vincent.

"He hasn't got them, Monsieur" said the breathless and worried looking Vincent as he arrived back.

"Mon Dieu! That stupid little bastard!" exclaimed Montreau as he realised that his 'good boy' had just driven off with the keys and left him locked out of his limousine.

"Shall I call a taxi, Monsieur?" asked Michel helpfully.

"Non! Call the Mercedes Agent and get someone out here with a spare set of keys!" said Montreau angrily as he turned and went back into the hotel followed by his entourage.

"Where's the bar?" Montreau demanded at the reception desk.

"Through the lounge, Monsieur" replied the nervous receptionist as she pointed in the general direction and Montreau strode away with Vincent with Marcel following closely. Michel stayed with Raphael at the reception whilst the young mademoiselle looked up the Mercedes Main Dealer's telephone number after Michel told her the name.

"I also have a Mercedes and have it serviced there" said Michel with a smile after Raphael gave him a quizzical look. The conversation with the service department assistant and then the service manager proved totally fruitless. Raphael hung up, looked at Michel and said "they don't carry spare keys, it's Mercedes policy that replacement keys have to be ordered on the factory at

Stuttgart, it's to stop car thieves."

"Oh, dear, Monsieur Montreau will be angry when you tell him" said Michel, enjoying every minute of the predicament.

"Mon Dieu" whispered Raphael as a Gendarme entered the lobby and approached the reception.

"Excuse me, Mademoiselle; do you know who the owner of the vehicle parked outside is?"

"I think these Messieurs may be able to help you, Monsieur Gendarme" she replied anxiously.

"Ah, bon" replied the Gendarme as he turned to Raphael and asked "is that your vehicle, Monsieur?"

"Non, it belongs to Monsieur Montreau" replied the notaire.

"Do you know where he is?"

"Oui, he's at the bar."

"He's drinking?"

"Oui."

"That's not to be encouraged when you're driving" said the Gendarme firmly.

"Non, shall I call him for you, Monsieur?" asked Raphael anxiously.

"Merci, Monsieur, if you would." Raphael nodded and hurried away towards the bar while Michel smiled at the Gendarme.

"It's a nice day" said Michel.

"Oui, it may be for some but not so good for others" the Gendarme replied.

"Oui, especially if you've parked your car in the wrong place."

"Quite so, Monsieur" nodded the Gendarme as Montreau arrived at the reception.

"What's all this about?" he demanded angrily.

"Are you the owner of the black Mercedes parked outside, Monsieur?"

"Oui, I am."

"It is causing an obstruction, so please move it to the hotel car park" said the Gendarme.

"I can't" replied Montreau.

"Why not, Monsieur?"

"It's locked and I haven't got the keys."

"Who has the keys, Monsieur?"

"My driver, but he's on his way to Lyon…"

"By public transport I presume?"

"Non, in my spare car…"

"You have a spare car but not a spare set of keys, Monsieur?"

"I do have spare keys but they are in my office in Lyon…"

"So, your driver has gone to get them?"

"Non, he's got the keys to my car outside, but he doesn't know that!"

"Monsieur, I'm becoming puzzled by you explanations, how long have you been drinking?"

"I've just gone into the bar and haven't had one yet!" Montreau exclaimed angrily.

"It is not necessary to shout, Monsieur" said the Gendarme calmly.

"I wasn't shouting!" shouted Montreau.

"Monsieur, under City Ordinance 527, I must advise you to move your car immediately as it is causing a blockage, or it will be removed and taken to the car pound at the Palace du Justice where you may collect it after paying the parking fine."

"Don't you understand, I can't move it, you bloody fool!"

"Enough, Monsieur, another outburst like that and I will arrest you under City Ordinance 632, that states clearly…" said the Gendarme.

"Raphael, do something!" exclaimed Montreau.

"Monsieur Gendarme, I'm sure we can sort this out…" began the notaire.

"Is someone from the Dealer bringing a set of keys?" interrupted Montreau.

"Non, Monsieur, they don't hold any spares…" replied the notaire.

"Why not?"

"It's Mercedes policy that replacement keys have to be ordered from the factory in Germany" said Raphael nervously.

"What!" exclaimed Montreau and Michel thought he was going to explode with anger or have a heart attack.

"It is obvious to me, Monsieur, that your vehicle can not be moved by you, so I must call the recovery lorry to come and remove it" said the Gendarme.

"Non!"

"Oh, oui, Monsieur, you can collect it later after you've paid the fine, bonjour" said the Gendarme before he nodded and casually wandered off across the lobby towards the revolving door.

"Shall I call a taxi, Monsieur?" asked Michel in his helpful voice.

"Non!" exclaimed Montreau.

"It makes sense, Monsieur" said Raphael mildly.

"I'll tell you what makes sense, while I go and have a good drink to calm my nerves, you call the office and tell Gabon that when that arsehole Nick arrives, send him straight back here with the bloody keys!"

"Oui, Monsieur."

"Then when he gets here, I'll tell him he's sacked!"

"Oui, Monsieur."

"And then you can take his place and be my driver, Michel" said Montreau before he walked off towards the bar as Michel whispered "mon Dieu."

"How long before Nick is back with the keys?" asked Raphael. Michel thought for a moment and replied "it's about two and half to three hours drive each way, depending on traffic, so, at the latest" he glanced at his watch "he should be back here by nine tonight."

"Well I expect it will be murder until then" said Raphael in a resigned tone.

"If he'd agree to a taxi, I can arrange a Mercedes with no problem" said Michel.

"Let him have a drink or two then I'll see if I can persuade him" replied Raphael.

"Right, meanwhile I'll just pop home to see how my wife is coping" said Michel and Raphael nodded before he went in the direction of the bar. Michel had just reached the revolving door when Vincent came running after him and called his name. Michel turned as Vincent caught up with him and said "Monsieur Montreau wants to talk to you."

"Right" Michel nodded and followed Vincent back to the bar, cursing quietly to himself.

"Michel, I've been thinking, we mustn't let this little inconvenience with my Mercedes set us back" said Montreau before he sipped at his scotch on the rocks.

"Non, Monsieur."

"So, as you know everything there is to know in Marseille, can you arrange the hire of something suitable for me to be driven around in?"

"Certainly, Monsieur."

"Bon, then arrange it, s'il vous plait."

"Oui, Monsieur" Michel nodded and hurried away to the reception desk.

Thirty minutes later, just as the Mercedes limousine was being driven away on the back of the Police recovery lorry, another Mercedes arrived from the dealership hire department. Michel produced his licence and signed the hire agreement before the driver handed him the keys. He then went to the bar in search of Montreau and announced that a new Mercedes awaited him. The Snake beamed and said "I knew I could rely on you, Michel."

"Oui, Monsieur."

"Now, we'll go to the Palace du Justice as planned, you stay here Marcel, when you phone Gabon at the club, tell him to call back as soon as Nick arrives there" said Montreau.

"Oui, Monsieur."

"I want to know exactly when the little shit will be back here with the keys" said Montreau angrily.

"Oui, Monsieur" nodded Marcel.

"What time do you think he'll get to Lyon, Michel?"

"I expect, depending on traffic, around six o'clock, Monsieur" replied Michel.

"So he'll be back here about nine?"

"Oui, Monsieur."

"Bon."

At the Palace du Justice, Michel waited in the Mercedes with Vincent as Montreau and Raphael tried to secure the release of George as well as Guy Descoyne. Michel knew that it was hopeless but he kept that fact to himself. He tried to engage Vincent in conversation but it was like talking to a dumb animal, so he gave up and turned his thoughts to Evette, waiting at Ricky's for him. He cursed himself for not telling Jacques that he had booked a room for her, as he feared she might arrange her own accommodation and he would be paying for an expensive empty room at the hotel. He sat and wondered what the plan was to arrest Montreau, making a mental note again that he would ask Evette as soon as he met her. It was nearly six o'clock when Montreau and Raphael appeared outside the Palace du Justice before walking slowly down the steps towards the parked car. Vincent jumped out and opened the door for Montreau, who slipped into the back seat. He looked angry and frustrated.

"They're being difficult, Monsieur?" asked Michel.

"Very."

"They hide behind the law, they're such cunning bastards in there" said Michel firmly.

"You're so right as always, Michel" replied Montreau.

"To the hospital now, Monsieur?"

"Oui, Michel."

Outside the Hospital de Timone, Michel waited alone as Vincent joined the other two in visiting Pierre. He gave them a five minute start before he parked the car and hurried in to see Mademoiselle Cressant. When she saw him enter the ward her face beamed.

"Michel, oh, Michel, ça va?"

"Oui, ça va, Helene?"

"Oui."

"This is just a fleeting visit to see how you are and to compliment you on your report in the 'Citizen'."

"Oh, merci, merci, I'm glad you think it was good" she smiled.

"I read every word and when I'd finished, I thought it was so well written and very accurate" he said as he held out his hand and touched hers.

"Oh, Michel…"

"So, tell me, how do you feel?"

"A lot better, merci."

"Bon, so we'll soon see you up and out of here…"

"Oui, you will, we've got a dinner date, remember?" she smiled.

"How could I forget that I'm going to have dinner with a famous reporter who only wants to talk about me and that's my favourite subject!" he replied and she laughed out loud.

"You're wonderfully funny" she said.

"So I've been told, now, I have to leave you as duty calls, but I'll come again soon, au revoir, ma petite" he said as he bent down and gave her a quick kiss on her forehead. She blushed before whispering "au revoir, Michel, and bon chance."

Michel arrived back at the car just as Montreau and the others emerged from the entrance.

"How is Pierre?" asked Michel when they were all in the Mercedes.

"As well as can be expected" said Montreau.

"He did have a very bad fall" said Michel in a sympathetic tone.

"Oui."

"Not only did he injure himself badly he did a lot of damage to the boat" said Michel as he drove off.

"I expect so" replied Montreau.

"The man who owns the boat is Monsieur Cousteau, and here are his details, he asked me to give them to you so you could pay for the damage" said Michel as he produced the envelope and handed it back to Montreau.

"Mon Dieu! I'm beginning to think Marseille is a very unlucky place to be!" exclaimed Montreau.

"Really, Monsieur?"

"Oui, Guy is arrested on trumped up drug charges, Pierre is injured and in hospital, George is arrested for fighting and carrying a gun, Raphael has also been arrested for fighting, my limousine has been stolen by the Police and everything is splashed all over the front pages of the 'Marseille Citizen'!"

"Your visit certainly has not got off to a good start, Monsieur."

"Non, the only person that has escaped all this trouble is you, Michel."

"Oui, Monsieur."

"And me, Monsieur" added Vincent.

"Oui, oui" said Montreau testily.

"And Marcel" Vincent droned on.

"Oui, alright, Vincent, that's enough."

"Where to now, Monsieur?" asked Michel.

"Back to the hotel, I want to know if that little bastard has arrived in Lyon yet."

"He should have, it's now gone half past six" replied Michel as he glanced at the dashboard clock.

Marcel was waiting anxiously in the lounge when they arrived back. He stood up as Montreau approached him and asked in an angry tone "well?"

"I phoned Monsieur Gabon as you told me, but he hasn't called back yet, Monsieur" replied Marcel.

"Get him on the phone now and let me speak to him" said Montreau.

"Oui, Monsieur" Marcel nodded.

"I'll come to reception when Gabon is on the line" said Montreau as he sat down in a comfortable arm chair. The lounge was filling up with guests and the bar was becoming busy with early evening drinkers. The presence of strangers around him appeared to annoy Montreau and Michel watched with interest as the irritable man's face became flushed.

"Get me a drink, someone" he said impatiently.

"Oui, a scotch as usual, Monsieur?" asked Vincent.

"Oui, and make it a double, and find out what everybody else wants" replied Montreau testily. Vincent nodded and looked at Raphael, who ordered a scotch, before turning to Michel, who shook his head and said "non, merci, I'm driving." As Vincent wandered off towards the crowded bar, Marcel arrived back.

"Monsieur Gabon is on the phone" he announced and Montreau then followed him to reception.

Michel caught up as Montreau demanded loudly down the phone "he's not arrived yet?" before slapping his forehead and shouting "mon Dieu! mon Dieu! Where is the little creep?" Michel imagined Monsieur Gabon at the other end of the phone struggling to placate his angry boss, but to no avail.

"Here, you talk to him, Ronay and see if you can get any sense out of him!" said Montreau as he handed the phone to a surprised Michel before striding back towards the lounge.

"Bonjour, Monsieur Gabon."

"Hello, Ronay."

"So there's no sign of Monsieur Nick yet?"

"Non."

"Well he could be caught up in traffic at this time of day" said Michel helpfully.

"Oui, but even so, I think he should have been here by now" replied Gabon in a weary tone.

"Possibly, of course there's always the chance that he's had an accident" said Michel.

"Mon Dieu! Don't say that…"

"Well, Monsieur Montreau's staff do seem to be accident prone at the moment" said Michel, turning the screw.

"I can do nothing from this end..."

"Oui, you can, contact the Gendarmerie and see if there've been any accidents reported on the autoroute this afternoon" advised Michel helpfully.

"Oui, alright."

"And I'll tell Monsieur Montreau that you'll call back when you've done that."

"Merci, Ronay."

"That'll put his mind at rest, au revoir, Monsieur."

Michel told Montreau what he had said to Gabon and the Snake looked anxious as he sipped his scotch. He nodded, said nothing and Michel could sense the apprehension in the others who were sitting around waiting for Montreau's next move. He finished his drink and said "we're going out now, you stay here Raphael and wait for Gabon's call, the rest of you'll come with me." They all nodded and followed Montreau out to the lobby whilst Michel went ahead to get the Mercedes from the car park. Montreau told Michel to drive to the house in the Rue du Aviateur where he had taken Guy Descoyne previously.

"You wait here, Michel" said Montreau as the car pulled up and he got out.

"Oui, Monsieur."

"And make yourself comfortable as we may be some time."

"Oui, Monsieur." Michel sat and watched the three men go into the house as he wondered what was going on behind the door of number 38, Rue du Aviateur. He settled down, put the radio on and thought about Evette for a while, then Josette for even longer. He decided to phone her from Ricky's and tell her that he had to stay in the hotel tonight. He knew she would be angry, but as Gerrard said 'sacrifices have to be made.' After a while he started the engine and put the heater on to warm himself up. He heard voices at last and glanced at the door of number 38, as the three men emerged, then he looked at the dashboard clock, it was nearly ten o'clock.

"Back to the hotel, Monsieur?" Michel asked as Montreau slid on to the back seat.

"Oui, Michel" replied the Snake as Vincent got in beside Michel and Marcel joined his boss in the back. They said nothing on the return journey to the hotel and Michel did not want to ask any questions. As they trooped into the lobby, Nick sprang up from a chair near the reception and Montreau fixed him with a steely gaze. But before he could say anything, the receptionist said "there's a phone call for you, Monsieur Montreau!" The Snake nodded and took the phone from the girl.

"Oui, oui, non, non, he's turned up here at last! Oui, oui, bon, Maurice, bon nuit" and Montreau hung up as he turned to face the pale faced driver.

"That was Monsieur Gabon telling me that you still haven't arrived in Lyon, so, where have you been with the keys to my limousine all this time?"

"I'm so sorry, Monsieur…" began Nick.

"You're sorry! You stupid little creep! Because of you, I've had to hire a car and my Mercedes has been towed away by the Gendarmes!"

"Oh, Mon Dieu!"

"So, you give me the keys right now, stay the night, get my Mercedes back from the car pound first thing tomorrow, and Vincent will go with you to see there are no slip ups!"

"Oui, Monsieur" Nick whimpered.

"Michel will drive my car from now on."

"Oui, Monsieur."

"You take the spare car back to Lyon and stay there until I return, then I'll decide what to do with you!"

"Oui, Monsieur."

"And tell me, where have you been?"

"Monsieur, I stopped at a service area on the autoroute near Lyon, for a coffee and when I went to pay for it, I found the keys in my pocket, so I turned round and came back immediately, I was here just before eight o'clock" replied Nick and Michel felt sorry for the young man.

"Alright, but do as I say in the morning."
"Oui, Monsieur."
"Raphael, let's have a meeting in my room."
"Oui, Monsieur" replied the notaire.
"Bon nuit, everybody, I'll see you all in the morning" said Montreau and he asked for his key before striding off with Raphael in tow. As the others wandered off towards the bar, Michel took the opportunity to tell the receptionist that he was popping out for a while and would be back later, the girl smiled then nodded.

He arrived at Ricky's and looked around for Evette before he went up to the bar.
"Bonsoir, Jacques, where is she?"
"Bonsoir, mon ami, in the passageway, dead drunk, thanks to you!"
"Me?"
"Oui, leaving her all alone this long…"
"But didn't you keep an eye on her?" interrupted Michel.
"I'm busy and I've got a bar to run, I can't babysit your lady friends all night!" replied Jacques.
"Mon Dieu!"
"Antone stayed for quite a while looking after her, but he'd had enough to drink and toddled off home about an hour ago."
"Is she alright?"
"I don't know, Antone put her back there, so you'd better see for yourself" replied Jacques. Michel went into the narrow passageway and found Evette huddled up on some cushions on the floor.
"Evette! Evette! Wake up, mon ami" he said as he shook her. Evette opened her eyes and smiled when she saw his out of focus face.
"Is that you, Michel?" she asked in a slurred voice.
"Oui, it's me."
"Bon, now are you taking me to bed somewhere nice?"
"Oui, I am."
"Bon, because I need a fuck!"
"Non, not tonight, ma petite…"
"Why not? What's the matter with me?"

"Nothing, nothing at all…"

"Bon, so let's go…"

"Oui, hold on to me" he said as he helped her up. She put her arms around him and murmured "you'll have to carry me…"

"Mon Dieu! What have you been drinking?"

"I don't remember, but some fat old man who says he's a friend of yours, he's called Antone, d'you know him at all?"

"Oui, I do…"

"Well, let me tell you, he can drink, oh, boy, can he…"

"I believe you, let's go."

"I could hardly keep up with him and I'm supposed to be on duty" she said slowly.

"Oui, you're never off" replied Michel.

"Don't tell Gendarme Gerrard…"

"I won't."

"Promise?"

"Oui, I promise." Michel struggled out into the bar with Evette as Jacques raised his eyebrows and sighed before saying "bon nuit, Michel." Once in the Mercedes she either fell asleep or unconscious and Michel drove quickly to the hotel. He parked outside and helped Evette into the lobby where one of her shoes fell off.

"Wait, wait, Michel, I've lost my shoe…"

"I'll get it in a moment after I've got you to the reception…"

"Reception?" she asked as she limped along with her arms around his neck.

"Oui, you're booked in here" he replied.

"Bon, it looks nice" she nodded as Michel half carried her to the desk where the receptionist looked distinctly anxious. Just as he was about to speak a voice he knew so well asked "and who's this then?" He turned to see Josette standing there, arms folded and foot tapping.

"Mon Dieu!" he exclaimed as he jumped at the sight of her.

"Well?" persisted Josette.

"She's a friend…"

"Michel!"

"She is, and she's booked in here and once I get her to her room I'm coming home with you" he said thinking very quickly.

"You're such a liar!"

"I'm not, I'll explain everything when we get home, just trust me, will you?"

"How can I?" Josette asked.

"Please just this once…"

"Who's this woman?" asked Evette.

"My fiancé, Josette…"

"Your fiancé?"

"Oui."

"I thought you were married?"

"I am…"

"That's only a temporary arrangement, we're getting married in May" said Josette firmly.

"Congratulations" replied Evette.

"Are you staying at the hotel, Mademoiselle?" asked the receptionist.

"I think so" replied Evette.

"She is…" said Michel.

"Name please?"

"Evette Gabrielle Jacqueline Ricard" she replied in slurred tones.

"Sign in please, Mademoiselle Ricard."

"I can't possibly do that…"

"Why not, Mademoiselle?"

"I can't see the book without my glasses and I don't know where they are" she replied.

"Just write something where my finger is pointing" said the receptionist, anxious to get Evette away to her room.

"Trés bien" said Evette and scratched something where the girl was pointing.

"You're in room 306, Mademoiselle" said the girl as she handed her the key.

"Bon, now take me there, Michel."

"Oui, Mademoiselle" he replied.

"I'll give you five minutes, Michel and then I'll be up there!" said Josette.

"I'll be back, don't worry" he replied as he helped Evette towards the lift.

"My shoe, Michel!" He nodded and left her whilst he ran across the lobby and retrieved her shoe.

"And where's my luggage?" she asked as he handed her the shoe.

"Luggage?"

"Oui, didn't you bring it?"

"Non, where is it?"

"In my car."

"Parked outside Ricky's I suppose?"

"Oui."

"I'll bring it in the morning."

"Bon, so, bon nuit, Josette, I'm glad I've met you!" said Evette loudly as Vincent appeared from the lounge.

"Hello, Ronay, who's this I wonder?" asked Vincent with a sly grin.

"A friend…"

"I've seen her before somewhere…"

"Don't think so, Vincent" said Michel hastily.

"Oui, she was with you at the club when you won all that money…" he grinned broadly as Josette overheard what he said and drew near, asking "what money is that, Michel?"

"I'll explain later, ma petite" replied Michel as the lift 'pinged' and the doors opened.

"You'd better" said Josette as Michel half carried Evette into the lift and smiled at his fiancé as the doors closed. He struggled with Evette along the corridor to her room and breathed a sigh of relief when he lowered her onto the bed.

"Bon nuit, Evette, I'll see you in the morning…"

"Aren't you going to undress me?" she grinned.

"Non, mon ami, not tonight."

"Shame, your fiancé could watch if she wanted to…"

"Bon nuit" said Michel before he left her room closing the door firmly as he went.

Michel tried to explain what had happened earlier as he drove his angry and upset fiancé back to the Rue du Camas.

"I phoned the hotel to find out where you were because I'm so worried about you and I don't know what to believe any more" she said through her tears.

"Oh, please don't cry, ma petite" he said as he stopped the Mercedes outside their flat.

"Michel, I only want us to be married and be happy…"
"I know, ma petite…"
"Is that too much to ask?"
"Non, of course not" he replied as he put a comforting arm around her.
"Why are you so involved with things all the time?"
"I don't know, they just seem to happen to me."
"Well, I wish they'd stop…"
"They will, once this is over, I promise…"
"You always promise but…"
"I know, but this time it's different" he interrupted.
"Why?"
"Because I love you and want to marry you in May…"
"Oh, Michel…"
"And then take you to Monte Carlo for a lovely, long honeymoon…" he said as his imagination came to his rescue.
"Oh, cherie" she purred.
"We'll stay at a luxury hotel near the casino, wander around the shops and buy you lots of nice things…"
"Shoes, I want lots of shoes…"
"Oui, you shall have them, ma petite."
"What else?"
"We'll go dancing every night, then walk by the sea in the moonlight and make love until the sun comes up and then do it all over again every day…"
"Oh, cherie" she whispered.
"I do love you, ma petite" he said before he gently kissed her.
"Let's go in" she whispered.
They went to bed happy and relaxed before making love gently then falling asleep in each other's arms.

CHAPTER 8

The next morning Michel hurried through his breakfast of croissants and coffee before leaving the flat. He knew that he had to get back to the hotel before Montreau and his entourage were about. As he drove quickly through the rush hour traffic he suddenly remembered that he had to get the keys to Evette's car and retrieve her luggage. He arrived at the hotel, rushed up to Evette's room and knocked on the door, but there was no response so he tried again.

"Evette! Evette!" He called as a muffled groan came from the room.

"Evette, c'est moi, Michel!" He waited as he heard movement and just as the door was opened by a dishevelled, half dressed Evette, Vincent and Marcel appeared in the corridor.

"Bonjour, Michel" they chorused as they wandered by with broad grins on their faces.

"Bonjour, mes amis" mumbled an embarrassed Michel.

"What do you want?" asked Evette.

"Your keys, to your car…"

"Why do you want my keys?"

"To get your luggage…"

"Oh, oui, come in while I try and find them" she said vacantly. As she wandered about looking for her handbag, Michel asked "can you meet me at Ricky's later and tell me the plan?"

"I'm not going in there again…" she mumbled.

"Why not?"

"I feel worse than death now and if I see the inside of that bar again, I'll die for certain…"

"Look, you have to tell me what the plan is…"

"I've already told you but you weren't listening!" she replied as she picked up her handbag from the floor.

"Oui, I know, but I was distracted at the time…"

"Get my case from my car and let me get sorted out, I'll find you later, alright?" she said as she handed him the keys.

"Okay."

"And by the way, do you know someone who can take a look at my car?"

"What's wrong with it?" asked Michel in an alarmed tone.

"It started making funny noises on the autoroute and when I stopped outside the bar the engine rattled, then there was a smell of burning oil."

"Mon Dieu" whispered Michel as he nodded.

"Don't be long" she said as he disappeared through the door.

He found Evette's Renault parked along from Ricky's, opened the boot and retrieved her case. After locking it he made a note of the registration number and hurried into the bar.

"Ah, Michel, ça va?" smiled Jacques.

"Ça va, Jacques…"

"A scotch?"

"Non, merci, it's a little early for a scotch, can I use your phone?"

"Oui, is it an emergency?"

"Oui" nodded Michel as he went into the passageway. He dialled Jean's number and waited.

"Hello, Gambetta's Garage…"

"Hello, Jean, c'est moi…"

"Ah, Michel, ça va?"

"Oui, ça va, Jean…"

"I suppose you're in trouble again…"

"Non, I'm not but a friend of mine is."

"So, that will be a woman with car problems then."

"Oui."

"It's so nice to be right all the time."

"It's a white Renault, parked outside Ricky's, I think it's got something wrong with the engine."

"And you want me to get it started?"

"Oui, if you can, but I think it may be serious" said Michel.

"Oh, how serious?"

"She said it made funny noises on the autoroute and smells of burnt oil."

"Well, I can usually fix funny noises but not sure about smells" replied Jean.

"Please help me, Jean, I'm in a bit of trouble at the moment…"

"You're always in trouble!"

"I'll leave the keys and the registration number with Jacques."

"Okay, I'll come and get it later."
"Merci, Jean."
"It sounds as if it'll be expensive…"
"It always is! Au revoir, Jean."

Michel returned the case to Evette and told her that Jean would be fixing her car in his specialist garage. She was grateful and promised that she would find him later so that they could go over the plan together. He then hurried down to the lounge to find Montreau and the others sitting around and drinking coffee.

"I hear you brought a woman into the hotel last night, Ronay…" said Montreau.

"Oui, Monsieur."

"Is she the same one that was with you at the club?" asked Montreau in a cold tone.

"Oui, Monsieur" replied Michel anxiously.

"Is she staying here?"

"Oui."

"Why has she followed you down from Lyon?"

"I asked her to come, Monsieur, you see, after my lucky evening at the club we became quite close, in fact, now she says that she can't live without me" replied Michel with a straight face.

"And you without her…"

"Oui, Monsieur."

"Ah, a ladies' man, well I'm not surprised" said Montreau with a crooked grin and the others smiled in unison as Michel looked suitably embarrassed before glancing down at the floor. He hoped that he had now removed any suspicious thoughts that Montreau may have had about Evette.

"Now, Messieurs, this is the plan for today, Michel, Nick, Vincent and Raphael will go to the Palace du Justice to collect the Mercedes, then Nick will go on with the spare car to Lyon and wait until I return" said Montreau as he glared at the young driver.

"Oui, Monsieur" whispered Nick.

"Raphael will stay at the Palace and try and get George released today, then Vincent and Marcel will come with me to Bandol" said Montreau.

"Are we going on your boat, Monsieur?" asked Vincent.

"Oui."

153

"You know I get seasick, Monsieur" said Vincent.

"I'm having a meeting on the boat but you'll be waiting on the jetty making sure I'm not disturbed" said Montreau firmly.

"Oh, bon, I'm alright as long as I don't go on a boat…"

"Oui, alright, Vincent, alright, now, after the meeting, we'll be coming back here and then calling on some business people, hopefully Raphael will be here with George" and Raphael nodded at that.

"So, off you go whilst I make some phone calls" said Montreau.

Michel called the car hire office, asked them to collect the Mercedes and left the keys with the reception before joining the others in the spare limousine. At the Palace du Justice the release of the Mercedes took much longer than expected and when they arrived back at the hotel, Montreau was impatient and angry.

"Mon Dieu! Those bastards are really causing me problems!" he exclaimed when Marcel told him what had happened.

"First of all, they said that they couldn't find your Mercedes" said Marcel indignantly.

"Couldn't find it?"

"Oui, Monsieur."

"Mon Dieu! It's bloody big enough, isn't it?" demanded Montreau.

"It is, Monsieur."

"It's a conspiracy, that's what it is" said Montreau and Marcel nodded.

"Oui, Monsieur."

"Now I'm late for my meeting at Bandol!"

"Oui, Monsieur."

"Michel, can you get me there by eleven thirty?" asked Montreau. Michel glanced at his watch and replied "I can try, Monsieur."

"Bon, let's go."

The powerful limousine was a delight to drive and it swept silently out of Marseille then along the coast road, passed Cassis, towards Bandol. Michel accelerated the big car to high speed whenever he could and made good time on the journey, occasionally glancing at the dashboard clock. It was just passed eleven thirty when he pulled up at the end of the main jetty in the harbour at Bandol. Montreau scrambled out and with the other two following, he hurried towards a large, elegant motor cruiser moored at the end of the jetty. Standing near the cruiser were a tall blonde woman and a stocky, grey haired man whom Michel vaguely recognised. They were greeted by Montreau before they followed him on board Michel parked the car and then wandered out along the jetty, admiring some of the luxury yachts and cruisers, as they bobbed at their moorings. As he drew close to Montreau's cruiser he estimated that she was about twenty metres in length with a spacious fly bridge and she looked brand new with her chrome fittings glistening in the sun. He noticed her name, it was 'Sea Serpent' and he thought that was very appropriate.

"She's a lovely boat" he said as he approached Vincent.

"Oui, but I don't like boats, I get sick just standing and looking at them" replied Vincent as he drew on his cigarette.

"Oh, shame."

"I'm not bothered" he replied as he exhaled his cigarette smoke.

"Do you think the meeting will be a long one?" asked Michel.

"How should I know?"

"Well, I saw a man and a woman go on board with Monsieur, and if they are friends of his, it might be some while before he's ready to go back to the hotel" said Michel, hoping that Vincent might know who they were.

"Don't think they're friends."

"Oh" said Michel with disinterest.

"Non, they can't be friends because they're either German or English, I can't tell the difference" said Vincent and Michel suddenly realised where he had seen them before. It was last August, when he was on the boating holiday, sailing along the Côtes d'Azure with Rene and Yvonne. They had moored up for the night and were in a restaurant in Cavalaire sur Mer when the couple, along with Edward Salvator, his wife and their son, Claude, came in for dinner. He remembered that Claude Salvator told him later that the blonde was English and her name was Ann. The grey haired man was her father and he was involved in drug dealing with the Salvators'.

It was obvious that Montreau was busy setting up new business links with the Englishman and his delightful daughter, now that Edward Salvator was dead and Claude was in prison.
Michel talked casually to Vincent for a while as he gazed across the harbour and to the gently rolling, blue Mediterranean beyond, glinting in the sunshine.

"I think I'll go back to the car and wait there for Monsieur."

"Okay" nodded Vincent as he lit another cigarette. Michel wandered back along the jetty and when he was out of sight he hurried to a phone kiosk by the Harbour Master's office.

"Monsieur Gerrard, c'est moi."

"Ronay, where are you?"

"In Bandol, you know who has a boat here and he's having a meeting on board with an Englishman and his daughter…"

"Do you know who they are?"

"Oui, I recognise them from when I saw them last year, they were with the Salvators'."

"Ah, I remember now, I contacted my bon amis at Scotland Yard at the time" said Gerrard.

"Bon, what did they say?" asked Michel.

"They said they would look into it."

"And?"

"I've heard nothing since, Ronay."

"Oh."

"I think I'll contact them again."

"Bon."

"Do you know their names?"

"Only that the daughter is called 'Ann'…"

"Trust you to know the woman's name" said Gerrard sharply.

"That's all Claude would tell me" replied Michel.

"Okay, now have you made contact with Ricard?"

"Oui, last night."

"Bon, keep up the good work, Ronay, and whatever you do, stick to the plan!"

"Oui, Monsieur" replied Michel lamely as he hung up. He stood thinking for a few minutes before phoning the hotel and was quickly put through to Evette's room.

"Hello."
"Evette, c'est moi."
"Michel, where are you?"
"At Bandol…"
"What are you doing there?"
"I'm here with Montreau."
"Bon, now before you do anything stupid…" she began.
"Believe me, I'm not doing a thing until I know what the plan is!"
"We haven't got time for that now…"
"Evette!"
"I'll tell you later, just do as I say."
"Mon Dieu" he whispered.
"Listen, Michel, play along with Montreau and do exactly what he tells you to…"
"Do I have a choice?" he interrupted.
"Not at the moment, I'll wait here until you get back and then I'll fill you in with all the details of the next part of the plan" she said.
"Bon, I look forward to that."
"Michel, be very careful, Monsieur Gerrard thinks that there are several moles at the Palace du Justice."
"Oh, bon, tell me, whose side are they on?"
"Just be careful, mon ami, au revoir."

He walked casually back to the car, deep in thought, wondering how he had managed to get so involved so quickly with Montreau. After the catastrophe in Le Touquet all he had to do was drive back to Marseille and resume his comfortable, disorganised life that he so enjoyed. The accident on the autoroute was all the Englishman's fault and he was to blame entirely for his predicament. Now he was in the mire he knew that he had to get out as quickly as possible and collect the reward on the way. Michel sat in the Mercedes, listening to the radio, for some while before Vincent suddenly appeared.
"Monsieur is coming now."
"Right" nodded Michel as he sat up and prepared himself.
Vincent opened the back door of the limousine as Montreau and the English couple arrived. The man spoke quite good French and

said "au revoir, Monsieur, I look forward to our next meeting" as he shook hands with the Snake.

"Au, revoir Monsieur, Mademoiselle" replied Montreau. The blonde smiled, shook hands and her gaze shifted to the Mercedes before she focused on Michel. A glimmer of recognition flashed across her face before she returned to smile at Montreau. The couple wandered off as the Snake got into the car followed by Marcel.

"Where to, Monsieur?"

"Back to the hotel, Michel."

"Oui, Monsieur."

When they arrived at the hotel, Michel excused himself and hurried to Evette's room.

"I'm glad you're back" she said as he sat down on her bed.

"So am I" he replied.

"Things may move quickly from now on."

"Before they do, tell me about the plan…" he began.

"There's no time at the moment, mon ami."

"Mon Dieu."

"Now, I need my car…"

"What?"

"I need my car" she repeated.

"What for?"

"I have to go undercover and try to find the women who framed Descoyne" she replied.

"Can't you take a taxi?"

"Non."

"Why not?"

"I've no money, besides it's not in the operational budget…"

"I'll lend you the money" interrupted Michel.

"Non, mon ami, I really have to have my car."

"Well I don't expect that Jean has been able to fix it yet."

"Phone him and find out" she said firmly.

"It's better that we go there" replied Michel knowing that a visit was likely to have a more positive outcome as Jean was a past master at stalling desperate customers who phoned for their cars.

"Okay, take me to his garage now, Michel."

"Alright, you wait here for five minutes then meet me in the car

park, it would not be good if we're seen leaving together."
"Oui."

As Michel was passing the reception desk he heard his name mentioned and he turned as the receptionist smiled and said "a call for you, Monsieur Ronay." He took the receiver from the girl and said "hello."

"Michel, ça va?"
"Oui, ça va, Helene?"
"Oui."
"Bon, how are you feeling today?"
"Lonely."
"Why is that?"
"The hospital have sent me home and I'm stuck here with my foot in plaster, hardly able to move" she replied.
"That's a shame."
"I need an intelligent man to talk to as well as pouring me a drink" she giggled.
"I think in that case you've called the wrong number."
"Non, I haven't."
"Really?"
"Oui, you're the top of my current list of men" she replied.
"I always enjoy coming top" he replied.
"So, come round to 23, Avenue des Mimosas, as soon as you can, Michel."
"Later, perhaps."
"There's no 'perhaps' about it, I always like certainty in my arrangements" she replied.
"Okay, I'll see you later for certain."
"Bon."
"But I can't stay long" he said.
"We'll see, au revoir" she replied as she gave a little giggle.

.

Michel knew he was taking a chance driving Evette to Jean's in the limousine, but he thought that he would not be missed for twenty minutes and he felt sure he could talk his way out of any problem that might arise. He pulled up outside the garage and was concerned to see Evette's Renault parked in the road.

"Bonjour, Jean" he said cheerfully as he entered the dusty

garage with Evette. Jean was under the bonnet of the damaged, rusty Renault and replied "bonjour, Monsieur trouble."

"How are you getting on with my friend's car?"

"I'm not" replied Jean as he came out from under the bonnet.

"Why?" asked Michel as Jean ignored him and smiled at Evette.

"Bonjour, Mademoiselle" he said.

"This is my friend, Evette."

"I guessed that" replied Jean as he tipped his beret back on his head.

"Bonjour, Monsieur, I'm sorry if my car is causing you a problem" Evette smiled.

"Nothing that can't be easily fixed" replied Jean.

"When might that be, Monsieur?" she asked sweetly.

"I can repair it in a few hours, once I get the parts."

"What is wrong with it, Monsieur?"

"You've blown the head gasket, Mademoiselle."

"Is that serious?"

"Non, I just have to remove the cylinder head and replace the gasket, so providing there's no other damage to the engine, I should be all finished by tomorrow lunchtime" he beamed.

"Oh, non, I really need my car now" she said in a concerned tone.

"I'm afraid that's not possible, Mademoiselle."

"Can you lend me a car until then?" she pleaded as she fluttered her eye lashes and like any man, Jean fell for it.

"Oui, I've just put a new starter on my Renault here, and if you can put with driving a car that Michel damaged, then you can have that" said Jean with a smile.

"Oh, Monsieur, merci, you really are so kind" she smiled and Jean blushed a little whilst Michel whispered "mon Dieu."

As Jean reversed the rusty Renault out into the road, Evette said to Michel "I expect that I'm going to be back late tonight, so wait up and I'll call your room."

"Are you going to tell me the plan then?"

"Oui."

"Bon, I look forward to finding out what I'm supposed to do…"

"I've already told you once but you didn't listen!" she interrupted as Jean stepped out of the Renault and held the door open for her. Evette smiled and sat behind the wheel, adjusted the driving mirror before giving them a wave as she drove away.

"What a lovely young woman" said Jean.

"You were putty in her hands" replied Michel.

"If only…" smiled Jean.

Michel hurried back to the hotel and went into the lounge to show his face, anxious in case he had been missed. He was relieved to find Vincent there, sitting alone, reading the paper.

"Hello, Vincent."

"Hello, Michel."

"Has everybody gone to lunch?" he asked as he glanced at his watch.

"Non, they've all gone up to Monsieur's room for a meeting."

"Oh."

"Monsieur said that we could take the afternoon off, but he wanted us back by six o'clock as we've got things to do tonight" said Vincent in a serious tone.

"Right, tell me, did Monsieur Raphael manage to get George released?"

"Non, and Monsieur is very angry about that, I can tell you."

"Oh, dear, well I'm off for some lunch and I'll see you later then" smiled Michel.

"Oui, and that reminds me, Monsieur told me to tell you to make sure the car is full of fuel as we may have a long trip tonight."

"Right" Michel nodded as he left Vincent.

Ricky's bar was quite busy when Michel arrived and after the usual exchanges with Jacques he ordered lunch then took his scotch to the back of the bar, sat down and waited for Antone. It was not long before the great man entered, ordered a drink, and then when he caught sight of Michel, he smiled and wandered over. Jacques followed with two baguettes as Antone eased his considerable frame onto a creaking wicker chair.

"Michel, ça va?"

"Oui, ça va?"

"I suppose you want something to eat as well?" asked Jacques as he put Michel's baguettes on the table.

"Not for the moment, ma petite" replied Antone.

"Please yourself, but you do need to eat, and it might improve your temper" said Jacques.

"I'll eat when I want to, thank you…"

"I'm only giving you my opinion" interrupted Jacques.

"Oh, please don't, you know how that exhausts me" replied Antone testily. Jacques then flounced away and Michel guessed that the lovers were not on the best of terms at the moment. Antone smiled and whispered "lovers tiff." Michel smiled and nodded.

"Now tell me everything that's happening with Montreau, and leave nothing out" said Antone. Michel went into great detail and the man listened carefully to every word. At the end, Antone let out a low whistle and said "tell Gerrard about the journey tonight and I'll have a few discreet words with people I know."

"Bon, I'm grateful, mon ami" said Michel as he knew that Antone had contacts at the very highest level, both in the Gendarmerie as well as the underworld. They had another drink together before Michel left Ricky's and drove round to 23, Avenue des Mimosas. He parked the Mercedes and rang the sonette.

"Oui?"

"C'est moi, the man at the top of your list!"

"Oh, Michel!" Helene exclaimed and the street door of the apartments clicked open. He hurried up the stairs and was welcomed into her spacious flat. She hobbled into her lounge then flopped down on the settee and put her plastered foot up on a cushion.

"I'm glad to see you, Michel, I was going out of my mind…"

"Why?" he asked as he sat down in a chair opposite her.

"I need to live on the edge all the time and I feel frustrated stuck at home like this" she replied.

"Shame."

"I know that I'm missing so much" she said in an impatient tone.

"I don't think so" he replied.

"Get us some drinks and then tell me how I can cope with this" she smiled and Michel made his way over to the drinks tray on the sideboard.

"Scotch?" he asked.

"Oui, a large one with a drop of water" she replied.

When they had said 'cheers', sipped their drinks and settled for a while, Helene asked "what's happening with Montreau and his gang?"

"I'm not at liberty to tell you at the moment."

"You promised me an exclusive interview" she said.

"Oui, I did, and you'll get it when the operation is over and Montreau is behind bars."

"Do you really think that he'll be arrested?"

"Oui, why not?"

"Well, he's such a slippery character and it's no wonder they call him the Snake" she replied.

"Don't worry about him, let's talk about you" Michel smiled.

"You do know how to cheer a poor girl up" she giggled.

"That's my one saving grace…"

"Don't you mean saving poor girls for yourself?" she laughed.

"Possibly" he grinned as he sipped his scotch.

"Well, I definitely need saving" she said mischievously.

"And I'm the man for the job."

"How long can you stay for?"

"I have to leave by about five" he replied and then she glanced at her watch.

"I wonder what we can do for the next two hours?"

"I have no idea…"

"I have" she smiled.

"Let me get you another drink" he said.

"Why not, we've plenty of time." They had another large scotch and talked about her plans for the future. She was ambitious and eventually wanted to be the Editor of the 'Marseille Citizen'. Michel was impressed by Helene and her positive outlook on everything. When she had finished talking and drinking, she fixed him with a glint in her eyes and said "kiss me for a while before you do it, then take it slowly and gently, so I relax completely…"

"Oui" he whispered.

"And mind my ankle."

"Oui."

"We'll be more comfy on the bed" she said and he nodded as he helped her struggle up from the settee. When she was standing, Michel put his arms around her before he kissed her passionately.

"Mon Dieu, that's a good start" she whispered.

"Oui, it was" he murmured before he helped her out of the room and in to the untidy bedroom across the hallway. She lay on the bed as Michel lifted her plastered ankle up and made her comfortable.

"I don't suppose you've ever made love to a cripple before" she giggled.

"Non, it's a new experience that I'm looking forward to" he replied. They lay for a while just kissing and whispering before he undid her blouse and lifted her breasts gently from her brassier, kissing the nipples until she murmured "oh, Michel, this is what I need."

"Trés bien" he whispered as slid his hand down to her skirt before lifting up and stroking her thigh.

"Have you really got to go at five?" she asked.

"Oui."

"What a shame" she said as his hand reached her panties.

"It is."

"Don't rush, Michel, I'm enjoying this."

"I won't" he replied as he ran his fingers along the outside of her panties.

"Kiss me some more" she said and he did until she was breathless.

"I'm ready now, Michel…"

"Bon" he whispered as he pulled her lace panties down to her ankles and free of her plaster. She opened her legs as far as she could before asking "can you manage?"

"Oui."

"Take your time" she said as he gently rolled on top of her and eased himself into her moist body. She gasped with pleasure as he slowly pushed right up into her.

"Mon Dieu, this is good" she said as he began a slow and gentle rhythm. Michel said nothing as he tried to concentrate his mind on other things to prevent the inevitable happening too quickly. He was determined to give her as much pleasure as he could without exhausting himself. He wondered where Montreau planned to go that night and he was concerned that it might be a very long journey. A Mercedes limousine with a full tank of fuel had a range that was only dreamed about a few years ago.

"Oh, Michel, Michel, now! Now!" her cries brought him back from his thoughts and he increased his speed towards the ultimate moment of pleasure. He felt her tighten on him as he released himself into her, then she screamed and he gasped.

"Mon Dieu! Mon Dieu!" he said between gasps.

"We must do this again" she whispered.

"I need a drink first" he said and she giggled. They lay on the bed, drinking scotch and chatting happily about friends, good times, bad times, and catastrophes for some while, before he glanced at his watch and saw that he had about half an hour left.

"I must go soon, ma petite."

"Not until you've taken care of my desperate need, cherie" she replied and he smiled. It was not long before he had penetrated her once again and begun his slow, gentle rhythm of ecstasy. He managed to carry on for some while before he at last gave in to the unstoppable surge and pushed her up to the headboard.

"Mon Dieu, I enjoyed that" she whispered.

"Bon."

"Now, what time are you coming tomorrow?" she asked.

"Tomorrow?"

"Oui, I need you every day until I'm well enough to go back to work" she replied.

"I can't promise that, ma petite."

"Try, just for me, Michel."

"Well…"

"You did enjoy it, didn't you?"

"Oui, of course…"

"Well then, sometime tomorrow, I'm not going anywhere so I'll be here" she said brightly.

"I'll try, but remember, I'm on undercover work and anything might happen…"

"Oui, but even crooks like Montreau have to sleep eventually and that's when you can come to me" she smiled and Michel shook his head. He wondered how he managed to get so involved all the time and asked himself 'is it me?'. He kissed her and after half hearted promises to call the next day, he left her apartment at five o'clock.

After re-fuelling the Mercedes at a garage near the hotel Michel then parked it close to the exit with the bent pole. He found Vincent still sitting in the lounge reading the paper.
"Hello, Vincent."
"Michel" he nodded.
"They're still having the meeting in Monsieur's room?"
"Oui, but I expect they'll be out soon."
"Any idea where we're going tonight?" asked Michel as he sat down opposite.
"Non, but possibly back to Bandol and then on somewhere else" he replied.
"Oh."
"It could be a long night so I hope you're up to it."
"Oui, of course."
"Bon."
"I'm going to my room for a wash and tidy up, I need to be feeling fresh for the journey" said Michel and Vincent nodded. As soon as he was in his room he phoned Gerrard.
"C'est moi, Gerrard."
"Bon, I'm glad you've called, Ronay, I've heard from the British Police…"
"Bon."
"The man and his daughter are well known to them…"
"Really?"
"Oui, and they have undercover officers following them all the time, so whatever you do, don't get in their way…"
"But how will I know who they are, Monsieur Gerrard?"
"I haven't got time to discuss operational details with you now, Ronay, just stick to the plan and everything will be okay…"
"Oui, the plan, but…"
"Tell me, what's Montreau up to now?" interrupted Gerrard.
"He's in his room having a meeting with the others, it seems we're going to Bandol tonight and then somewhere else…"
"Where, Ronay?"
"I don't know!"
"Call me as soon as you get there, I'm not leaving my office tonight and I need to know!"

"Oui, Monsieur." As Gerrard hung up Michel felt vulnerable and alone. He had a shower and felt better as he relaxed on the bed, waiting for the call from Montreau that would take him on another adventure that would probably last all night.

CHAPTER 9

The bedside telephone rang and awoke Michel from a doze.
"Oui, Michel Ronay…"
"Cherie, c'est moi" said Josette.
"Ma petite…"
"Are you coming home tonight?"
"If I can, but I've got to drive to Bandol soon and then somewhere else…"
"Where?"
"I don't know yet, Montreau hasn't told me."
"Oh, Michel, when is this nonsense going to stop?"
"Soon, ma petite."
"I hope so, now, have you seen that woman again?"
"What woman?"
"The drunk one at the hotel, you must remember!"
"Oh, that drunk woman…"
"Oui, that one! Or is there more?"
"Of course not, ma petite…"
"There had better not be!"
"Trust me…"
"This time will be the last time" she interrupted.
"I must go now, ma petite…"
"Phone me as soon as you can, cherie."
"I promise, au revoir." Michel had just put the phone down when it rang again.
"Hello."
"Hello, Ronay" said Vincent.
"Ah, Vincent…"
"Monsieur wants to leave soon, is the car ready?"
"Oui, it's fuelled and waiting."
"Bon, have it outside the hotel at seven sharp."
"Right."

At exactly seven o'clock, Montreau, Raphael and Vincent came out of the hotel and got into the waiting limousine.
"Where to, Monsieur?"
"Bandol, Michel, s'il vous plait."

"Oui, Monsieur" nodded Michel before he accelerated away into the evening traffic. None of them spoke on the journey and Michel wondered about the meeting in Montreau's room. Raphael looked worried whilst Montreau appeared detached and deep in thought. Vincent had a fixed grin and just looked stupid all the time. The Mercedes responded, silently and powerfully to the lightest touch on the accelerator and they arrived at Bandol in very good time. Michel stopped by the jetty as instructed and Montreau, with his men, left the car and hurried to his boat. Michel got out and stretched his legs as he waited in the cold night air for them to return. Twenty minutes later they appeared, each carrying a suitcase which they put in the boot of the car. When they were all seated comfortably inside, Michel asked "where to now, Monsieur?"

"Monte Carlo…"

"Monte Carlo, Monsieur?" asked Michel in a surprised tone.

"Oui…"

"That's a long way away, Monsieur…"

"I know, Michel, so you'd better drive as quickly as you can" replied Montreau firmly.

"Mon Dieu" whispered Michel as he accelerated away from the jetty, heading for the centre ville and then out towards the autoroute. Once passed the péage on the A8, Michel settled the Mercedes to a high cruising speed and wondered what was in the suitcases. He thought that the contents were most likely to be drugs and guessed that they were on their way to meet the Englishman and his elegant daughter. He watched the signs on the gantry above the road flash by as the limousine effortlessly maintained its high speed. The exit for Toulon came quickly followed by Hyeres then Cannes, finally, Nice on the 160 kilometre dash to Monte Carlo. No one spoke on the journey and Michel was glad when he turned off the autoroute and headed for the centre ville of the fairy tale principality.

"Where to, Monsieur?"

"The Hotel Excelsior, it's on the Boulevard Charlotte, do you know it?"

"Non, Monsieur."

"I'll guide you then." Montreau then gave directions and they were soon at the hotel.

"Vincent, you wait here with Michel" said Montreau as he left the car with Raphael carrying his briefcase.

"Oui, Monsieur" nodded the dumb one and Michel sighed.

"I'll stretch my legs" said Michel as he got out and breathed the cool night air.

"Okay."

Twenty minutes later, Montreau appeared without Raphael and slipped into the Mercedes.

"Now take me to the Casino" said Montreau and Michel nodded as he pulled away. When they arrived at the famous gambling house, Montreau said "park the car, Michel, then come with me, Vincent, you stay here and don't move until we come back."

"Oui, Monsieur" replied Vincent. Michel found an empty bay and eased the limousine into a space between a Bentley and a BMW before switching off the engine. He removed the keys and followed Montreau into the Casino.

"Are we meeting someone, Monsieur?" he asked when he caught up with the Snake.

"Oui, and I want you to be your charming, lucky self, tonight."

"Oui, Monsieur."

"It's important to me."

"Oui, Monsieur" replied Michel as they hurried through the main entrance and into the bar. Michel spotted the Englishman and his daughter seated at a table in the far corner.

"Ah, there they are" said Montreau as he headed towards the couple. The man stood as they approached and smiled.

"Bonsoir, Monsieur Montreau" he said as he held out his hand.

"Bonsoir, Monsieur Carter and Mademoiselle" replied Montreau as he gave a little bow.

"So this is your lucky man?" asked Carter.

"Oui, Monsieur Michel Ronay, the only man who's ever beaten the tables at the Jardine Bleu" replied Montreau and Michel blushed before shaking hands with Carter.

"My daughter, Ann, who always comes with me to France because she loves it so" said Carter as Ann nodded at Michel.

"I'm pleased to hear it" said Michel as he gazed at her flawless complexion, blue eyes and long blonde hair. Her low cut black dress enhanced her neat figure and her diamond ear rings with a matching necklace complemented her understated beauty.

"Now, let's have some champagne" said Carter.

"Oui, I think a little celebration is called for" nodded Montreau as Carter raised his hand at a passing waiter.

"Tell me, Monsieur, is he here yet?" asked Montreau in a whisper.

"Non, not yet, but be patient, Conrad, he'll be here later" replied Carter.

"So, time to play the tables then, Roger?" asked Montreau.

"Oui, and it will give a good impression if he sees us relaxed and enjoying ourselves."

"Bon, and if Michel does his usual trick of winning a fortune, he'll be even more impressed!" said Montreau with a grin.

"He will indeed" nodded Carter.

"Do I know this Monsieur?" asked Michel as the Môet Chandon arrived.

"Non, but you will do, his name is Monsieur Zarabowski" replied Montreau as the waiter eased the cork and poured the sparkling elixir into the flutes.

"So, who is Monsieur Zarabowski?" asked Michel.

"He's a Russian billionaire businessman, and he has moored in the harbour one of the biggest yachts you've ever seen" replied Carter.

"How nice" said Michel anxiously as they picked up their glasses.

"Here's to business with friends" said Montreau before they touched flutes and drank to the toast.

"So, are you feeling lucky tonight, Monsieur Ronay?" Ann asked in good French.

"Oui, Mademoiselle, and please call me Michel."

"That's good, Michel, because I'm feeling lucky as well, and if we play together I know our combined luck will make sure that we beat the Casino" she smiled.

"We can try, Mademoiselle."

"Ann, s'il vous plait" she smiled.

"Oui, I'm sure we'll win, Ann" replied Michel.

"Bon, now if you'll excuse me for a moment" said Ann as she got up from the table and they all stood politely before she slipped away towards the ladies room.

"Will we have a meeting on his yacht tonight, Roger?" asked Montreau anxiously.

"Oui, I understand that is what he has planned" replied Carter.

"Bon."

"Michel, whilst we're having the meeting, I'd be glad if you would look after Ann for me" said Carter and Michel beamed.

"My pleasure, Monsieur."

"Bon, we'll all be on the yacht but it's so big I'm sure you'll find a bar somewhere on board where you can sit and enjoy a quiet drink" said Carter and Michel smiled at the thought.

"I'm sure, Monsieur."

"Michel has a way with the ladies" grinned Montreau.

"Has he indeed, well I best warn Ann in that case" replied Carter in an anxious tone.

They sat and talked about the long term business opportunities but Michel did not get a clear understanding of what the business consisted of before Ann returned.

"Shall we go and try our luck, Michel?" she smiled.

"Why not?"

Montreau and Carter followed them into the ornate gaming room where Michel found two vacant seats at a Roulette table. Once they were seated, Carter put a bundle of Bank notes in front of Ann whilst Montreau did the same for Michel. The money was passed to the croupier who quickly counted it before issuing chips to the players. The other players at the table glanced at the couple before the croupier called "Mesdames and Messieurs, place your bets, s'il vous plait!"

"Bon chance, Michel" Ann whispered as she put chips on red twenty three and black thirteen.

"Merci, and bon chance" he replied as he placed on red seven. Montreau and Carter watched with interest as the croupier spun the wheel before dropping the ball. It clattered for what seemed an eternity to Michel before it settled into red seven.

"Rouge, sept" called the croupier and Michel could not believe his luck.

"What did I tell you, Roger?" beamed Montreau as the croupier piled the chips in front of Michel.

"He's a lucky man to have around" smiled Carter and Montreau nodded.

"Mesdames and Messieurs, place your bets, s'il vous plait!" called the croupier and Ann placed chips on red seven and on black thirteen.

"It's my turn to win now, Michel" she whispered as he put chips on red twenty three. The wheel spun, the ball clattered and then landed.

"Rouge vingt trois!" exclaimed the croupier, the players gasped and Carter said "mon Dieu."

"He's unbeatable" whispered Montreau.

"I think I need a drink" said Carter.

"I'll join you" said Montreau and they wandered back to the bar.

"You really are a man of mystery" whispered Ann as she leaned close to Michel and he caught the scent of her perfume.

"Non, just lucky" he whispered back.

"Are you lucky in love?" she asked.

"All the time" he replied.

"How nice."

"Mesdames and Messieurs, place your bets, s'il vous plait!"

"I'm with you this time" said Ann.

"Okay" nodded Michel as he placed his chips on red twenty six and Ann followed suite. The wheel spun and the ball clattered before landing on black thirteen.

"All good things come to an end" smiled Michel and Ann laughed.

"Don't tell me that you're giving up?" she said.

"Non, I never give up on anything" he smiled as he looked up from the table and noticed a man standing behind the players opposite, a man he thought he recognised. The face was somehow curiously familiar but the mop of ginger hair, bushy eyebrows and droopy moustache confused him. Suddenly the man winked at him as the croupier called for them to place their bets. Michel glanced down at the table and placed chips on red thirty six as he struggled with his thoughts about the winking man. He looked up again but the man had disappeared, much to his relief. The croupier spun the wheel and the ball landed in red eighteen, the losing players sighed as Michel shrugged his shoulders. Suddenly a hand appeared beside him on the table with a folded slip of paper, Michel glanced to his right and was horrified to see the face of the hairy man grinning at him.

"Monsieur" whispered the man through his moustache before he disappeared. Michel unfolded the note and it read 'meet me in the toilet'.

"What's that?" asked Ann.

"Just a lucky message" replied Michel.

"You've a system to win?" she whispered excitedly.

"Non…"

"Let me see it!"

"You wouldn't understand…" he began.

"Please, Michel." He gave in and showed her the note.

"It's in code" she said as the croupier called them to place their bets. Michel took the easy way out and nodded as he placed his chips on red seven.

"How fascinating" whispered Ann as she followed and put a large pile of chips with Michel's. The wheel spun and the ball clattered.

"Rouge sept!"

"Mon Dieu! It works!" said Ann.

"Oui, now please excuse me, I'll only be gone for a few minutes" said Michel.

"Tell me what numbers I should bet on while you're away" said Ann.

"Thirteen, twenty four, thirty two and thirty six" replied Michel confidently as he plucked the numbers out of the air, hoping that that would convince her that there was a system to his winning streak.

"Merci" she whispered.

"Bon chance" he replied as he left the table and headed for the toilets.

The ornate men's room was attended by a smart young man, who checked the pristine towels folded neatly by each wash basin, ensured that every gentleman was brushed down and for a tip, sprayed a discreet puff of enchanting Eau de Cologne in the general direction of the client. Michel entered and looked about for the ginger haired man before nodding to the attendant and positioning himself before a shaped, porcelain petite cubicle, to relieve himself. He was only there for a few moments when the hairy one appeared next to him and also began to relieve himself. Michel hardly dare look at the man who suddenly whispered "Ronay, c'est moi."

"Cyril, I didn't recognise you, what are you doing here?"

"I'm undercover and following Montreau, don't you remember that it's all part of the plan?" hissed Gerrard.

"Oh, oui, of course" nodded Michel, confused as ever.

"So?" asked Gerrard.

"What?"

"So what's going to happen next?" whispered Gerrard anxiously.

"The Englishman is called Carter and his daughter is Ann…"

"We know that, Ronay!" interrupted Gerrard.

"Bon."

"And?"

"They're going to a meeting tonight with a Russian business man called Zarabowski, on his yacht" replied Michel.

"Where is this yacht?"

"Here in the harbour…"

"Bon, now the British police are here undercover, following Carter, so whatever you do, don't get in their way and stick to the plan otherwise everything will go wrong!"

"Oui" said Michel as he wondered what the plan was and what could go wrong.

"My men are everywhere, Ronay, so you're in no immediate danger…"

"Immediate danger! Mon Dieu! What does that mean?"

"You're safe for the time being, but watch yourself…"

"Gerrard…"

"Shh! You don't know who's listening, bon chance!" said Gerrard as he zipped up his trousers and went to wash his hands. Michel hurried after him in an attempt to ask more questions but the Gendarme quickly rinsed and wiped his hands on a towel whilst the attendant brushed him down. He then searched in his pocket for a tip and after a quick puff of Eau de Cologne Gerrard disappeared through the door, leaving Michel uncertain of what to do next.

"Would Monsieur like to wash his hands?" inquired the attendant and Michel nodded.

When Michel arrived back at the table, Ann had amassed a huge pile of chips and smiled broadly when he sat beside her.

"Don't tell me" he said.

"Oui, every number came up" she whispered and Michel was suddenly conscious of all the other players watching him closely.

"I think I need a drink" he said as Montreau and Carter arrived back from the bar.

"Mon Dieu" said Montreau when he saw the pile of chips in front of Ann.

"I don't believe it" whispered Carter as he leaned forward and kissed his daughter's head.

"Neither do I, Daddy" she said as she turned to face her delighted parent. At that moment Carter looked across the table at two men who had just arrived. They were both heavily built with cropped, iron grey hair and the older man was wearing gold rimmed spectacles which hardened his appearance. The croupier called for bets to be placed but neither Ann or Michel did so as Carter nodded and said "bonsoir, Monsieur Zarabowski."

"Bonsoir, Monsieur Carter, you seem to be enjoying a lucky moment, don't let me disturb you" replied Zarabowski with a smile.

"Non, I think my daughter and her companion had just finished playing for the moment" said Carter.

"Bon, so perhaps we could have a drink in the bar and you could introduce me to your friends" said the Russian as he peered over his spectacles.

"Of course" nodded Carter and he moved the chair for Ann to get up. The croupier gathered all her chips as well as Michel's and placed them in separate velvet bags before returning them to the couple. They followed Zarabowski and his man through into the bar where an empty table was quickly found for the party.

"Monsieur Zarabowski, may I present Monsieur Montreau and his associate Monsieur Ronay" said Carter.

"Monsieur Montreau" said Zarabowski as he shook Montreau's outstretched hand.

"And lucky Monsieur Ronay" he said as Michel shook hands.

"Monsieur Zarabowski."

"I do like a lucky man, wasn't it Napoleon who asked, before promoting a General, 'is he lucky?'" smiled the Russian.

"Oui, it was" beamed Montreau as he gave a little bow. They then all sat at the table and Carter waved for more champagne. The Môet Chandon duly arrived and toasts were made to 'new business friends' before they settled down to discuss the plans for the evening.

"I would be pleased if you would all be my guests aboard my yacht, we can relax and discuss business opportunities in more privacy whilst enjoying a drink" said Zarabowski.

"Delighted" nodded Montreau.

"Oui, merci, I think my daughter and Michel have won enough at Roulette tonight" smiled Carter.

"Oui, if Michel stays at the table much longer he'll bring the Casino to its knees!" exclaimed Montreau.

"Oh, I do like the sound of that" said Zarabowski and they all laughed. The light hearted conversation continued as Michel caught a glimpse of Gerrard occasionally hovering in the background. At last the Russian decided that it was time to return to his yacht and leaving Igor, his large companion, to show them the way, he set off to prepare to receive his guests. Michel cashed in their winnings and joined the party as they followed Igor out into the cold night. The Carters squeezed into the Mercedes with them, then Michel followed Igor and his driver in a similar limousine, down to the harbour. Eventually they stopped by a lit gangplank that lead up to the deck of a truly awe inspiring ocean going yacht. Michel estimated that it was at least fifty metres in length and appeared to have several spacious decks, all beautifully lit by concealed lights which made the white superstructure gleam and the chrome fittings glisten.

"Mon Dieu" he whispered as he followed the excited party aboard the billionaire's yacht. Vincent was instructed by Montreau to wait in the car and he pulled a face at that. Igor lead the way to the splendid day cabin which looked more like the drawing room of the Czar's Winter Palace in St. Petersburg. The plush, deep pile cream carpet gave a lightness to the enormous cabin which contrasted with the gleaming black concert grand piano and the dark wood of the tables and chairs in the dining area.

The settees and chairs were covered in matching red damask inlaid with gold thread, which to Michel appeared a touch tacky and unsophisticated. As they entered the cabin, Zarabowski, dressed in a red silk dressing gown, stepped forward to greet them.

"Welcome aboard my little indulgence" he smiled as he waved them to be seated.

"Mon Dieu, Monsieur Zarabowski, my mind boggles at the prospect of any large indulgence you may have" said Montreau as he sank down into a plush chair and the Russian laughed.

"Wealth is very useful and can be used for the benefit of oneself as well as others" replied Zarabowski with a smile and Michel thought 'oui, as long as you are one of the oneself's'. As they sat down two waiters appeared and served them all with glasses of champagne and large bowls of Caviar.

"Mon Dieu" whispered Montreau as he helped himself to a bowl.

"My Caviar is the finest available and I hope that your discerning French pallet's will be satisfied with it" beamed the Russian, obviously eager to make an impression on Michel and Montreau.

"Oui, I'm sure" replied Montreau.

"But first a toast… to success" said Zarabowski as he raised his glass. They had just echoed his words and taken a sip when the figure of a large woman in a long pink dress, covered in sequins, entered the cabin. Zarabowski saw her immediately and said "ah, Svetlana, my dear, come and meet my new friends." The large woman smiled and wobbled towards them. Michel was quite taken aback and sat with his mouth open as he gazed at the apparition. Svetlana had shoulders that would have put her in the front row of the French National Rugby team, arms that belonged on an Olympic swimmer and hands that she could box with. Her heavily made up face was square and over rouged, her eyelashes were hideously false and her lipstick looked as if it had been applied with a roller. Her diamond necklace and pendulum ear rings were undoubtedly real but so large and sparkly as to appear false. Her low cut pink dress just managed to contain her large bosom and the split up the side showed a thick, muscular leg to the onlookers. Her white high heeled shoes struggled to maintain her undoubted weight and Michel breathed a sigh of relief when she sat down on a settee next to Zarabowski.

"Svetlana is my dearest companion and we are very close" beamed the Russian as he gave a little pouting kiss to the apparition in pink who smiled coyly. The introductions were made and when Michel shook hands with Svetlana it confirmed his thoughts that she would be more at home driving a large tractor on a farm in Georgia. He made a mental note to never go on an ocean voyage with Svetlana on board, just in case they were shipwrecked alone on a remote desert island. Svetlana could manage a little French but often had to refer to her lover in Russian and he quickly translated for her. They all chatted happily as they consumed the champagne and caviar until a while later Zarabowski said "Svetlana, my dear why don't you show Ann and Michel around whilst we men talk boring business for a moment." The apparition nodded and struggled to her feet as Zarabowski put a helping hand on her large bottom to give support. Michel looked at Ann, who smiled as he winked at her, and they followed the unsteady Svetlana to the sliding doors at the back of the cabin. The cold night air struck them as they wandered out onto the spacious rear deck and Ann shivered a little which gave Michel the opportunity to slip his jacket off and place it around her shoulders.

"Merci, Michel" she whispered and he smiled. Svetlana was totally unaffected by the cold, and Michel put her hardiness down to long winter nights in Mother Russia.

"Monte Carlo is beautiful" said Svetlana as she waved her huge arms expansively at the myriad lights cascading down from the floodlit pink castle on the hill.

"Oui, Madame" replied Michel as he and Ann joined the Russian by the rail at the rear of the deck.

"Please call me Svetlana, comrade" she smiled.

"Merci, I will and call me Michel" he replied

"It's nice to be out here" she said.

"Oui, it is."

"I get bored with all that business talk, don't you Michel?"

"Sometimes, but it depends what it is" he replied hoping that Svetlana would let something slip.

"I always get bored, it's the same old thing all the time, money, money, money" she said, shaking her head and slurring her words as the champagne loosened her tongue.

"Well, you can never have too much" said Michel helpfully.

"I suppose not, but this time it's all American dollars, I mean, why can't they talk about Roubles, that's what I want to know..."

"Or Pounds" said Ann.

"Da, or pounds" nodded Svetlana.

"What's so special about dollars then?" asked Michel.

"Oh, Vladimir has got cases full..." replied Svetlana.

"Really?"

"I don't know why he has to talk to his friends about it all, it's no secret that he's going to give them the dollars any way" she blurted out.

"How nice" said Michel.

"Da"

"Why is he being so generous?" he asked.

"I don't know, probably because he's got so many" she replied.

"That's very kind" said Michel and Svetlana nodded.

"Now, I'm supposed to be showing you around this boat."

"Oui."

"This is the rear deck."

"Oui."

"And there's another one below this one."

"Bon."

"And there's two more at the front of the boat."

"Par excellence."

"So, that's all there is" she smiled.

"Fascinating" replied Michel.

"Now I've shown you around, shall we go in?" asked Svetlana.

"Why not" said Michel and he put his arm around Ann before they followed Svetlana back into the cabin. Zarabowski looked up as they entered and remarked "that was a quick trip around, my dear."

"Da, but you know I can't walk far in these shoes" Svetlana replied as she lowered herself onto the settee beside him.

"You have a lovely yacht, Monsieur" said Michel hoping to remove any tension from the moment.

"I'm glad you're impressed" replied Zarabowski.

"I need another drink" said Svetlana in Russian and instantly one of the waiters rushed forward with a bottle of champagne. When he had filled her glass and topped everyone up, Svetlana smiled and said "friends" before downing the contents in one go.

"She's normally used to drinking Vodka, I'm afraid" said Zarabowski apologetically.

"At least I can hold my drink, not like you" she replied and they all sensed that the tone was turning unpleasant.

"Da, my dear, but I think you now may be getting a little tired and emotional…" began Zarabowski.

"I'm not, I'm getting ready for a good drink before I let my hair down!" she replied and Michel cringed at the prospect.

"Now, now, my dear…"

"I'm going to the bathroom, I'll leave you to make excuses for me! Coming Mademoiselle?" commanded Svetlana and Ann nodded before following the large Russian. When they had left the cabin, Zarabowski smiled at Montreau and said "between you and me, she's a little nervous at the moment."

"Why is that, Monsieur?"

"Please keep this confidential…"

"Of course, Monsieur" interrupted Montreau whilst Michel nodded.

"Svetlana is booked into a clinic in Geneva next week…" said the Russian in a whisper.

"Nothing serious I hope" whispered Montreau in reply.

"Well it may be…"

"Mon Dieu."

"Her operation is for gender re-assignment…"

"Oh!"

"At the moment she's hung like a donkey and it's upsetting her" whispered Zarabowski and Michel did not know whether to laugh or cry so he did neither.

"Mon Dieu" whispered Montreau.

"I'm sure that you'll be glad when it's all over, Monsieur" said Michel helpfully.

"Oui, and Svetlana will be as well" nodded the Russian.

"That's understandable" nodded Michel.

"Oui, hopefully it will end her violent mood swings."

"Oui, I'm sure…"

"She often used to frighten the crew" said Zarabowski and Michel believed him.

"How upsetting" said Montreau.

"Oui, but when I told them that she used to be a peasant farmer with a wife and ten children in the Ukraine, they accepted her and understood" said the Russian.

"Trés bien, that's what comrades are for, moral support in difficult times" smiled Montreau.

"Now, you, Michel and Monsieur Carter are the only people, apart from the crew, who know our little secret" said Zarabowski.

"Our lips are sealed" said Montreau.

"Merci" smiled Zarabowski as the ladies re-entered the cabin.

"I hope you've all been talking about me" said Svetlana as she sat beside her lover and waved at the waiter for more champagne.

"Of course, my dear" smiled Zarabowski.

"Bon, let's drink to that" she replied as the waiter filled her glass then topped them all up once again. She emptied her glass in one go and then giggled. But before anything else was said, Carter stood up, nodded at Svetlana and said to Zarabowski "my driver will be waiting so I really would like to conclude my business with Conrad before it gets any later, Vladimir."

"Of course, Roger."

"And we should be heading back to Marseille" said Montreau.

"Oui, that's understandable, we've all got busy days ahead" replied Zarabowski.

Michel was relieved to be leaving and he followed them all down to the limousine parked by the illuminated gang plank. They stood for a moment saying 'au revoir' when a Jaguar car appeared. Carter waved at the driver who then drew alongside the Mercedes. The driver got out and opened the boot as Montreau directed Vincent to open the boot of the limousine. The three cases were quickly removed from the Mercedes and placed in the Jaguar.

"See you back home guv'nor" said the driver.

"Yes, have a good trip, Charlie" replied Carter as he waved before the Jaguar sped away.

Michel guessed that the cases contained drugs and were now on their way back to London. He wondered where all the US dollars were and what was going to happen next. Carter and Ann had been invited to stay on the yacht with Zarabowski until all the business had been completed, whenever that might be.

Michel drove the limousine steadily back to Marseille after

collecting Raphael from the Hotel Excelsior. Little was said on the journey and they arrived at four o'clock in the morning. Michel parked the car after they had all got out and wandered up to his room. He thought of calling Evette but changed his mind, the details of the plan would have to wait. He undressed quickly, fell into bed and was asleep the moment his head touched the pillow. It seemed that he was asleep for only a moment when he was suddenly awakened by the telephone.

"Oui" he mumbled.

"Michel, c'est moi."

"Who?"

"Evette…"

"Mon Dieu, go back to sleep" he mumbled.

"It's nine o'clock, so wake up, I need to talk to you."

"Oh, non."

"I'll come to your room now…"

"I'm still in bed!"

"That doesn't matter, just get up and open the door in a minute" she said.

"Okay" he replied and hung up. He struggled out bed and made his way unsteadily to the door and opened it when he heard her knock. Evette strode into the room, he closed the door and stood looking at her. She stared at him for a moment before he asked "what?"

"You look awful, just awful…"

"So would you if you'd just got to bed after driving to Monte Carlo and back, after having too much champagne to drink whilst trying to be polite to a Russian billionaire and his overweight Ukrainian transvestite!"

"Mon Dieu!" she whispered.

"I tell you, Mademoiselle Gendarme, I'm earning every Franc of the reward!"

"Oui, but I haven't got time to discuss all that now…"

"You're beginning to sound like Gerrard!"

"Oui, we're both Gendarmes serving France!" she replied.

"And where does he get those ridiculous disguises from?"

"What do you mean?"

"He met me in the Casino toilet looking like a mad, ginger haired hippie!"

"In the toilet?" she asked with a puzzled look.
"Oui."
"His methods are very successful…"
"You may think so, but everyone looks at him with total disbelief!"
"We haven't got time for all this now, it's important that you know what the plan is…"
"Oh, oui, I'm looking forward to this!" he replied as someone knocked on the door. Michel grimaced and opened it to reveal Vincent standing there.
"Bonjour, Ronay."
"Bonjour Vincent."
"Monsieur says be ready to go in ten minutes…"
"Ten minutes?"
"Oui, you heard" grinned Vincent.
"I've only just got out of bed…"
"Ten minutes, Ronay, so say 'au revoir' to your lady friend and get dressed!" exclaimed Vincent with menace before he walked off down the corridor.
"Mon Dieu" whispered Michel as he closed the door.
"I wonder where you're going now" Evette mused.
"I'd like to go back to bed, but I think I'm going to die soon so it doesn't matter" he said as he slumped down on a chair.
"You've only got ten minutes so you'd better hurry" she said.
"I will be glad when this is all over."
"Oui."
"While I'm getting dressed, tell me about the plan" he said.
"There's no time now" she replied.
"Why not?"
"Now I've got important phone calls to make before you leave with Montreau."
"Fine, just leave me in danger, hanging out to dry, mon Dieu, never again will I help the police" he mumbled.
"I'll catch you later, au revoir and bon chance, mon brave" said Evette as she left the room.

It was fifteen minutes later when Michel arrived in the lounge and sat down with Montreau and the others. After greeting one another, Montreau said "as we all had a late night, I think we should have some coffee before we set off again."

"Merci, Monsieur" nodded a relieved Michel. An attentive waiter took the order for coffee and croissants as they all relaxed for the moment.

"Where are we off to this morning, Monsieur?" asked Michel.

"We're going to Bandol, Michel" smiled Montreau.

"Oh, bon."

"Then you and Vincent will come with me on another little trip" said the Snake.

"Oh, very nice" nodded Michel as he wondered where he was going next. The coffee eventually arrived and after they had all finished their breakfast, Montreau told Michel to get the Mercedes. When he was waiting outside the hotel, he saw Evette talking to two men in a BMW, which then drove off. Montreau, accompanied by Vincent and Marcel, strode out of the entrance and they all slipped into the limousine. Michel took the coast road to Bandol and enjoyed the relaxed ride as Montreau did not seem to be in a hurry. When Michel occasionally glanced in his rear view mirror, he saw that the BMW saloon following was the same one that he had seen outside the hotel. He was sure that the two occupants must be undercover police and he felt relaxed knowing that they were close behind. They arrived at the jetty in Bandol and as Montreau left the car, Michel asked "shall I park the car or wait here, Monsieur?"

"Leave the car and come with me" replied Montreau.

"I can't leave it here, Monsieur…"

"Arrangements have been made, so do as I say" said Montreau. Michel shrugged his shoulders and slipped from the driver's seat, whereupon, Marcel took his place behind the wheel, which made Michel distinctly nervous.

"Don't be concerned, Michel" smiled Montreau as he turned and headed towards his boat, accompanied by Vincent. The limousine then pulled away and disappeared into the morning traffic. Michel caught up with Montreau as he boarded the 'Sea Serpent' and noticed the look of disquiet on Vincent's face as they followed him into the day cabin. A dark, swarthy man was standing near the command position and nodded at Montreau as he wished him 'bonjour.'

"Now, mon amis, this is Louis, who is my captain, and he will be taking us on a little trip to rendezvous with Monsieur Zarabowski" said Montreau.

"Mon Dieu" whispered Michel.

"You know I get sea sick, Monsieur" wailed Vincent.

"You'll be alright, I've got some pills you can take" said Montreau.

"Are we going far, Monsieur?" asked Michel anxiously.

"Non, Michel, but far enough to keep away from the undercover police that have been watching our every move" smiled the Snake and Michel shivered as he realised that he might be in deep trouble.

"A good plan, Monsieur" he said with a nod.

"I think so, now, Louis, is Pascal aboard?"

"Oui, Monsieur."

"And we've plenty of fuel and food?"

"Oui, Monsieur."

"Bon, now we can go" said Montreau and Louis went out onto the deck and called "Pascal!" A young man appeared and after a brief conversation he went to the bow as Louis came inside and started up the engines. The throbbing noise of two diesel engines on start up invaded the cabin and Montreau went outside followed by Michel. Pascal came aft and cast off as Louis engaged drive and the 'Sea Serpent' moved slowly away from her berth.

"It's a lovely day for a cruise" said Montreau.

"Oui, Monsieur."

"I hope you like sea trips, Michel."

"I do, Monsieur" he replied as he thought of the wonderful time he had had with Rene and Yvonne last August. However, this trip was unlikely to be as pleasant.

"Where are we going to meet Monsieur Zarabowski?" asked Michel as Vincent joined them on deck.

"Somewhere that is convenient, Michel, but that need not concern you" replied Montreau.

"Right."

"But, what I will tell you is that after we've rendezvoused with Monsieur Zarabowski, we will be staying on board and returning by way of the Rhone to Lyon."

"Does that mean we'll be on the boat for days, Monsieur?" asked Vincent in an apprehensive tone.

"Oui, Vincent, it does."

"Mon Dieu" whispered Vincent.

"So we're not going back to the hotel in Marseille then?" asked Michel.

"Non, Marcel has driven back to collect Raphael, who has booked us out with all our luggage and they will be in Lyon when we eventually arrive on the 'Sea Serpent'" replied Montreau with a grin.

"That's a very good plan to keep the Gendarmes off our back" said Michel helpfully.

"Exactly, they can't follow us at sea, now let's have a drink to celebrate our future success" said Montreau before he returned to the cabin. Michel looked at Vincent, who shrugged his shoulders and went into the cabin. The 'Sea Serpent' made progress slowly out beyond the harbour and then Louis increased the power to the engines and the bow raised as the boat began to shudder as it ploughed into the gently rolling green Mediterranean.

CHAPTER 10

Michel relaxed with a glass of champagne as he sat back on the large bench seat, on the aft deck of the 'Sea Serpent' as it moved purposefully through the glinting water. The sun was quite strong and it felt warm for the time of year. Montreau sat close by on the seat, occasionally glancing out at the receding coastline, whilst Vincent stood by the rail looking decidedly green.

"This is very pleasant, Messieurs" said Montreau.

"Oui, Monsieur" replied Michel whilst Vincent nodded.

"After all our latest setbacks, a nice quiet sea trip will make us feel much better" said Montreau with a smile.

"Oui, Monsieur" replied Michel and as the Snake appeared to be in a relaxed mood, he decided to ask a question or two.

"Tell me, Monsieur, are we going to Monte Carlo?" The Snake looked at him coldly, sipped his champagne and replied "you ask too many questions for your own good, Michel."

"Sorry, Monsieur, I only asked out of interest" replied Michel before he calmly sipped his champagne.

"I will tell you when the time is right what is of interest to you and what you need to know" said Montreau with a touch of menace.

"Oui, Monsieur" nodded Michel and he looked away towards the open sea, realising that any further conversation with Montreau was pointless. The 'Sea Serpent' began to turn slowly in an easterly direction and Michel tried to guess where they were going to rendezvous with Zarabowski. He remembered from his delightful sea trip last August with Rene and Yvonne that there were many places to anchor up near picturesque islands all along the Côte d'Azure. He thought that was most likely, as a meeting in the harbour at Monte Carlo would be easily observed. Montreau was right; police surveillance was very difficult, if not impossible at sea with so many pleasure craft enjoying the sunlit Mediterranean. The cruiser carried on for another hour or so before Pascal came out on deck and asked "are you ready for lunch, Monsieur?"

"Oui, Pascal."

"Bon" he nodded and went back into the cabin. Twenty

minutes later, Pascal appeared again and summoned them in for lunch. They sat at the large table and enjoyed a crisp, fresh chicken salad with all the trimmings, followed by a chocolate gateaux smothered in thick cream. Coffee and brandy finished the meal and Michel felt quite light headed as the champagne, mixed with brandy, took effect. Vincent managed to just finish the meal before he declared that he would have to go to his cabin and lie down. Montreau nodded at Vincent and then invited Michel up to the fly bridge. He followed the Snake unsteadily up the chrome ladder to the open top of the cruiser, where the wind was bracing. They sat in the command seats and enjoyed the vista all around the boat.

"Don't touch the controls up here" said Montreau.

"Non, Monsieur."

"They are a duplicate of what Louis has in the main cabin, and he is in command."

"Oui, Monsieur" replied Michel as he glanced at the panel before him and noticed the compass heading was 110 degrees, confirming that they were travelling in a south easterly direction. He guessed that the rendezvous would be near the Iles d'Hyères, a group of three small islands just off the picturesque town of Hyères. The islands lie about one third of the way to Monte Carlo from Bandol and it seemed a logical place to meet Zarabowski on his magnificent yacht. Michel relaxed and turned his thoughts to Josette, Evette, Monique and Mademoiselle Cressant. What a story he would have for the ambitious reporter, if he should survive the adventure, and he glanced at the Snake as his spine tingled with apprehension. Montreau looked cruel and Michel knew that the crook was ruthless. He hoped that Gerrard was somehow keeping tabs on their movements and would intervene to save him if things went horribly wrong. Then he wondered if a Gendarme who could hide behind a ginger wig, false eyebrows and droopy moustache thinking that was an adequate disguise, had the for sight to take swift and direct action in a crisis; somehow he doubted it.

"We'll be at our rendezvous point in about an hour or so, Michel" said Montreau as he looked at his watch.

"Oh, bon, Monsieur" replied Michel, now sure that they were to meet somewhere close to the Iles d' Hyères.

"Then after we've unloaded some special cargo from Monsieur

Zarabowski's yacht, we can set off back to Lyon" beamed Montreau.

"Excellent, Monsieur" replied Michel, not daring to ask what the Russian cargo was, but guessing it consisted of the US Dollars that Svetlana had mentioned.

"Oui, it will have been a most satisfactory and enjoyable sea trip."

"Oui, Monsieur."

"And very profitable too" smiled Montreau.

"Trés bien, Monsieur."

"I think I'm ready for another drink, how about you, Michel?"

"Oui, Monsieur."

"We'll go back down; it's too windy to stay up here." Michel nodded and followed the Snake back to the aft deck where they sat once again on the bench seat that stretched right across the stern of the boat. Michel poured the champagne that had been sitting in the ice bucket and said "salut" to Montreau.

After an hour or so, the first island in the chain of the Iles d' Hyères came slowly into sight and Michel braced himself mentally for the next part of the adventure whilst wondering whether it was all part of the plan that he knew nothing about. When the 'Sea Serpent' was within about three hundred metres of the rocky beach, Louis called to Pascal to drop the anchor as he cut both engines. The cruiser slowed, then came to a stop and wallowed gently as the anchor was released with a clatter from the chain. Louis appeared on the aft deck and announced "we've arrived, Monsieur."

"Bon, well done, Louis."

"Merci, Monsieur."

"You've made good time" said the Snake as he glanced at his watch.

"Oui, Monsieur."

"Our Russian friend should be here in about an hour or so" said Montreau.

"Right, Monsieur."

"Then after we've loaded the cargo, we can set off for Lyon."

"Oui, Monsieur."

"You and Pascal have a good rest now and something to eat;

you've got a long night ahead."

"Merci, Monsieur" said Louis before he returned to the cabin and called Pascal.

An hour passed and then another with no sign of the Russian yacht. Montreau went up to the fly bridge with a pair of binoculars and spent the next half hour vainly searching for a sight of the yacht. Michel followed him and wished he hadn't, as Montreau's patience was slowly ebbing away and being replaced with anger.

"Where has that stupid Russian got to?" he said with menace as he handed the binoculars to Michel, who shrugged his shoulders.

"See if you can find him, Michel."

"Oui, Monsieur." There were many small boats and pleasure craft sailing in the late afternoon sun, but there was no sign of the Russian luxury yacht.

"I'm going below, so have one last good look then come down in a minute, I need to talk to you and Louis."

"Oui, Monsieur."

Michel did as he was asked and then joined Montreau in the main cabin with Louis.

"Messieurs, we have a problem, our Russian friend has not appeared and I can only assume that he's either forgotten where the rendezvous is, or he's lost!" said Montreau.

"Shall we try to contact him by radio, Monsieur?" asked Louis.

"I wanted to avoid that if at all possible."

"Why, Monsieur?"

"Because our conversation will be monitored by the coastguard and our position known" replied Montreau.

"If you want to find the Russian, it's a chance we'll have to take, Monsieur" said Louis.

Montreau looked thoughtful for a while and nodded "oui, I suppose you're right, Louis, see if you can make contact on the radio."

"Oui, Monsieur."

"But be brief, just find out where the Russian yacht is and give her our position."

"Oui, Monsieur" nodded Louis before he went forward to operate the radio at the command console. Michel sat quietly and tried to hear what Louis was saying but he could not quite understand what was being said as there appeared to be interference accompanied by crackling. Louis then raised his voice and Michel heard him say "west of the Iles d' Hyères, west... hello... hello, I say again, west..."

"It seems Louis is having problems, Monsieur" said Michel and Montreau nodded.

"Nothing goes smoothly" replied Montreau with a sigh as Louis rejoined them in the main cabin.

"I'm sorry, Monsieur, there's some interference on the radio, so I'm not sure if my message was understood, but it seems that the Russian yacht has been waiting at the east of Iles d' Hyères..."

"That stupid bastard!" exclaimed Montreau angrily.

"I confirmed that we were at the western side of the islands..." began Louis.

"I knew that Zarabowski was drunk and wasn't listening to me when we arranged the rendezvous, I expect he's got it all wrong!" interrupted Montreau.

"Oui, Monsieur."

"Get the engines started, Louis, and let's get to the other end of the islands before the stupid Russian makes another mistake and confuses his captain again!"

"Oui, Monsieur" replied Louis before he hurried away and called for Pascal.

Within a short while the 'Sea Serpent' had started her engines, raised the anchor and was at full speed towards the eastern end of the chain of islands. Montreau told Michel to accompany him to the fly bridge and help in the search for the Russian yacht. It was getting late in the afternoon and the sun was setting behind them as the cruiser made good time towards its destination.

"I just hope that he stays put until we get there" said Montreau as he handed the binoculars to Michel.

"Oui, Monsieur" replied Michel whilst he had doubts about that. If the radio message was misheard then Zarabowski might believe that it was he who had to make a speedy journey to the west to rendezvous with the 'Sea Serpent'. Michel thought that the situation might develop into a giddy sea chase around the Iles d' Hyères all night long and he smiled to himself when he imagined how Mademoiselle Cressant would relish the details. He could see his picture on the front page of the 'Marseille Citizen' accompanied by banner headlines announcing that he had foiled a plot at sea to…? Then he wondered what the plot was and if he was sticking to the plan to bring Montreau and his accomplices to justice. He felt confused and lonely as he scoured the horizon through the binoculars for the billionaire's yacht.

The 'Sea Serpent' eventually arrived off the most easterly point of the Iles d' Hyères when it was almost dark. There was no sign of the yacht and Montreau became so angry that Michel thought he was going to have a seizure.

"Mon Dieu! Where is that stupid, drunk, idiot of a Russian?" he shouted.

"Obviously not here, Monsieur" said Michel.

"I can see that, mon Dieu! I'm surrounded by idiots!"

"Perhaps Louis should try and make contact on the radio" said Michel.

"Oui, go and tell him to do that whilst I stay up here and keep looking" replied Montreau.

Michel left the fly bridge and went down to see Louis. After a while contact was made with the yacht, which was now cruising at full speed in a westerly direction well passed the islands, searching for the 'Sea Serpent'.

"Mon Dieu, they went to the south of the islands looking for us as we came here by the northern route, that's how we missed them and now they're on their way to Marseille!" exclaimed Louis.

"Tell them to stop and turn round, Monsieur will go mad if we lose them" replied Michel. Louis tried again but was unsure if his message was received and understood amongst the crackling static of the signal.

"We'd better get after them, Louis."

"Oui, will you tell Monsieur what has happened?"

"Oui, but I think he's already guessed" replied Michel with a smile.

Louis turned the cruiser on to a westerly heading and applied full power to the engines whilst Michel tried to placate the inconsolable Montreau after informing him of the Russian yacht's present position.

"Shall we go down to the cabin and have a drink, Monsieur?" asked Michel soothingly.

"Oui, Michel." They went down to the cabin and found Vincent sitting quietly, looking decidedly unwell.

"Is anything happening?" asked Vincent innocently and Michel thought that Montreau was going to kill him.

It was an hour later when Michel returned alone to the fly bridge and spotted the Russian yacht through the binoculars. She was all lit up in the darkness, cruising at full speed towards the 'Sea Serpent' so Michel hurried down to the cabin to break the good news to Montreau whilst warning Louis that a collision was likely if he did not alter course.

"Mon Dieu! Call them on the radio to stop, Louis!" exclaimed Montreau in alarm. Pascal took over at the helm whilst Louis switched on the radio and attempted to contact the yacht. Fortunately the signal was good and clear communication was established, much to their relief.

Michel followed Montreau up to the fly bridge to watch the yacht slowly approach the 'Sea Serpent'. Louis had cut the engines to a tick over and Pascal had gone out on the forward deck to be ready to tie up alongside the Russian yacht. The two cruisers edged ever closer and Montreau became excited at the prospect of concluding his lucrative business with Zarabowski.

"Once this is over, Michel, we can relax" said the Snake.

"Oui, Monsieur."

"I think a champagne celebration will be in order before we set off for Lyon."

"Trés bien, Monsieur."

"Then I'm going to bed."

"Oui, Monsieur."

The gap between the cruisers narrowed until they were close enough for a crewman on the yacht to throw a line down to Pascal. The young man caught the rope and quickly made it fast as the 'Sea Serpent' gently bumped the side of the yacht. Zarabowski suddenly appeared and called to Montreau.

"Bonsoir, Conrad!"

"Bonsoir, Monsieur."

"At last we meet!"

"Oui."

"What an adventure."

"Oui, Monsieur."

"But never mind, I'm sure you didn't mean to make a mistake over our rendezvous plan…"

"I didn't! You're the one who got it wrong…" interrupted Montreau in an angry tone.

"Well, it doesn't matter as we're here now, are you ready for the transfer?"

"Oui, Monsieur."

"Bon, tell my crew where you want the cases" shouted Zarabowski.

"Oui, on the rear deck, s'il vous plait, Monsieur" called Montreau.

"Tell my crew" he called and disappeared from view. Then several men appeared at the side of the yacht and looked down at Montreau on the fly bridge. Michel hoped that they would understand instructions in French and nothing would go wrong in the transfer of the cargo.

"Unload the cases onto the rear deck" called Montreau as he pointed towards the stern of the 'Sea Serpent'. One of the men nodded and called out "da" before he pointed towards the stern of the yacht.

"What does he want, Michel?"

"I've no idea, Monsieur."

"Onto the rear deck, comrade" said Montreau as he pointed once again.

"Da" came the reply as the man waved his hand towards the rear of the yacht.

"I think he wants us to move along for some reason, Monsieur" said Michel.

"Quick, let's go down to the deck and make him understand that's where we want the cases" said Montreau before he hurried away and down the ladder to the aft deck. Michel followed him and by the time they had reached the deck, a small davit had been swung out from the yacht with a large case suspended beneath. The davit was near the stern of the yacht and Michel realised that they would have to manoeuvre the 'Sea Serpent' along from its present position so that the case could be lowered onto the deck.

"Louis! Slacken the ropes so we can get under the case" commanded Montreau.

"Oui, Monsieur" he nodded and made his way forward. The rope was released and the cruiser drifted slowly back along the hull of the yacht until the aft deck was positioned under the swinging case. Louis tied up securely and joined them on the deck. By now the slight swell of the sea had become a little more substantial and the case began to swing too much in Michel's opinion. The crew man waved down and shouted "da" before the case was lowered towards the deck of the cruiser. When it was within their grasp, Louis, Pascal and Michel grabbed at it and steadied it down safely.

"Bon" said Montreau as Vincent arrived to help them carry the case into the cabin. Three more cases were successfully unloaded and placed on the floor of the cabin. When they returned to the deck to receive the next case, the swell had increased, Vincent's face had grown pale and Zarabowski appeared by the davit with Svetlana.

"This is the last one, Conrad" said the Russian.

"Bon" replied Montreau and he gave a wave. As the case was being lowered it started to swing alarmingly and to help steady it, Svetlana leaned out and caught the rope. Unfortunately, even her mighty shoulders could not hold the swing of the heavy case and she was plucked from the side of the yacht and plunged into the sea between the two vessels. Michel just caught a glimpse of her muscular body in a flowing white gown as it flashed downwards.

"Svetlana! Svetlana!" shouted Zarabowski.

"Quick, one of you save her!" shouted Montreau as they all rushed to the side of the cruiser and peered down. Then, without hesitation, Pascal jumped into the sea where Svetlana was struggling to keep afloat. The young man quickly caught hold of her and swam towards the back of the 'Sea Serpent' where the fixed boarding ladder descended below the water line. Svetlana struggled up the ladder to where Louis and Michel's outstretched hands grasped her thick arms and hauled her on deck.

"Merci, merci" she gasped between breaths as they hurried her inside the warm cabin.

"I'll get some towels and blankets" said Louis as Pascal staggered in.

"Well done, mon brave" said Montreau.

"Merci, Monsieur" nodded Pascal before he started to undress. Then Svetlana undid her gown and let it fall to the floor, revealing her underwear. She was not a pretty sight with her blonde hair straggled about her face and makeup smeared in every direction. Montreau excused himself and went out on deck to inform Zarabowski that his beloved was safe and unhurt. Louis arrived back with towels and blankets and soon the transvestite, along with her rescuer, were warm and dry. Brandy was given to them both and they appeared to be unharmed by their ordeal. Whilst they were recovering, the last case was lowered successfully and brought into the cabin.

"Bon, now all we have to do is get you safely back on board your yacht, Mademoiselle Svetlana" said Montreau.

"Da, and how will you do that?" she asked.

"I think it best if Monsieur Zarabowski makes that decision" replied Montreau.

"Da, if you say so, although I'm in no hurry to go" she smirked and Montreau winced at that.

"I'm sure you'll be more comfortable when you've changed into fresh clothes and rested…" he began.

"Non, I can take everything off now and just keep a towel wrapped around me whilst I relax with Pascal and have another drink" she interrupted and Michel shivered at the thought whilst Pascal looked positively frightened.

"I'm sure you need to rest after your ordeal" ventured Montreau.

"Non, I feel like having a party to celebrate my rescue, and besides, I haven't had a chance to thank Pascal" she purred and Michel whispered "mon Dieu" as he imagined Pascal helplessly locked in some ghastly sexual embrace with the Ukrainian transvestite.

"Mademoiselle…" began Montreau when he was interrupted by the arrival of Zarabowski. They all turned to face him as he stepped into the cabin and said "Svetlana, my dear, thank God you're safe!"

"Da, Vladimir, and it's all thanks to young Pascal, he's so brave and so strong, I just want to hold him close and…"

"Alright, my dear, alright, now let's get you back on board"

interrupted Zarabowski and they all sighed with relief.
"Only if we can have a little party, Boushka" she pouted.
"Of course, of course, anything to make you happy, Svetlana" Zarabowski beamed and the despair showed on all their faces.
"We'd love to come to your party, Mademoiselle Svetlana, but we really must make our way to Lyon, now that we have concluded our business..." began Montreau.
"Make them all come to my party, Boushka" interrupted Svetlana with a pout and Zarabowski nodded.
"Messieurs, please be our guests for a little while, it will make my little petal so happy" pleaded the Russian and Montreau felt that he was obliged to agree.
"Certainly, just a quick drink then, to celebrate Mademoiselle's safe rescue" smiled the Snake.
"Bon."
"Then we really must leave you" said Montreau.
"Of course" nodded Zarabowski.

It was decided that Louis and Vincent would remain on the 'Sea Serpent' whilst the rest of the party would go aboard the yacht. They followed Zarabowski out onto the aft deck where his personnel platform stood waiting to winch them up to the deck of the yacht. The platform was large enough to transport them all and once they were safely on it, Zarabowski gave the command to lift. Michel hung on tight to the surround rail as the platform swung from side to side as it was winched up to the landing area on the yacht. They then followed Zarabowski into the grand cabin whilst Svetlana excused herself. As they arrived, the two waiters plied them with champagne before the Russian waved them all to sit.
"Thank you so much for coming, it means so much to Svetlana, she's very tense at the moment, I'm sure it's the worry of the operation that's affecting her" said Zarabowski.
"Of course, it's understandable" smiled Montreau.
Dishes of caviar appeared once again, along with toast slices and biscuits. They had more to drink and Michel listened whilst Zarabowski and Montreau talked in vague terms about future business. Then the Russian let it slip.
"The Americans are such fools and easily mislead..." he said.
"Really?"

"Da, you only have to tell them that you're a new democracy that needs help and they pour millions of Dollars in, thinking that they can buy their way to your hearts and minds" laughed Zarabowski.

"It's the same old story" nodded Montreau.

"So we take the money and laugh at them behind their backs" the Russian giggled.

"They're so naïve" said Montreau as Svetlana entered the cabin and Michel gasped. She was wearing a long red wig, her makeup was horrendously Gothic and she was wearing a red silk Susie Wong dress with a slit up to her thigh. She smiled as Zarabowski said with a sigh "here's my lovely Moushka." She walked purposefully across the cabin and sat down beside her lover as a waiter presented her with a glass of champagne on a silver plate. She raised the glass and looked at a horrified Pascal and murmured "to my lovely rescuer, Pascal." They all raised their glasses and joined in the toast to the pale faced young man.

"Are you alright now, my petite Svetlana?" asked Zarabowski.

"Da, and I feel like singing to my Pascal" she replied and Michel winced as Pascal went even paler.

"Of course" murmured Zarabowski. He left his seat, went over to the grand piano and sat at the keyboard whilst Svetlana tried to follow gracefully, tottering on her high heels. When she had placed her back against the side of the piano and extended both arms along the top in a provocative sexual pose she began to sing 'I've got you under my skin' as Zarabowski attempted to follow her, tinkling slightly off tune. Michel thought she sounded like a cross between Marlene Dietrich and a cement mixer. He looked at Montreau whose face was transfixed and then at Pascal who appeared emotionally dead. When she had finished murdering that song she started singing "are the stars out tonight? I don't know if it's cloudy or bright, for I only have eyes for you..." Michel finished his champagne and waved at the waiter for more. Montreau did the same whilst Pascal remained transfixed. Michel wondered if they would ever escape from the clutches of the Russians and he longed for a tranquil moment with Josette in Ricky's bar. The Ukrainian ended her repertoire with 'The lady is a tramp' and they all sighed with relief as they applauded her.

"Did you enjoy that, da?" she enquired as she resumed her seat.

"Oui, bravo, Mademoiselle Svetlana" said Montreau.

"I sing some more for you later…"

"Non, Mademoiselle, we really have to be going now" interrupted Montreau.

"Make them stay, Boushka" she pouted and Zarabowski looked pleadingly at Montreau.

"Okay, just for a little while" nodded the Snake and Michel guessed that the large cases must contain millions of US Dollars for Montreau to be so compliant with Svetlana's demands.

"Da, let's drink Vodka from now on and let our hair down, da?" she beamed and Michel suddenly lost the will to live.

Michel had consumed a number of Vodka's, accompanied each time by a toast from Svetlana, before his body could take no more and he drifted off into an alcoholic stupor. He thought he heard singing at one point as he vaguely came round before sinking once more into oblivion. Later he surfaced again and glanced around the cabin to see Zarabowski slumped in a chair with his head lolling to one side, snoring, Pascal pinned down on a settee underneath Svetlana, who was kissing him passionately and Montreau sitting bolt upright in a wide eyed catatonic state. It reminded him of a friend who was hit on the head by a golf ball whilst on holiday in Spain, and the accident turned him into a vegetable. Michel closed his eyes once again and wished that the cabin would stop spinning round.

"Michel, Michel, wake up" Montreau's voice penetrated his brain and Michel opened his eyes.

"Leave me to die, Monsieur" he mumbled.

"Come on, we have to go…"

"Leave me…"

"You can sleep all you want once we're back on my boat" said Montreau angrily. Michel blinked at the daylight streaming through the cabin windows and sat up before glancing at his watch. It was just after eight.

"Mon Dieu" he whispered.

"Let's get off this floating catastrophe right now!" exclaimed Montreau as Michel looked around for Pascal. The young man was sitting up on the settee, wearing only his underpants, and

Michel wondered what the Ukrainian had done to him. There was no sign of Zarabowski or Svetlana and Michel was relieved at that.

"I'm with you, Monsieur" said Michel as he stood up and tried to balance himself. The three of them made their way unsteadily out onto the deck and one of the crew helped them into the passenger platform. They were lowered gently onto the deck of the 'Sea Serpent' and waved to the helpful crewman on board the yacht.

"Louis, get us free from that bloody Russian boat and underway to Lyon before you make a large pot of black coffee!" shouted Montreau.

An hour later Michel was sitting on the bench seat on deck, drinking more coffee with Montreau. Pascal had gone to his cabin and Michel decided to ask him later if the Ukrainian had interfered with him. He was curious and besides, he reasoned, it would make interesting reading in the 'Marseille Citizen'. The fresh sea air helped with Michel's recovery from the night of excess and he was determined that he would never mix champagne with vodka again. His mind wandered, he thought about Josette, Monique and Evette before thinking about his escape from Montreau. No matter what the reward was, he wanted to be free from this nightmare as soon as possible. He just wanted life to be as it was before he set off to start the futile business with cousin Henri in Le Touquet. The accident on the autoroute, caused by the silly Englishman, had been the reason for all his troubles and involvement with the Snake. Michel thought about his late Mother and her favourite saying when things went wrong 'you never know what life has in store for you and there's the proof'.

Vincent came out on deck looking a little better than when Michel last saw him.

"Do you want me to open the cases for you to check, Monsieur?" he asked Montreau.

"Oui, Vincent, that's a good idea" replied the Snake and he stood up and followed Vincent into the cabin. Michel was curious and he waited for a while before he made his way in, by then Vincent had forced open two of the large cases which were filled with US Dollars. Michel thought that there must have been millions contained in the cases and wondered what sort of deal Montreau had done with the Russian.

"Well, what do you think, Messieurs?" asked the Snake with a grin.

"Formidable, Monsieur" said Michel.

"Oui, formidable" echoed Vincent.

"Oui, it's a shame it's not all mine" said Montreau.

"Really, Monsieur?"

"Non, Michel, I'm just passing it all through the club for Zarabowski" replied Montreau. So Michel knew then that the business deal was money laundering the cash through the 'Jardine Bleu' and sending big cheques to Zarabowski. No doubt he had a Swiss bank account in which to make deposits, whilst the Snake skimmed off a nice handling fee. On the amount of money in the cases that would represent a huge sum for Montreau. It had obviously been misappropriated from the generous funds provided by the American Government to aid the fledgling Russian democracy. That is how some Russians become billionaires in one giant leap from their usual rewards from petty crimes. Vincent opened the rest of the cases and Montreau stood with a fixed grin as he surveyed the vast amount of money before him. Michel and Louis were spellbound by what they saw and just remained silent, watching in wonder.

"Shall I close the cases now, Monsieur?" asked Vincent

"Non, leave them open, it will be a constant reminder to me of my success as an international business man" replied Montreau.

"Oui, Monsieur."

"Let's have some champagne to celebrate" said Montreau.

"Non, merci, Monsieur, I'll stick to coffee until later" replied Michel.

"What about you, Louis?" asked the Snake.

"Not just yet, Monsieur, I'll wait until we have reached the river" replied Louis.

"How long will that be?"

"We're cruising at fifteen knots, so in about four hours, Monsieur" replied Louis. Montreau glanced at his watch and announced "then at one o'clock, Messieurs, we'll have a celebration champagne lunch!"

"Trés bien" said Michel and Louis nodded before returning to the helm. Michel followed Vincent out on deck whilst Montreau remained in the cabin feasting his eyes on his new found wealth. Michel wondered if the Russian knew exactly the total amount of money contained in the cases and guessed that Montreau would make certain 'adjustments' in his favour. As it appeared that Zarabowski had so much money a few misappropriated sums would hardly be missed.

The sun shone on the blue green sea which glinted as the waves gently rolled and caused the tops to break into fine spray. Michel relaxed on the bench seat alongside Vincent for a while and watched some of the yachts sail by and he occasionally glanced up at a helicopter that buzzed along, back and forth, over the beaches. No doubt the pilot was gazing at the hardy sun worshippers, and Michel smiled when he remembered sailing naked on Rene's little yacht. After a while he decided to try and engage Vincent in some conversation.

"This is pleasant, Vincent."
"Oui, but I'll feel happier when we've reached the river" he replied.
"Not too long to go."
"Another four hours, Ronay, which is too long for me because I can't swim and anything could happen in that time" said Vincent.
"Like what, for instance?"
"I don't know, but I think this whole adventure down here is jinxed" he replied gloomily.
"Why do you say that?"
"Ronay, are you blind?"
"Non, I don't think so."
"We've got Pierre in hospital with a broken leg, Monsieur Descoyne and George in police custody facing serious charges as well as reports in the papers about Monsieur being in Marseille!"
"Oui, you have a point" nodded Michel.
"And this was supposed to be a quiet visit to start up business with Salvator's people."
"Oui."
"Now we're on Monsieur's boat with a load of money that's on show!"
"True" nodded Michel.

"Something is bound to go wrong" said Vincent as he shook his head and gazed at the distant coastline. They sat in silence for some time, each deep in thought.

Pascal emerged from his cabin below and asked them if they wanted coffee.

"Oui, s'il vous plait, Pascal" smiled Michel and Vincent nodded.

"Trés bien, Messieurs" replied Pascal. Michel thought that he looked a lot better since last he saw him. Montreau came out on deck and joined them before Pascal arrived with their coffee. They all remained quiet and watched the coastline drift by for some time before the 'Sea Serpent' began to turn on a northern heading as they passed Cap Couronne. When they reached Port-St-Louis, the mouth of the River Rhone was before them and Louis came out on deck to announce that their sea trip was almost over.

"Bon, I always feel that we're almost home when we arrive in the River" beamed Montreau.

"It's a relief to me" mumbled Vincent.

"Let's go up to the fly bridge and enjoy the scenery before we have our champagne lunch" said Montreau. Vincent declined the invitation but Michel followed the Snake up to the open deck and sat at the command console, enjoying the view.

"It's a pity that Vincent suffers with the mal de mer" said Michel. "I think it's a bit like being a passenger in a car"

"How do you mean?"

"Well, if you're driving the car you don't feel ill, but as a passenger, you often do" replied Michel.

"Do you suggest that I let Vincent take control of my cruiser?"

"Well I don't think it would do any harm, Monsieur." Montreau thought for a moment and replied "I suppose I could let him just steer it for a bit, now we've almost reached the river."

"Oui, Monsieur, I'm sure it would make him feel a lot better" said Michel with a smile.

"Alright, I'll let him have a go for a little while after lunch" said Montreau.

The 'Sea Serpent' had actually entered the Rhone when Pascal came up to announce that lunch was ready. In the cabin, the table was almost groaning under the weight of food dishes that Pascal had placed upon it. It was a buffet lunch that was supreme in every detail and the two bottles of champagne in ice buckets were the final enhancement.

"I'm ready for this, Messieurs" said Montreau as he helped himself to a plate of prawns in a rich cream sauce.

"Oui, Monsieur" said Michel and Vincent nodded before he picked up a petite cheese baguette.

"Come on, Vincent, enjoy yourself" said the Snake.

"I won't be able to do that until we've reached Lyon, Monsieur" replied Vincent.

"Will you feel any better if you take command on the fly bridge after lunch?" asked Montreau. Vincent looked surprised and replied "you'd let me drive the boat?"

"Oui, for a short while, that'll give Louis a break" nodded Montreau.

"Oh, merci, Monsieur" replied Vincent with a smile on his face.

"Bon."

Pascal poured the champagne and they all drank to Montreau's success before settling down to enjoy the lunch. After consuming another two bottles of champagne, they made their way unsteadily up to the fly bridge. Louis accompanied them and once Vincent was seated behind the controls, Louis gave him instructions on the handling of the 'Sea Serpent'. Michel and Montreau sat on the bench seat at the back of the deck and gazed lazily out over the calm water of the Rhone. Michel heard Louis say clearly that Vincent was to stay in mid stream of the river and avoid the marker beacons that warned of underwater obstructions. Vincent nodded and then Louis left the fly bridge to enjoy his lunch with Pascal. For a while the cruiser made smooth and steady headway and other than a helicopter buzzing along the far side of the river from time to time, nothing disturbed their tranquil cruise. Vincent decided as all was going so well and he was enjoying himself, a light touch on the throttles would be fun as well as reducing the journey time to Lyon. That sort of initiative always pleased Montreau and Vincent knew that his boss would be delighted to be back in Lyon sooner than expected. The Snake did not notice the slight increase in speed as Vincent gently eased the throttles forward and the noise of the powerful diesel engines rose. Michel began to feel a little anxious but said nothing as Montreau closed his eyes and began to doze in the warmth of the afternoon sun. Vincent, now accustomed to his new found power, decided to increase speed just a little more. The 'Sea Serpent' raised her bow and began to plough through the water at considerable speed as her momentum built up. Vincent was busy looking at the helicopter and so missed seeing the small marker in front of the cruiser. Louis realised what was happening and was halfway up the ladder to the bridge, shouting to Vincent, when the cruiser hit something very substantial below the surface of the water. Montreau awoke as there came a shattering crash and the 'Sea Serpent' shuddered from stem to stern. The engines raced for a moment then stopped abruptly as the cruiser lost all forward momentum and began to sink slowly by the stern.

"Mon Dieu!" shouted Louis as he arrived on deck. Vincent stood up, white faced and began to shake visibly as the 'Sea Serpent' slowly tilted backwards. Montreau leapt from his seat and grabbed Vincent by the throat.

"You stupid idiot! You bloody stupid idiot!" he screamed as he struggled to choke Vincent to death.

"Monsieur, it's important we abandon ship now, you can kill him later!" exclaimed Louis. Michel nodded and followed Louis down to the aft deck where the dinghy was suspended on davits. The cruiser was settling quickly in the water and Michel guessed that her hull had been ripped open so badly that there was no hope of saving her. Pascal joined them on the deck and began to release the dinghy for their escape from the sinking cruiser. Montreau struggled down with Vincent behind him as the water gushed over the side and onto the deck. Water began to pour into the cabin and Michel could see the open cases of money begin to float up from the floor. When Montreau saw what was happening he suddenly went red in the face and then almost as quickly his countenance changed into a distorted, pallid look before he groaned out loud and clutched at his chest.

"Mon Dieu! He's having a heart attack!" exclaimed Michel and he rushed towards Montreau as he collapsed in the ankle deep swirling water. Louis and Vincent helped Michel get the Snake into the dinghy just as it floated free in the rising water. They then all clambered aboard, shocked by what had happened and the suddenness of the accident. As the cruiser sank lower, Michel could see the cases floating up to the roof of the cabin and tipping over, spilling their contents into the water. Louis slowly paddled the dinghy away from the sinking cruiser and they all watched with horror as the beautiful, sleek craft, sank beneath the surface of the river with a gurgle accompanied by the hiss of cold water on the hot engines. In a moment the vessel had completely disappeared and other than a few US Dollar notes and various odd items floating about, there was nothing left of the 'Sea Serpent'.

CHAPTER 11

It was not long after Louis paddled slowly away from the scene of the disaster that the first rescuers arrived. A small cabin cruiser powered by an outboard motor with a crew consisting of a man, woman and an excited dog approached before drawing alongside the dinghy.

"Mon Dieu, mon amis, are you alright?" asked the rescuer.

"Non, help us get this Monsieur to the port, he's very ill" replied Michel, convinced that Montreau was dying.

"Oh, mon Dieu" said the man as he caught hold of the rope that Pascal handed up to him. Then willing hands lifted Montreau up and onto the cabin cruiser as another larger vessel arrived.

"Do you need any help?" called a man from the bow of a cruiser, similar in size to the 'Sea Serpent'.

"Non, merci, Monsieur" called Michel.

"We saw you go down, what a catastrophe" said the man shaking his head.

"Oui, it was."

"We'll stay close just in case you need us" said the man and Michel nodded his thanks as the others carried Montreau into the cabin. The cabin cruiser then set off at a fast pace back towards Port-St-Louis, where they could get the medical care that the Snake obviously needed. As they made their way along the river, the helicopter flew at low level parallel to them but at a distance, and Michel wondered if they were just being inquisitive or whether they were the police watching them.

He went into the cabin and looked down at the pale lifeless figure of Montreau laying on the bench seat. The woman was trying to administer some brandy to him and when it reached his lips, he coughed then opened his eyes. Michel was relieved that he was still alive, but he wondered for how much longer and he glanced at Louis, who slowly shook his head. They went out to the rear deck and Michel said "I think he's had it."

"Oui, I agree, and it's all Vincent's bloody fault!" replied Louis.

"Oui" nodded Michel.

"That arse has sunk the cruiser and killed Monsieur" said Louis sadly.

"Oui."

"I loved the 'Serpent', she was a delight to handle and I was so happy when Monsieur employed me to look after her" wailed Louis and Michel nodded, feeling some sympathy for the man. He then glanced at the large cruiser that was following them at a safe distance when suddenly the helicopter attracted his attention by increasing its speed and heading towards Port-St-Louis. Michel then felt sure that the police were in the helicopter watching their every move.

In a short while they arrived in the harbour and as soon as they had moored the cabin cruiser, Louis hurried off to advise the harbour master of the accident and summon urgent medical help. It was not long before the ambulance arrived and the attendants lifted Montreau from the cabin onto a stretcher before giving him oxygen. It was decided that Michel would go with Montreau to the Hospital de Timone in Marseille, whilst the others stayed at Port-St-Louis to help with the investigation into the loss of the 'Sea Serpent'.

As Marseille is only some forty kilometres distant from Port-St-Louis, the ambulance arrived at the Hospital, with its siren still blaring, in just over twenty minutes and Montreau was rushed into the Accident and Emergency Department. Michel stood by the reception desk watching the Snake as he disappeared down the corridor on a trolley, surrounded by Doctors and attentive nurses. He then gave the receptionist all the relevant details regarding Montreau before going to the pay phone and making his first call.

"Hello" said Josette.

"Hello, ma petite…"

"Michel! Where are you?"

"At the hospital…"

"Mon Dieu! Are you alright?" she demanded anxiously.

"Oui, oui, I'm fine."

"What are you doing there then?"

"It's a long and complicated story…"

"It always is where you're concerned" she interrupted.

"I'm just calling you to let you know that I'm alright and I'll be home for dinner tonight."

"Oh, cherie, I'm so glad, I've missed you…"

"I've missed you too."
"What time will you be home?" she asked.
"I'm not sure…"
"How will I know when to start cooking dinner then?"
"I'll be home by eight" he replied with a sigh whilst wondering why women always demanded to know the details of everything. He thought 'why can't she be content with the fact that I'm coming home?'
"I'll see you then, cherie" she replied.
"Oui, ma petite."
"I love you, cherie…"
"And I love you too" he murmured.
Michel decided to have a cup of coffee from the vending machine before he phoned Monique.
"Hello…"
"Monique, c'est moi."
"Oh, Michel, where have you been?"
"It's a long story…"
"It always is!"
"I'll be back home later this afternoon and I'll tell you everything then."
"Bon, what time will you be here?"
"In an hour or so" he replied.
"Bon."
"How is Mama?"
"She's okay for the minute."
"Bon, I'll see you soon" he said.
"Oh, Michel, ma cherie, I do love you…"
"And I love you too, ma petite."
He then called Mademoiselle Cressant.
"Hello…"
"Helene, c'est moi."
"Michel!"
"Oui…"
"Where are you?"
"At the hospital…"
"Are you alright?" she asked anxiously.
"Oui, I'm fine…"
"Bon, now, what's been happening?" she asked excitedly.

"Plenty!"

"Oh, bon…"

"I've got a story for you that will make you the most famous reporter in France!"

"Oh, trés bien! It's exclusive, I hope?"

"Oui, of course."

"Bon, when are you coming to see me?"

"Tomorrow…"

"Oh, Michel, are you going to make me wait all that time?"

"I'm afraid so."

"Oh, Michel…"

"Just be patient, it'll be all worthwhile."

"Okay, what time are you coming tomorrow?"

"Mid morning."

"Bon, then you can stay for lunch!"

"Oui, I look forward to that."

"Au revoir, cherie."

"Au revoir, Helene."

After another cup of coffee, Michel called the hotel to speak to Evette, but she had left and was not expected back until later. Then he called Gerrard but he was also unavailable and away from his office. Michel was just about to make inquiries at reception about Montreau when a Doctor approached him.

"I understand that you accompanied Monsieur Montreau to the hospital, is that so, Monsieur?"

"Oui, Doctor."

"Are you a relative?"

"Non, I'm a business associate."

"Can you contact his wife?"

"I don't know if he's married, Doctor."

"Well somebody then who is his next of kin."

"I only know his manager in Lyon" replied Michel.

"Would you please contact him urgently because Monsieur Montreau is very seriously ill."

"Is he going to die?"

"We can't be sure at this stage, he's suffered a major heart attack and we'll have to wait for a while to see how he stabilises, Monsieur."

"Mon Dieu" whispered Michel.

"So, make that call to his manager, s'il vous plait" said the Doctor before he hurried away.

Whilst Michel was busy searching for the number of the 'Jardine Blue' in the phone book, Gerrard and Evette arrived in reception.

"Ronay" said Gerrard in a whisper which made Michel jump and clutch his chest. He whirled round to see the two Gendarmes standing before him.

"Mon Dieu! You made me jump, Cyril."

"Call me Monsieur Gerrard, we're on police business, Ronay."

"Very well, bonjour Monsieur Gerrard and Gendarme Mademoiselle Ricard" said Michel with a slight bow and a touch of sarcasm.

"We have to talk, Ronay."

"Oui, of course, but tell me, how did you know that I was here?" asked Michel.

"I was in the helicopter watching your every move and when Montreau's boat sank I just followed you to the port and then contacted the harbour master" replied Gerrard.

"Bon, it's good to know you were there" said Michel.

"Oui, it was all part of the plan."

"Really?"

"Oui, now we'll discuss matters in Gendarme Ricard's car, it's parked outside" said Gerrard in a serious tone.

"First I have to call Gabon at the club in Lyon to let him know what has happened to Montreau" said Michel.

"Be quick, Ronay."

"There's no hurry, Monsieur Gerrard, Montreau is very ill and not going anywhere" replied Michel.

"Listen, Ronay, Montreau's illness is not part of the plan, and it only complicates things!"

"The man is almost dead! How can that complicate things?"

"That's not what we want" replied Gerrard.

"Non, and I don't think Montreau wants to be dead either!"

"Listen, Ronay, this is very serious and a great deal of police resources have been used in this plan, it has got to succeed!"

"If Montreau dies, then your plan to make sure he doesn't take over Salvator's crooked business is immaterial!"

"We can't stand here arguing, Ronay, call Gabon and then come outside" said Gerrard before he turned and walked away followed by Evette.

Michel found the number of the 'Jardine Bleu' and eventually got through to Gabon. He told the anxious manager everything and Gabon was lost for words when Michel had finished.

"Mon Dieu! I'll let Madame Montreau know what has happened" said Gabon.

"Bon, and you'd better get Marcel to drive her down here to the hospital as soon as possible" said Michel.

"Oui, I'll do that, Michel."

"Bon."

"And thank you for all you've done for Monsieur."

"My pleasure."

"I'm sure he's grateful to you."

"Oui" replied Michel whilst thinking 'I'm banking on that'.

Michel wandered out of the hospital and found Gerrard sitting with Evette in her Renault. Obviously Jean had managed to repair it and all was well. Michel expected that the bill would be presented to him as he knew that Jean was a pushover where young women were concerned. They only had to flutter their eyelashes and look vulnerable and all thought of charging them for their car repairs disappeared from his mind. However, Michel suspected that the cost of the repairs were spread over other customers invoices but he still wondered how the rumour ever got started that Jean Gambetta was the richest man in Marseille.

"So, Ronay, tell us what you know so far" said Gerrard as Michel sat in the back of the Renault. Michel related all the events leading up to Montreau's admittance to hospital. Other than gasps and whispered "mon Dieu's" at appropriate moments from Evette and Gerrard, they did not interrupt his flow. When he finished there was a stunned silence.

"Well, Monsieur Gerrard, what now?" asked Michel.

"Er, I'm just thinking how to get the plan back on track..."

"Never mind about that, Monsieur Gerrard, Montreau is almost dead and his men are either in hospital with him or in custody with you, so I reckon I've done my job and all I want now is the reward before I resume a normal life once more!"

"Ah, not so fast, Ronay, we've got to recover the money from the boat first" replied Gerrard.

"Why?"

"It's vital evidence, Ronay."

"Well, Monsieur Gerrard, I suggest that your colleagues in the maritime department get diving pretty quick because I need the reward money!"

"Mon Dieu! The investigation has only just begun and you want the reward now?"

"Oui, I'm broke and I've got to pay Mademoiselle Gendarme Ricard's hotel bill..." Michel began.

"What!" interrupted Gerrard as Evette looked distinctly uncomfortable.

"I booked Mademoiselle Ricard into the hotel so she could keep a close eye on Montreau, wasn't that part of the plan?" Michel asked cheekily.

"Non, it most certainly was not!"

"Oops!" smiled Michel and Evette giggled.

"This is not funny!" exclaimed Gerrard.

"This master plan of yours seems to be a sort of 'make it up as you go along'" said Michel.

"Have you any idea what you're talking about, Ronay?"

"Non, Monsieur..."

"I despair of you, Ronay."

"Listen Monsieur Gerrard, it's all over and your plan is now unimportant, Montreau is almost dead, you've got his men and soon you'll have the money from the river, so, please arrange to pay my reward as soon as possible" said Michel firmly.

"It's not that easy" said Gerrard.

"Well it had better be, I put my life on the line to help you, so other than making a full statement, it's finished as far as I'm concerned!"

"Ronay..."

"I'm going home now and then tomorrow I'm going back to Lyon to collect my car" interrupted Michel.

"I need you to come to my office and give me all the details about the Russian..."

"After I've been to Lyon, Monsieur, for once I'm putting myself first!"

"Be in my office tomorrow morning at ten o'clock, Ronay, otherwise I'll have you arrested!"

"Alright, Monsieur Gerrard, I'll be there, but make sure your chief has my reward cheque, s'il vous plaît!"

"Mon Dieu" whispered Gerrard.

"Now, I think I need a drink before I go home, so would you please drive me to Ricky's, Mademoiselle?"

Evette looked at Gerrard who nodded and she started the Renault then glanced at Michel in the rear view mirror. He caught her glance and smiled as she winked at him. They dropped him outside his favourite bar but declined his invitation to join him in a drink to celebrate the outcome of the Montreau adventure in Marseille.

"We have important police work to complete, Ronay, we've no time to relax" said Gerrard.

"Oui, Monsieur, I understand" smiled Michel.

"Oui, I'm glad you do, now when you get back from Lyon, I want you to come to my office again, I need to outline the next phase of the plan to you with my chief" said Gerrard.

"I look forward to that, Monsieur, especially if he's got your sense of humour!" exclaimed Michel and Evette began to giggle.

"Ronay!"

"Au revoir, Monsieur, Mademoiselle."

Ricky's was busy with late lunch drinkers who overlapped the early evening customers, in fact, the bar was so popular that it was full almost all the time.

"Ah, Michel, ça va?" beamed Jacques.

"Oui, ça va, Jacques?"

"Bon, your usual, mon ami?"

"Oui, and make it a double, s'il vous plaît."

"Oui" nodded Jacques and poured a large double brandy.

"Is Antone here?"

"Oui, and he'll be as pleased as I am to see you safely back where you belong."

"Merci, Jacques" Michel nodded before he lifted his glass and gulped a good measure of brandy.

"Oh, mon Dieu, you're back" said Antone as he approached Michel who turned to face the great man.

"Antone, ça va?"

"Oui, I'm so pleased to see you obviously unharmed after

being caught up with that Snake for so many worrying days" said Antone as he leaned his considerable frame against the bar.

"Oui."

"Jacques, pour me a brandy, I've become giddy with relief" said Antone and Michel smiled.

"Oui" nodded Jacques.

"Now, Michel, tell us all about your frightening time with Montreau" said Antone.

"I'll just give you the broad picture for the moment as I have other things to do" replied Michel.

"Of course, we understand."

"I must go home…"

"To Monique or Josette?" interrupted Antone.

"Both…"

"How very difficult for you, Michel, and I do sympathise."

"Then I've got to go back to Lyon…"

"Mon Dieu! You're not going back there surely?" asked Antone in a concerned voice.

"Oui, to collect my car, if it's been repaired yet."

"Mon Dieu, you face constant danger from Montreau's people" said Antone as he shook his head.

"Oui, I do, and I certainly deserve the reward that Gerrard promised me" said Michel.

"Have no fear, I will personally speak to the Chief and insist that you are paid in full, any citizen who gives such service as you have done deserves his reward" beamed Antone as he drank his brandy in one gulp.

"Merci, Antone" replied Michel knowing that the close relationship that the great man had with the gay Chief of Police would ensure that the reward was paid.

"I'll talk to him tomorrow night, he's invited me round to see some new video's of young Bulgarian men sunbathing in the mountains you know, so he'll be in a good mood" smiled Antone.

"Merci."

"Have another drink with me, Michel."

"Oui, merci." Jacques poured two brandies and they talked for a while before Michel decided to call Auto Peintures S.A. in Lyon to see if his Mercedes had been repaired. He went into the private passage behind the bar and phoned Monsieur Trouville, the manager, who was pleased to inform him that the car was ready for collection. Michel explained that business matters would keep him in Marseille for the next day but he would collect the Mercedes at lunchtime the day after. When Michel returned to the bar, Rene had arrived and was talking to Antone, but when he saw Michel his face lit up with a broad smile.

"Michel, ça va?"
"Oui, Rene, ça va!"
"Oui, have a drink…"
"Non, merci, Rene, I've had enough, perhaps when you're ready you'd give me a lift home?"
"Oui, certainly, which home do you have in mind?"
"Montelivet first, then Rue du Camas, s'il vous plait" replied Michel and Rene laughed whilst Antone shook his head.

On the way to Montelivet, Michel asked Rene to take him and Josette to Lyon to collect the Mercedes.
"Oui, of course" replied Rene with a smile.
"Bon."
"And when you eventually arrive back in Marseille for good, perhaps you'll come over for one of Yvonne's special dinner parties" said Rene.
"Oui, I will."
"Bon, she's been getting so restless recently and needs attention, so a good night in with both of us will make her feel so much better."
"Oui."
"And you know how she likes dressing up" said Rene with a smile.
"Oui" nodded Michel as he began to feel aroused by the thought of Rene's statuesque wife in one of her tantalising costumes. He knew that a good dinner party with plenty to drink followed by unbridled sex was always to be recommended as it gave such pleasure to all those involved. After all, that's what close friends are for, he reasoned.

Rene waited in his cab whilst Michel paid a fleeting visit to Monique and explained that he was just attending to some unfinished business before returning from Lyon for good. She was relieved to know that and Michel told her that her patience would be rewarded. After kisses and 'au revoirs' he left his long suffering wife before Rene drove him back to his flat in the Rue du Camas.

Josette kissed him passionately and held on to him for some while after he arrived at the flat.
"You're not leaving tonight are you, cherie?"
"Non, ma petite" he replied.
"Bon."
"We'll have a nice relaxed evening before we go to bed and I'll tell you everything that has happened" he smiled.
"Bon" she replied and kissed him again.
Josette prepared dinner for them and then after a leisurely brandy or two, when Michel described his adventures, they went to bed where they made love gently until they fell asleep in each other's arms.

The next morning Michel phoned for a taxi to take him to the Palace du Justice for his meeting with Gerrard and his Chief, Monsieur Devine. Michel was shown up to Gerrard's office where the Gendarme was sitting at his paper strewn desk.
"Bonjour, Monsieur Gerrard."
"Bonjour, Ronay."
"Will this interview take long?" asked Michel.
"Possibly, why do you ask?"
"I've other people to see this morning" replied Michel as he glanced at his watch.
"Who?"
"Well, first I'm going to the hospital to see how Montreau is and then I'm having lunch with Mademoiselle Cressant…"
"Listen, Ronay, police business comes first!" interrupted Gerrard as his Chief entered the office.
"Bonjour Messieurs" said Chief Devine. Gerrard stood up and the introductions were made.
"So, it seems everything has gone to plan" said Devine.
"Oui, Monsieur Chief" nodded Gerrard.
"And I understand that we have to thank Monsieur Ronay here for the part he played" said the Chief and Michel nodded.
"Oui, Monsieur Devine, and the reward will come in very

handy" said Michel.

"Reward? What reward?" asked the Chief with a puzzled look.

"It's all been arranged by Monsieur Gerrard" said Michel quickly before the open mouthed Gendarme could say anything.

"We'll talk later about this, Gerrard" said the Chief firmly.

"Oui, Monsieur" whispered the Gendarme.

"Now tell us all you know about this Russian" said Monsieur Devine. Michel gave a full account of everything that had happened and what he had observed whilst Gerrard took notes. When Michel had finished the Chief thanked him and asked "is there anything else we should know, Monsieur Ronay?"

"Oui, the Chief of Police will be recommending my reward, so Monsieur Gerrard was only carrying out his wishes by telling me, Monsieur Devine" said Michel with a smile.

"Oh, er, oh…"

"I just thought you should know that Monsieur Devine."

"Oui, well, oui, thank you, er, if the Chief of Police has sanctioned it then that's alright" replied Devine anxiously. Gerrard smiled and shook his head as Michel winked at him.

Michel took a taxi to the hospital and went to the reception where he asked after Monsieur Montreau.

"He is still in intensive care and Madame Montreau is with him now" said the receptionist.

"Merci, is it possible that I can speak to the Doctor who's treating him?" asked Michel but before she could answer a voice he recognised said "bonjour, Michel." He turned to see Marcel standing there.

"Bonjour, Marcel, have you been here long?"

"I drove Madame down late last night and she's been with him ever since" replied Marcel

"Mon Dieu, it's really serious then?"

"Oui, as far as I can make out, if he survives, he'll be an invalid for the rest of his life…"

"Mon Dieu!"

"We're all very shocked…"

"Oui."

"It's all that arsehole Vincent's fault!" exclaimed Marcel with feeling.

"Oui, it was" nodded Michel.

"What really happened on Monsieur's boat?" Marcel asked.

"Let's get a coffee and sit down for a moment then I'll tell you everything" said Michel, Marcel nodded and followed Michel to the vending machine.

Half an hour later when Michel had finished his tale of woe, embroidered here and there for effect, he glanced at his watch.

"I have to go now, please give my best wishes to Madame and tell her that I'm thinking of her and praying for him" said Michel with a straight face.

"Merci, Michel."

"And would you let Monsieur Gabon know that I'm going up to Lyon to collect my car tomorrow and I'll call in at the club to see him."

"Oui, certainly, Michel" smiled Marcel.

Helene Cressant was delighted to see Michel and gave him a big kiss when he arrived at her flat.

"Now you are staying for lunch?" she asked as she hobbled into the lounge.

"Oui, of course."

"Bon, we can take our time then" she smiled.

"Oui."

"Pour us some drinks, cherie" she smiled as she sat down on her sofa and placed her plastered ankle up on a cushion.

"Brandy?"

"Oui, and then we can get started…"

"It's too soon, besides I want to eat before we make love" interrupted Michel and she laughed.

"And I want the exclusive story of what you've been up to before lunch and an hour on the bed will only be afterwards, if you're good" she grinned.

"Oh, I'm very good, Mademoiselle Top Reporter and an hour on the bed is not long enough " he chuckled as he poured the brandy.

"Oh, that sounds promising!"

"I'm here to serve" he smiled as he handed her the brandy. They drank to each other and their respective futures. She then produced a large note pad and told him to begin. He left nothing out and went into every detail of his days with Montreau. Helene wrote quickly and other than the occasional "mon Dieu!" followed by laughter, she did not interrupt him. When he had finished, she asked him many questions, which he did his best to answer and when she was satisfied she looked at him.

"Mon Dieu, what an adventure you've had with that crook" she said.

"Oui, and it's not over yet" he replied.

"He's finished, isn't he?"

"Oui, he is, but who knows what his wife will do?"

"Mon Dieu, will she carry on?"

"It wouldn't surprise me, I mean, she will inherit a business that makes plenty of money and you can never have too much of that, can you?"

"Non, I suppose not."

"And married to him, I expect she's got expensive tastes" said Michel.

"Oui, I'm sure you're right."

"Gerrard wants another meeting with me when I get back from Lyon tomorrow" said Michel.

"What for?"

"Another phase of his plan is to be revealed to me."

"Mon Dieu, this story could run and run!" she said excitedly.

"Oui, it could, now how about lunch?"

They enjoyed a large bowl of spaghetti bolognaise with a bottle of burgundy followed by cheese and then fruit salad with cream. Michel then led her slowly into the bedroom and made her comfortable on the bed.

"This is the way I like to be interviewed by reporters" he said as he lay beside her.

"Really?"

"Oui."

"So, how many other reporters do you know who do this?" she asked with a smile.

"Not many" he grinned before he kissed her. They made love gently and slowly before the inevitable climax that left them both breathless.

"I think I should do more interviews at home" she whispered.

"Only with very special people" he smiled.

"Oui, you could be a regular contributor to my column" she smiled.

"I'd like that."

"Oui, so would I."

"How much would I get paid?" he asked.

"Nothing, because I'm the reward" she laughed.

"What about expenses then?"

"Possibly" she nodded.

"In that case I'll think about it" he smiled before he kissed her passionately.

Josette had finished preparing dinner when he arrived home.

"I'm sorry I'm late, ma petite, but the things I had to do took longer than expected" he said as he kissed her.

"I was getting anxious about you, Cherie."

"Never worry about me, I'll always arrive eventually" he said.

"Bon, now pour us a drink and tell me what you've been doing" she smiled.

Michel sat with her, sipping brandy as he went through all the day's events, enhancing the meeting with Gerrard and his Chief, embellishing the hospital visit before playing down the interview with the ace reporter from the 'Marseille Citizen'.

"I'm so proud of you, cherie" she said when he had finished.

"Merci, ma petite."

"I'm glad it's all over now."

"Oui, it is."

"After we've collected the car tomorrow and come back here, promise me that we're never going to go away again" she said firmly.

"Non, we never will" he replied.

"Bon, and promise me that we can get married in the spring…"

"Well, ma petite…"

"Michel, it's important to me because I think I'm pregnant" she interrupted.

"Mon Dieu."

CHAPTER 12

Michel spent a restless night worrying about the complications that Josette's pregnancy would bring to his life. He felt horribly trapped by this latest turn of events and he had decided that Josette's condition should remain confidential until they announced the date of their wedding in the spring and she agreed. Michel knew that he must get divorced from Monique before then and he thought that might be a little tricky. However, as she was expecting him home later that day, he decided that if there was a lull in the conversation he might take the opportunity to slip in his request for a divorce. 'While there's life, there's hope' he thought.

Michel left Rue du Camas with Rene at nine o'clock the next morning and headed out towards the autoroute to Lyon. They were accompanied by Josette and Yvonne who decided that as the journey would be a leisurely affair, they should also enjoy a nice day out.

"Are we going to have lunch somewhere nice, cherie?" asked Josette.

"Oui, bien sur, I found a lovely petite place in Lyon, called the Bistro Romaine" replied Michel.

"Bon" said Josette with a smile.

"And it's my treat" said Michel.

"Merci, Michel" said Rene.

"We'll collect my car first of all, then have lunch."

They chatted amiably all the way to Lyon and it was just before twelve that they arrived outside Auto Peintures S.A., in the Rue du Commerce. Michel went in alone and twenty minutes later he drove out of the customer's car park in his fully restored Mercedes taxi. Josette jumped out of Rene's car and joined her fiancé in his, she gave him a kiss before Michel waved to Rene and Yvonne to follow them to the Bistro Romaine in the Boulevard Chavre for lunch.

They enjoyed a meal that was the very best of French cuisine, enhanced by several bottles of rich Burgundy. At the end, they all felt full and a little light headed, which made driving unwise until they had consumed more coffee and taken a stroll outside. When

Rene and Yvonne were ready to return to Marseille, they said 'au revoir' outside the restaurant before driving off.

"Now I have to see Monsieur Gabon at the club" said Michel as he slipped behind the wheel of his taxi.

"Will you be long, cherie?" asked Josette.

"Non, ma petite."

Michel drove to the Avenue Foche and parked close to the 'Jardine Bleu', then he kissed Josette and promised he would not be long. Once inside the club he was shown up to Maurice Gabon's office, where the manager welcomed him with open arms.

"Marcel phoned and told me that you were coming, I'm so glad you did" said Gabon as he waved Michel to a seat.

"Bon, Maurice, now tell me, how is Monsieur?"

"Little has changed, I'm afraid, he remains very ill and in intensive care" sighed Maurice.

"Mon Dieu, what a catastrophe."

"Oui, and it could all have been avoided" replied Maurice as he shook his head.

"Oui, everything was going so well, Monsieur had finished his business with Monsieur Zarabowski and we were on our way back here, cruising along in the sunshine after a champagne lunch" said Michel.

"What actually happened, Michel?"

"Well, Monsieur and I were sitting on the top deck enjoying the view, Vincent was driving, and, quite honestly, he wasn't looking where he was going…"

"Mon Dieu!"

"He'd been told by Louis to watch for the beacons that marked things under the water but the stupid idiot wasn't paying attention."

"I wonder why Monsieur let Vincent anywhere near the controls, the man is just a thick, stupid fool" said Maurice with feeling.

"Quite, then the next thing I knew, the boat had hit something and was sinking…"

"Mon Dieu" whispered Maurice.

"It's lucky that no one was drowned, we went down so quickly and that's when Monsieur had his heart attack."

"What a catastrophe!"

"I helped Monsieur down to the deck where the dinghy was and then got him safely on board that…"

"Oh, Michel, we're all very grateful to you" interrupted Maurice.

"Monsieur's safety was my only concern" replied Michel modestly.

"He and Madame will be so grateful…"

"It's enough to know that I did everything possible to save Monsieur."

"Michel, we at 'Jardine Bleu' will always remember what you did for Monsieur, and if there's anything we can do for you, then just let me know" smiled Maurice.

"Well, there is something you could help me with…"

"Name it, Michel."

"As I will be in Marseille for a while now, just until Monsieur is well enough to return to Lyon, you understand."

"Oui, of course" nodded Maurice.

"And as I will not be at the club spending my winnings, I'd be grateful if you could let me have a million Francs in cash to take away now" said Michel with a smile.

"Well, er, I…" stammered Maurice a little taken aback.

"It would help me as I'm getting married soon and my fiancé is pregnant." On hearing that Maurice looked stunned for a moment but gathered his composure and nodded.

"Of course, Michel, I'm sure that if Monsieur were here, he would sanction that" he smiled.

"Bon."

"I'll have the cashier bring the money up right away, meanwhile, would you like some coffee?"

"Oui, merci" smiled Michel.

Twenty minutes later he was back in his Mercedes with Josette and a million Francs in a briefcase.

"What have you got in there, cherie?"

"Some of my winnings, ma petite."

"How much?"

"A million Francs…"

"Mon Dieu!"

"Exactly!"

"Oh, Michel, what a wedding we'll have!"

"Oui."

"And then anywhere in the world for a honeymoon!"

"Except Le Touquet!" he replied and she laughed before kissing him.

"I agree" she smiled.

"Now, I've just got to call in at the hotel I stayed at to settle my bill and then we can go home" he said to his fiancé who smiled as he started the Mercedes.

The Hotel Arnaux in the Rue Benoir still looked run down and shabby as Michel pulled up outside.

"Is this where you stayed, cherie?" asked Josette. "It doesn't look very special."

"Non, but the people who own it are friends of Gerrard…"

"That explains it" interrupted Josette.

"Oui, I'll be as quick as I can" he said as he slipped out of the car carrying the briefcase.

Madame Veron was behind the reception desk and when she saw Michel, her eyes opened wide.

"Monsieur Ronay!" she smiled.

"Bonjour, Madame…"

"Gabrielle, s'il vous plait" she lowered her head and fluttered her eyelashes.

"Gabrielle, it's so nice to see you again."

"Oui, tell me, are you back staying with us for a while, your room is still available" she said.

"Non, I'm afraid not…"

"Oh, shame, I looked forward to getting to know you better" she pouted and Michel remembered her in his bed, which gave him a little shiver.

"I'm disappointed too, but duty calls and I have to return to Marseille now to help Cyril, in fact I'm seeing him this afternoon…"

"Oh, bon, give him my regards" she interrupted.

"I will, now, I'd like to settle my bill" he smiled and she nodded before preparing l'addition. She presented it and he took the money from his wallet and paid her.

"Merci, Monsieur."

"Now, is there somewhere we can go which is more private?" he asked and her eyes lit up.

"Oh, oui, follow me" she replied as she stepped from behind the desk. Michel followed her across the hallway to a door marked 'private'. It was small but comfortable with a sofa and an armchair, the blinds were drawn which gave it a cosy atmosphere.

"I come in here when I want to escape from Jacques" she said as she lowered herself onto the settee.

"How nice and private" said Michel as he sat beside her.

"Now, what can I do for you, Monsieur Michel Ronay?" she asked in a suggestive tone.

"It's more like what I can do for you, Madame Gabrielle Veron…"

"Oh, I like the sound of this" she interrupted before she made a lunge at Michel to kiss him.

"Just a moment, Gabrielle…"

"You're not going to disappoint me, are you?"

"Non, never!"

"Bon."

"I have to tell you that I think you're a very attractive, mature woman who needs attention…"

"Oh, I do, I really do!" she whispered.

"Unfortunately, as I am called away, I'm unable to give you what you want today…"

"Oh, shame" she half gasped.

"But, let me give you this as a little token of my regard for you and I hope you will spend on yourself, on a holiday perhaps" he said as he opened the briefcase.

"Mon Dieu!" she exclaimed when she saw the money.

"My winnings" he said as he gave her ten thousand Francs.

"Oh, Michel, Michel" she whispered as she took the money, wide eyed with astonishment

"For you and I hope that it brightens up your life a little…"

"Oh, oui, it does, I can go away for a week or two and leave Jacques to run the place" she said.

"I hope you meet someone nice who will look after you."

"Merci, Michel, I can't thank you enough."

"My pleasure."

"I must give you a little reward" she smiled.
"Non…"
"Just a 'quickie' here on the sofa!"
"Non, merci…"
"It won't take a minute, I'm not wearing any knickers and I'm ready…"
"I can't stop, honestly."
"You're such a tease" she said.
"Look, I'm sure I'll be coming back to here soon, I'll ring you, book a room and then I promise you I'll give you exactly what you want…"
"What I need, Michel."
"Oui, what you need, Gabrielle."
"Bon, I look forward to it" she smiled.

Michel left the Hotel Arnaux hoping that he had given some hope to Madame Veron for the future, but knowing that he would never stay there again.

"There, all done" said Michel as he slipped behind the wheel.
"Bon, now we're free to go home" smiled Josette.
"Oui, ma petite."

They drove out of Lyon and onto the slip road of the autoroute. Michel was deep in thought about the future. He had promised to go home to Monique as well as calling at Gerrard's office, but when he glanced at the clock on the dashboard he knew that the Gendarme would have to wait until tomorrow. Then Evette came into his mind followed by Helene, could he manage to keep these attractive women in tow? And did he really want to? He glanced at Josette and he knew deep down how much he loved her. She looked radiant with happiness, obviously looking forward to her wedding and her first baby. Michel knew he could not let her down, but he also knew that there were many complications ahead before everything was settled.

"Now, ma petite, where were we before I crashed into that stupid Englishman's caravan?"
"On our way home!" she laughed.
"Oui, our return to Marseille!" he exclaimed.

Follow Michel and Josette in

SPRING IN MARSEILLE

Printed in the United Kingdom
by Lightning Source UK Ltd.
124079UK00001B/133-141/A